Autumn: The City

Also by David Moody

Hater

Dog Blood

Autumn

Autumn: The City

David Moody

THOMAS DUNNE BOOKS

ST. MARTIN'S GRIFFIN ✳ NEW YORK

THOMAS DUNNE BOOKS.
An imprint of St. Martin's Press.

AUTUMN: THE CITY. Copyright © 2011 by David Moody.
All rights reserved. Printed in the United States of America.
For information, address St. Martin's Press,
175 Fifth Avenue, New York, N.Y. 10010.

www.thomasdunnebooks.com
www.stmartins.com

ISBN 978-0-312-57000-2

10 9 8 7 6 5 4

Prologue

There were no warnings and no explanations. We were conditioned to respond at speed. The alarm sounded and we were up and on the move in seconds. The routine was familiar from a thousand drills, but I immediately knew this was different. I knew this was for real. I could sense panic in the early morning air and I had a sickening feeling in the pit of my stomach that something was happening which was about to change everything.

In silence we collected our kit and assembled at the transports. I saw trepidation and uncertainty in the faces of everyone around me. Even the officers—those experienced, battle-hardened men and women who controlled and directed our every action—appeared bewildered and scared. Their fear and confusion was unsettling. They knew as little as the rest of us.

We were on the road in minutes and the journey took less than an hour. The early morning darkness began to lift as we approached the city. We brought chaos to the rush hour, bulldozing through the traffic and delaying people getting to their schools, offices, and homes. I saw hundreds of people watching us, but I didn't allow myself to look into any of their faces. If the rumors we were starting to hear were true, they didn't have long. I forced myself to concentrate on trivial, pointless details: counting the rivets in the floor by my boots, the number of squares in the wire mesh covering the windows . . . anything to avoid remembering that, somewhere out there in the fragile normality of this morning, were the people I had known and loved.

We tore through the heart of the city, then out through the suburbs, following major roads and motorways which eventually ran deep into green and uncluttered countryside. The sky was gray and heavy and the light remained dull and low. Major roads became minor roads, then rough and uneven gravel tracks, but our speed didn't reduce until we reached the bunker.

We were some of the first to get there. Within fifteen minutes of our arrival the last transport sped down the ramp and into the hangar. Even before its engine had stopped I heard an officer give the order to shut the doors and seal off the base. Whatever it was that was happening to the world outside, I knew it was a disaster of unimaginable proportions.

The very last shard of daylight disappeared as the bunker doors were sealed. I picked up my kit and walked deeper underground.

PART I

1

For most of the last forty-eight hours, Donna Yorke had hidden under a desk in a corner of the office where she'd worked since the summer. On Tuesday morning, without any warning, her familiar surroundings had become alien, nightmarish, and cold. On Tuesday morning she had watched the world around her die.

Along with the rest of her colleagues, Donna worked an early shift one week in four. This week it had been her turn to get in first and open the post, switch on the computers, and perform various other simple tasks so that the rest of her team could start processing as soon as they arrived at their desks at nine. She was glad it had happened so early in the day. As it was she'd only had to watch four of her friends die. If it had happened just half an hour later she'd have had to watch the other sixty-or-so people in the office suffer the same sudden and inexplicable suffocating death. None of what had happened made any sense. Cold and alone, she was too terrified to even start trying to look for answers.

From her ninth-floor vantage point she had watched the destruction wash across the world outside like an invisible tidal wave. Being so high above the city she hadn't heard anything, and the first sign that anything was wrong had been a bright explosion in the near distance, perhaps a quarter of a mile away. She'd watched with morbid fascination and genuine concern as a plume of billowing fire and dense black smoke had spewed up into the air from the gutted remains of a burning petrol station. The cars on the road nearby were scattered and smashed. Something huge had clearly plowed through the traffic, crossed the dual carriageway, and crashed into the pumps, immediately igniting the fuel stores. Had it been an out of control truck or tanker perhaps?

But that had just been the beginning, and the horror and devastation which followed had been relentless and on an unimaginable scale. All across the heavily industrialized east side of the city she saw people falling to the ground. She could see them writhing and squirming, then dying. And more vehicles were stopping too—many crashing into each other and blocking the roads, others just slowing to a gradual halt as if they'd run out of fuel. Donna watched as the chaos moved nearer. Like a shock wave it traveled quickly across the city below her, rolling relentlessly toward her building. With fear making her legs feel heavy with nerves, she stumbled back and looked around for someone who could offer explanations and reassurance. One of her colleagues, Joan Alderney, had just arrived to start work but by the time Donna found her she was on her hands and knees, fighting for breath. Joan looked up at her with huge, desperate eyes and her body shook with furious convulsions as she fought to draw in one last precious breath. Her face quickly drained to an ashen, oxygen-starved blue-gray but her lips remained crimson red, stained by blood from numerous swellings and sores which had erupted in her throat.

As Joan lay dying on the ground next to her, Donna was distracted by the sound of Neil Peters, one of the junior managers, collapsing across his desk, showering his paperwork with spittle and blood as he retched and choked and fought for air. Jo Foster—one of her closest friends at work—was the next to be infected as she walked into the office. Donna watched helplessly as Jo clawed at her neck, then mouthed a hoarse and virtually silent scream of pain and fear before falling, dead before she'd even hit the floor. Finally Trudy Phillips, the last member of this week's early shift, panicked and began to stumble and run toward Donna as the searing, burning pain in her throat increased. She had only moved a few meters forward before she lost consciousness and fell, catching a cable with her foot and dragging a computer monitor off a desk. It crashed to the ground, just inches from her face. Once the sound had faded and Trudy had died, the world became terrifyingly quiet.

Donna's instinctive reaction was to get out of the office and look for help, but as soon as she was outside she regretted having moved. The lift provided a brief enclosed haven of normality as it carried her down to the ground floor lobby, but the sliding doors then opened to reveal a scene of death and destruction on an incomprehensible scale. There were bodies all around the lobby. The security guard who had flirted with her less than half an hour ago was dead at his desk, slumped forward with his face pressed up against a CCTV monitor. One of the senior office managers—a short, overweight man in his late forties called Woodward—was trapped in the revolving door at the very front of the building, his wide gut wedged against the glass. Jackie Prentice, another one of her work friends, was sprawled on the floor just a few meters away from where Donna stood, buried under the weight of two more men, both dead. A thick, congealing dribble of blood spilled from Jackie's open mouth and had gathered in a sticky pool around her blanched face.

Without thinking, Donna pushed her way out through a side door and onto the street. Beyond the walls of the building the devastation appeared to have continued for as far as she could see in every direction. There were hundreds of bodies whichever way she looked. Numb and unable to think clearly, she walked away from the building and farther into town. As she approached the main shopping area of the city the number of bodies increased to such an extent that, in places, the pavements were completely obscured—carpeted with a still-warm mass of tangled corpses.

Donna had naturally assumed that she would find others like her who had survived the carnage. It seemed unlikely— impossible even—that she could be the only one who was left alive, but after almost an hour of picking her way through the dead and shouting for help, she had heard nothing and seen no one. She kept walking for a while longer, convinced that she might turn the next corner and find everything back to normal as if nothing had happened, but the ruination was apparently without end. Numbed by the incomprehensible magnitude of the inexplicable catastrophe, she eventually gave up, turned around, and made her way back to the tall office block.

The family home was a fifty-minute train journey away—more than two and a half hours by car. She could have gone back to her flat, but there didn't seem to be much point. Three months into a one-year work experience placement from business school, Donna had chosen to live, study, and work in a city over a hundred and fifty miles away from virtually everyone she knew. What she would have given to have been back with her parents in their nondescript, little three-bedroom semidetached house on the other side of the country. But what would she have found there? Had the effects of whatever happened here reached as far as her hometown? Had her parents survived like she had, or would she have found them dead too? She couldn't bear to think about what might or might not have happened to them.

The fact of the matter was, she eventually forced herself to accept, she was where she was and there was very little she could do about it. As impossible and unbelievable as her circumstances now were, she had no option but to try and pull herself together and find somewhere safe to sit and wait for something—anything—to happen. And the most sensible place to do that, she decided, was back in her office. Its height provided some isolation, she knew the layout, and it was clean, spacious, and relatively comfortable. She knew where she could find food and drink in the staff restaurant. Best of all, security in the office was tight. Access to the working areas was strictly controlled by electronically tagged passes, and from a conversation she'd had with an engineer who'd been running tests last week, she knew that the security system itself ran independent of the main supply. Regardless of what happened to the rest of the building, therefore, power to the locks remained constant, and that meant that she was able to securely shut out the rest of the world until she was ready to face it again. The advantage might only have been psychological, but it was enough. During those first few long hours alone, that extra layer of security meant everything to her.

Much of the rest of the first day had been spent collecting basic necessities, initially from just around the office, later from several of the closest city center shops. She found herself some warmer clothes, a mattress, a sleeping bag, and gas lamps from a camping store, enough food and drink to last her a while, and a radio and portable TV. By early evening she had carried everything up the many flights of stairs (she deliberately avoided the lifts—what if the power failed and she got stuck, she'd thought) and had made herself a relatively warm and comfortable nest in the farthest corner of her office. As the light faded at the end of the day she tried every means available to make contact with the outside world. Her mobile phone didn't work. She couldn't get anything more than a dial tone on any of the office phones (and she tried more than twenty different handsets) and she couldn't find anything other than static and silence on the radio and television. The streetlights around the building came on as usual, but with no one else left alive, the rest of the city remained ominously dark. Eventually Donna gave up trying and buried her head under her pillow.

The first night took an eternity to pass and the second day even longer. She only emerged from her hiding place on a couple of occasions when she absolutely had to. Just after dawn she crept around the perimeter of the office and looked down onto the streets below, initially to check whether the situation had changed, but also to confirm that the bizarre events of the previous day actually had taken place. During the dragging hours just gone, Donna had begun to convince herself that the death of many thousands of innocent people couldn't really have happened so swiftly, viciously, and without any apparent reason.

From where she was hiding underneath the desk, Donna caught sight of her dead friend Joan Alderney's outstretched right foot. Seeing the woman's corpse unnerved her to the point where she couldn't tear her eyes away. The close proximity of the body was a constant, unwanted reminder of everything that had happened and eventually she plucked up enough courage to do something about it. Fighting to keep her emotions and nausea in check, one at a time she dragged the bodies of each of her four work colleagues—stiff, inflexible, and contorted with rigor mortis— down to the far end of the office where she lay them side by side in the post room and covered them with a large dust sheet taken from another floor where decorators had been working.

The third morning began in as bleak and hopeless a manner as the second day had ended. Feeling slightly more composed, Donna crawled out from underneath the desk again and sat down in front of the computer that she used to use, staring at the monochrome reflection of her face in the empty screen. She had been trying to distract herself by writing down song lyrics, addresses, the names of the players in the football team she supported, and anything else she could remember on a scrap of paper, when she heard something. There was a noise coming from the far end of the office floor; the first noise she'd heard in hours. It was a tripping, stumbling, crashing sound which immediately made her jump up with equal measures of unexpected hope and sudden concern. Was her painful isolation about to be ended? She crept cautiously toward the other end of the long, rectangular-shaped building, her heart pounding.

"Hello," she said, her voice little more than a whisper but sounding uncomfortably loud, "is anybody there?"

There was no response. She took a few steps farther forward and then stopped when she heard the noise again. It was coming from the post room. Donna pushed open the heavy swinging door and stood and stared. Neil Peters—the manager she had watched fall and die in front of her just two days earlier—was moving. Swaying unsteadily on clumsy, barely coordinated feet, the dead man dragged himself across the room and thumped heavily into the wall, then turned around awkwardly and walked the other way. Instinctively Donna reached out and grabbed hold of him.

"Neil?"

The body stopped moving when she held it. There was no resistance or reaction, it just *stopped*. She looked deep into Neil's emotionless face. His skin was tinged with an unnatural green hue and his eyes were dark and misted, the pupils fully dilated. His mouth hung open, his lips puffed and cracked, and his tongue swollen like an oversized slug. His chin and neck appeared bruised, flecked with dried blood. Petrified, Donna released her grip and her dead manager immediately began to move again. He tripped over one of the bodies of the other three office workers on the floor, then slowly picked himself up. Donna stumbled back out through the doors, which swung shut after her, trapping the moving corpse inside. She glanced over to her right and pulled down on the top of a filing cabinet, bringing it crashing down in front of the door and blocking the way out.

For a while Donna stood there, numb with disbelief, and watched through a small glass window as Neil Peters's shell-like remains staggered around the room, never stopping. By chance the body occasionally turned and moved in her direction. Neil's dry, unfocused eyes seemed to look straight through her.

Breathing hard and trying not to panic, Donna left the office floor and stood on the stairs to put some distance between herself and what she'd just seen. The corpse of Sylvia Peters, the office secretary, lay in front of her, spread-eagled across the landing where she'd died earlier in the week. As she neared the body, a slow but very definite movement caught her eye. Donna watched as two of the fingers on the dead woman's left hand trembled and occasionally spasmed, clawing at the floor involuntarily. Sobbing with fear, Donna ran back to her hiding place on the ninth floor, pausing only to glance out of a window she passed and look down onto the world below.

The same bizarre and illogical thing was happening again and again down at street level. Most bodies remained motionless where they'd fallen but many others were now moving. Defying all logic, bodies which had laid motionless for almost two days were now starting to move.

Collecting up her things, Donna hurriedly made her way to the tenth floor (where she knew there were no bodies) and locked herself into a small, square training room. On her way back up the stairs, she realized that Sylvia Peters's body had gone.

2

Every door and window in the small, end-terraced house was either locked or blocked by furniture. Jack Baxter stood in silence in the corner of his bedroom and peered out from behind the curtain as yet another corpse tripped down the street and staggered away into the inky-black darkness of the night. What the hell was going on?

Returning home from a night shift early on Tuesday morning, he had been surrounded by people when all this had begun. Jack worked at a warehouse just outside the city center. The bus route which he took home followed a rough figure-eight loop past the warehouse, through the center of town, over to the suburb where he lived, then back again. At that time of morning the bulk of the passengers usually got off when they reached the center of the city, their working days just beginning, and, when it had happened—whatever *it* was—he had been one of only eight people left on board.

The first sign that something was wrong had been when an

old man, sitting on the same side of the bus, two rows in front of him, had started to wheeze and cough uncontrollably. His condition deteriorated dramatically in just a few seconds. Initially haunched forward, the pensioner had thrown himself violently back in his seat, fighting to breathe, his body convulsing uncontrollably. Jack had been out of his seat and about to help him when a young woman had yelled out in agony from the back of the bus. Her three children had been screaming and crying too. Helpless, he ran toward them but stopped and turned and ran back the other way when he realized that the driver of the bus was now also coughing and choking. He sprinted the length of the suddenly lurching vehicle and reached the driver, who was retching and gagging on the blood that was running down his throat. Jack tried to grab the wheel as the driver lost consciousness and slumped forward but he was too late to stop the bus from swinging out in a clumsy arc across the carriageway, smashing through the traffic coming the other way and eventually crashing into the front of a pub. The sudden impact threw him to the ground, his head smacking against the metal base of one of the seats and knocking him out cold.

He had no idea how long he'd been unconscious. When he finally came around his vision was blurred and he'd struggled to regain his balance. The driver and the rest of the passengers were dead. Using the emergency release lever he'd managed to force the door open and he stumbled out onto the street into a world suddenly filled with unparalleled and completely inexplicable carnage. As the people on the bus had died so, it seemed, had everyone else for as far as he could see in every direction. Numb with shock, Jack stood motionless in the middle of it all, his body remaining still while his eyes darted around the macabre scene, never daring to settle on anything for too long. He began to count the bodies—ten, twenty, thirty, and then more and more . . . the destruction appeared endless. For a while he'd waited expectantly for the silence to be shattered by the wail of approaching police, fire, and ambulance sirens, but none had come. With each passing minute the ominous quiet worsened. Eventually he'd been able to stand the eerie stillness no longer and he ran.

A breathless ten-minute sprint through a suddenly alien landscape had got Jack home. Things and places which had appeared ordinary, familiar, and nondescript when he'd left for work the previous evening had been transformed into twisted, bizarre, and grotesque sights. The supermarket where he'd done his shopping yesterday was on fire, unchecked flames devouring the entrance doors through which he'd walked a thousand times before. In the playground of the primary school at the end of his road he had seen the fallen bodies of parents surrounded by the smaller, uniformed corpses of their children. A car had driven into the front of a house seven doors down from his own. Through the rubble and dusty debris he'd seen the body of the owner of the house slumped dead in her armchair in front of the TV. What had happened made no sense. There were no obvious explanations and there was no one else left to ask for answers. Apart from Jack there didn't seem to be anyone else left alive. Somehow, in the midst of all this death and destruction, he alone had survived.

Jack had lost his wife Denise to cancer some fifteen months earlier. In some ways having suffered such an acute and immense loss back then made it easier for him to deal with what was happening now. He was used to coming home to a cold, quiet, and empty house and spending hour after hour alone, talking to no one. Even now, four hundred and thirty-seven days after she'd passed away (he still counted each day he spent without her), the memory of the physical and mental pain his wife had endured was a thousand times worse than anything he'd felt since everyone else had fallen and died.

Once he'd arrived back home, Jack had tried to make contact with the rest of the world. He'd tried every one of the thirty or so phone numbers in his address book but no one answered. He'd listened to the radio for a while. He'd expected to hear hissing static, but for a long time there was nothing, just an empty, endless silence. One station he'd found was still playing music. He listened hopefully and nervously as the last few notes of the final song faded away, only to be replaced by the same relentless quiet that was everywhere else. In his mind he pictured radio presenters, newsreaders, and engineers lying dead in their studios, by default still broadcasting the aftereffects of whatever it was that had killed them all.

Since then he had spent much of the time sitting upstairs, watching the world outside, hoping that this illogical nightmare would end as quickly as it had begun. But it hadn't. Looking out from one of the back rooms, Jack could see the body of his elderly neighbor, Stan Chapman, lying facedown and motionless in the middle of his lawn, still dressed in his pajamas. No one but Jack himself, it seemed, had been spared.

Because of his unsociable working hours, Jack's days had long operated in reverse to most everyone else's. In spite of everything, by noon on the first day he was having trouble staying awake. He had dozed through a long and disorientating afternoon and evening and had then spent what felt like forever sitting on the end of his bed in the darkness, wide awake, alone and petrified. And the next day had been even harder to endure. He did nothing except sit in silence and think frightening thoughts and ask himself countless questions which were impossible to answer. For a while he had contemplated going outside and looking for help but he had been too scared to venture any farther than halfway down the staircase before turning back and returning to the relative safety of the upstairs rooms. As the early light of Thursday morning began to creep across the ravaged landscape, however, what remained of Jack's world was turned on its head once again.

Just before seven o'clock a sudden metallic crashing noise had shattered the oppressive silence, the clattering sound taking forever to fade away into nothing. For a few seconds Jack hadn't dared move, paralyzed with nerves. He'd waited desperately for something to happen but, now that it finally had, he was almost too afraid to go and see what it was. Forcing himself to move, he slowly made his way down to the front door and, after crouching down and peering through the letterbox and seeing nothing, he opened it and went outside. In the middle of the road was a metal dustbin. Strangely relieved, Jack took a few steps toward the end of the drive, and looked up and down the deserted street. But it wasn't deserted. In the shadows of the trees on the opposite side of the road a solitary female figure was slowly moving away. Suddenly more confident, he sprinted the length of the street and grabbed hold of the woman's shoulder. She stopped moving instantly and just stood there, her back to him. Overcome with emotion, he hadn't stopped to wonder why she hadn't heard him or reacted to him in any other way. Instead he simply turned her around to face him, desperate to talk to someone else like him who had survived. But it was immediately obvious that this woman was just another victim of the scourge which had torn across the city. His shock and disbelief was such that he hardly reacted to her nightmarish appearance. She might have been moving, but this poor soul was as dead as the thousands of bodies still littering the silent streets.

Jack stared into her black, emotionless eyes, looking for an explanation. In the low light her yellowed skin appeared saggy and loose. Her mouth hung open as if she no longer had the energy to keep it shut and her head lolled heavily to one side. He let the body go and it immediately stumbled away, now moving in the opposite direction. Jack turned, sprinted back to his house, and locked and bolted the door behind him. He staggered into the kitchen and leaned against the sink for support, staring out into the garden and trying to make sense of what he'd just seen. His dark and disjointed thoughts were disturbed by the sudden appearance of his dead neighbor's drained white face at the window. The body had stumbled through a missing panel in the fence which Jack had been meaning to replace for the last three summers.

More than twelve hours had passed since Jack had seen the first body moving. He'd spent the rest of the day upstairs, hiding in his bedroom again. He packed a bag with clothes and food but when it came to leaving the house he was too scared to go. He knew he'd have to go outside again eventually, but for now the familiarity and relative security of his home was all he had left.

Even now he could hear the body of his elderly neighbor, crashing relentlessly around the back garden, never stopping.

3

Another endless night and morning alone was all that Jack could stand. He sat at the top of the stairs and reached the inevitable conclusion that he had to get out and try and find out what was happening, and the sooner he did it, the sooner he could get back. With his rucksack already packed he nervously locked up his home and left shortly after midday.

For a few precious minutes the autumn day felt reassuringly normal. It was typically cool and dry, yet threateningly dull and overcast. A brisk, gusting wind was fresh and welcome, blowing away the smells of death and burning which hung heavy in the air like an acrid fog.

When he reached the end of his road, Jack stopped, turned around, and took a few hesitant steps back toward his house, already craving the safety of being on the right side of a locked door again. Too frightened to move forward, but equally afraid of the consequences of turning tail and hiding alone in his home for days, possibly even weeks on end, he didn't know which way to turn. He stood in the middle of the street and sobbed like a child who'd lost its parents.

Jack eventually reached a compromise with himself. He decided he would walk a little way farther toward the city center, and after half an hour he would turn around and come back home. Tomorrow he would venture a little farther, then farther still the next day and the next day after that until he found other people like him. There had to be others, didn't there? He started walking again, wishing that he'd learned to drive like just about everyone else he knew had done as soon as they'd turned seventeen. He would have felt much safer in a car.

Jack stopped walking when he was halfway down Turnhope Street as the first moving body he'd seen since leaving the house slowly stumbled into view. He was just about able to cope with the corpses lying motionless on the ground, but the ones which moved were a different matter altogether. Despite the fact that they ignored him and didn't react to anything he did, he still felt threatened by their unnatural presence and impossible mobility. As the body (the stooping, uniformed remains of a male traffic warden) approached, he instinctively stood still and pressed himself against the wall of the nearest building, hoping that he would blend into the background unnoticed. The corpse staggered past without even lifting its head. It dragged its feet along the ground unbearably slowly and Jack watched as it listlessly walked away, its arms hanging heavy at its sides, swaying in time with its shuffling steps.

The intense silence was unbearable, almost completely uninterrupted. Apart from the occasional gust of wind blowing litter down the empty streets he heard nothing: no cars, planes, music, voices . . . and the quiet made everything else louder. The sound of his feet as they scuffed along the pavement sounded as if they'd been amplified a thousand times. Once or twice he cleared his throat, ready to shout out for help, but at the last moment he decided against it. As much as he wanted to find other people like him, he was more frightened of drawing attention to himself. And despite the fact there didn't seem to be anything or anyone else left but him, he didn't have the balls to take any chances. He was too scared. No, he wasn't just scared, he was damn well terrified.

Jack walked the length of Portsdown Park Road, which ran into Lancaster Road, which in turn led into Haleborne Lane and then merged with Ayre Street, one of the main routes into the heart of the city. In his allotted thirty minutes, Jack had barely covered a mile and a half. He hadn't seen anything or anyone apart from another thirty or so of the silent, stumbling bodies. Some of them—the majority, in fact—he had managed to ignore and pass with little difficulty. They looked, to all intents and purposes, relatively normal from a distance, just a little disheveled and unkempt and lacking in color, almost monochromatic. Once in a while, however, one of them would come along, which instantly filled him with nervous nausea and dread. The reanimation of the dead, it seemed, had been completely random and without any obvious logical criteria. Five minutes ago Jack had passed a body which had clearly been involved in a horrific accident. It had been male, he thought, but he couldn't be completely sure. The virtually naked body was burned from head to toe. There didn't appear to be a single patch of skin which hadn't been charred beyond recognition. The hair had been

23

burned away from the scalp and the face—or the black hole where the face had been—was unrecognizable, just a mangled, carbonized mass. Some strips of clothing still hung around the creature's emaciated frame, flapping in the breeze. Most of it, however, had either burned away or melted and fused with its blackened flesh. But somehow it kept moving. Ignorant to the damage and deformation it had suffered and oblivious to any pain or shock, the bloody thing just kept on moving. Its eyes were burned-out, empty sockets and it had no coordination, but still it kept on dragging itself forward, clumsily crashing into walls, parked cars, and other obstructions. It was the smell more than anything which tipped Jack over the edge. He'd caught a taste of the scent of scorched flesh on the breeze and had immediately dropped to his knees and emptied the contents of his stomach into the gutter.

Although he'd decided to turn back if nothing happened, the desperate desire to find someone else still alive kept Jack moving toward the center of town. As he neared the heart of the city, the full enormity of what had happened was made painfully apparent. The small and insignificant suburb where he lived had been brutally scarred by the devastation but that was nothing compared to the city center. Here, where there were far more shops, offices, factories, and other buildings, the scale of the destruction was overwhelming. Nothing seemed to have been left untouched by the silent and invisible killer which had struck early on Tuesday morning.

Walking down one side of a wide dual carriageway, he finally plucked up enough courage to shout out.

"Hello!" he yelled, frightening himself with the sound of his own voice. "Hello . . . Is there anybody there?"

Nothing. No surprise. He tried again.

"Hello . . ."

He stopped shouting and listened as his words echoed around the desolate street, bouncing off the walls of the empty buildings. Now that he seemed to be its only occupant, the world suddenly felt vast and he felt insignificant. In the far distance he heard a lone dog howling mournfully.

"Hello . . ." he shouted again.

Dejected, he wondered whether it was worth going on. He'd left his home with a minimal amount of hope, but now even that had evaporated away to nothing. But how could he possibly be the only one left? Out of millions—possibly billions—of people affected, how could he have survived when everyone else had died? Did it have anything to do with where he'd been when it had happened? Did he have a natural, inbuilt immunity? Was it because he worked nights? Was it the curry he'd eaten at the weekend, or the tablets for depression he'd been taking since Denise died? Nothing seemed beyond the realms of possibility anymore.

He was getting closer to the dead heart of the city with every step. Just one more minute then I'll turn back and head home, he repeatedly told himself. The main road gradually narrowed to a single lane in either direction and the sudden closeness of the tall buildings on either side made him feel trapped. He decided against shouting out again. There were even more bodies up ahead, a group of them. Or was it a gaggle of corpses?

25

he wondered. Or a clutch? He managed to walk past them with a newfound nonchalance, even plucking up the courage to push one of them out of the way when it staggered randomly into his path.

A door opened, and Jack froze instantly. He began to stagger quickly backwards as one of the creatures—a young girl dressed in a grubby, crumpled school uniform—emerged from inside a dark building and moved toward him at speed, arms outstretched. He tripped up the curb and barely managed to keep his balance, doing all he could to distance himself from the body which suddenly threw itself at him.

"Help me," the girl said, and he caught her in his arms. She was warm and she sobbed as he held her. She wasn't like the other corpses he'd seen: she had control and strength and she could speak and . . . and it took him almost a minute to accept that he had, at last, found another survivor. He held her tightly as if he'd known her for fifty years and not seen her for ten. He was no longer alone.

Suddenly feeling even more exposed than before, Jack checked around anxiously, then took the girl's hand and led her toward the entrance to the nearest building. It was a dental surgery—a cold, dark, and claustrophobically small private practice which still smelled slightly of antiseptic and mouthwash. The two of them sat down together on hard plastic seats in the waiting room, alongside three motionless corpses which had been waiting to be seen by the now-dead dentist since early Tuesday morning. A dental nurse was slumped across the counter to their right. The presence of the bodies didn't seem to matter anymore.

At first neither of them knew what to say.

"I'm Jack . . ." he eventually stammered awkwardly.

"I heard you shouting," she replied, still crying. "I didn't know where you were. I heard you but I couldn't see you, and then . . ."

"Doesn't matter," he whispered, stroking her hair and gently kissing the top of her head, hoping she didn't mind. "It doesn't matter."

"Have you seen anyone else?"

"No one. What about you?"

She shook her head, pushed herself away from him slightly, and sat up in her seat. He watched as she wiped her face.

"What's your name?"

"Clare Smith."

"And are you from around here, Clare?"

She shook her head again. "No, I live with my mum in Letchworth."

"So how did you end up in this part of town?"

"I'd been stopping at my dad's this weekend. We didn't have any school on Monday so I stayed with him an extra day and . . ."

She stopped talking and Jack watched helplessly as her sobs became a relentless stream of tears.

"Look," he said, trying to make it easier for her, "you don't have to tell me anything if you don't want to. If you want we could just—"

"What happened?" she asked suddenly, cutting across him and looking deep into his face for the first time. "What did this?"

Jack sighed and stood up and walked away.

"No idea," he replied, bending down and looking over the nurse's body through a frosted-glass hatch into a small office. "I was on my way home when it happened. I didn't see anything until it was too late."

"Dad was driving me to school," Clare said quietly, staring down at her feet. "He lives right on the other side of town so we were coming back through the city center . . ." She paused to wipe her eyes and clear her throat. "We stopped for the traffic lights and Dad just started to choke. I tried to help him but there was nothing I could do. He drove into the car in front and the car behind hit us. Dad just kept coughing and shaking until he died and I couldn't do anything to help him . . ."

Clare began to cry uncontrollably. Jack walked back to her and knelt down in front of her chair. She grabbed hold of him, burying her face in his chest. Still feeling a little awkward and unsure, he put his arms around her again and rocked her gently. She wiped her eyes and continued to talk between heavy sobs.

"I got out of the car to try and get some help, but it had happened to everyone. Everything had stopped and everyone was dead. We were stuck in the middle of the biggest crash you've ever seen. There were hundreds of cars all smashed into each other. I had to climb over them just to get to the side of the road . . ."

"It happened so quickly, Clare. No one had any time to react."

"So why are we still alive?"

"Who knows. I was just sitting on the bus trying to get home and . . ."

He stopped talking suddenly.

"And what . . . ?" Clare pressed.

"Shh . . ." he hissed, lifting a finger to his lips. He could hear something. He walked out of the waiting room, beckoning Clare to follow close behind. A twisting wooden staircase led up from the ground floor to the rest of the surgery. At the very top of the staircase were three doors leading to separate consulting rooms. Jack pushed the nearest door and it swung forward, revealing a small square room with a dead patient slouched in a large treatment chair, a dental nurse's corpse lying at his feet. On the other side of the room the stuporous body of a dentist—his once-clean white overalls now covered with seeping yellow and bloody brown stains—was trapped, its path blocked by the chair, the dead nurse, and an overturned trolley of medical equipment. The corpse staggered helplessly from side to side, going nowhere.

"Let's get out of here," Jack said quietly. He grabbed Clare's hand and led her back out onto the street.

4

Almost a hundred feet above the city center, Donna watched the world around her slowly begin to crumble and decay.

Although she felt constantly on the verge of panic, she somehow managed to maintain a surprising degree of control and, generally, was able to continue to think and act relatively rationally and sensibly. She wondered whether it was because she was in the place where she used to work. She had become used to switching off and detaching herself from her emotions in this gray and oppressive environment. In the same way she'd spent the last few months here processing customer instructions and paperwork, she now found herself having to process the remains of her life. Had she been at home with its familiar comfort and memories, she felt sure she'd have been overwhelmed by everything by now.

Hunger and other more rudimentary needs eventually forced her out from the training room at the far end of the tenth floor of the office block. At some point (she wasn't exactly sure when), the power in the building and surrounding area had failed. She found a collection of safety lamps and torches in a cabinet in the building manager's office on the ground floor which, she presumed, would have been used in the event of an emergency or a building evacuation. She added the lamps from downstairs to the collection of lighting equipment she'd already gathered and then, slowly and methodically, she spaced them around the windows on the tenth floor, eventually managing to work her way around almost three-quarters of the perimeter of the building.

There was a newfound determination to her actions.

Just after seven o'clock when the evening light began fading rapidly, she lit every lamp and switched on every torch. Her plan was simple. She was desperate to find other survivors but she didn't want to go outside and look for them. She guessed that anyone else left alive in the city would probably feel the same way. Rather than risk going out where she would be looking for a needle in a haystack, she instead decided that the most sensible thing she could do would be to stay put and let the rest of the world know where she was.

In the otherwise utter blackness of the night skyline, the lights in the windows of the office block lit up her location like a beacon.

It worked.

Paul Castle, a music store sales assistant in his early twenties, was painfully hungry but had been too afraid to leave the store where he'd worked and where his customers and colleagues had died in agony last Tuesday morning. He'd searched the entire building and, until now, had been able to find enough scraps to survive on. He'd known all along that going outside was inevitable, but he'd done all he could to put it off for as long as possible. Now he had no choice but to leave. It was that or starve.

Paul waited until nightfall before venturing out. He figured that the darkness would offer him some protection from the wandering bodies that he had seen staggering aimlessly up and down the streets outside. In their present state they didn't seem to pose much of a threat to him, but the additional camouflage that the night provided brought some welcome comfort and reassurance. As long as he managed to avoid dwelling on the fact that they had lain dead at his feet for the best part of two days before rising again, he was just about able to keep his fragile emotions in check.

In the low light of early evening, it became slightly easier to ignore the condition of the rest of the world. From across the street a staggering dead body looked almost the same as someone who was still alive and who still possessed control, coordination, and independence of thought. He had seen more than enough drunkards, addicts, and down-and-outs in the city center at night to be able to convince himself that this was just more of the same. Despite his nervousness, his comparative speed and agility made it possible for him to move among and around the bodies as if they were normal people trapped in a bizarre slow-motion replay of their lives.

There was little in the way of supermarkets or food stores in the city center. This was a place where people had worked and shopped for gifts and luxuries, where they had studied and partied and where they had been entertained in cinemas, theaters and clubs. Paul ran down a long concrete ramp close to the music store and then turned right and sprinted across the road in the direction of a newsagent and a high-class department store, Bartram's, where he knew he'd find a fairly well-stocked food hall.

Now that he was outside, Paul found the darkness unexpectedly unnerving. It unsettled him to see so many huge shop fronts and expensive window displays standing dark and unlit. Even the streetlights were off around here. He found himself running through blackness and into more blackness. He stopped for a moment to catch his breath and climbed up onto the top of a tall lump of concrete-and-steel street art. Light rain fell around him as he stood there with hands on hips, looking down over miles and miles of lightless city, right into the suburbs. Breathless, he peered as far as he could into the distance, desperate to see something that might give him a little hope.

Feeling empty and numb, Paul continued on toward the store and forced his way into the building over a heap of dead shoppers stuck in the doorway. He followed unlit signs to the food hall, where he filled several plastic carrier bags with food and drink, then loaded them into a shopping trolley. Pausing only to allow another one of the pitiful cadavers to drag itself past the front of the building, he weaved around the corpses in the door, pushed the trolley back out into the night, and wearily began to work his way back to his store. For a while he thought about trying to get home. He'd considered it a few times before but it seemed too far to try and travel alone while the situation remained so uncertain. Truth was he was a coward looking for excuses not to take risks, but it didn't matter. There was no one left to criticize or condemn him. Maybe he'd find a car and try and drive home in the morning—but then again, maybe not.

The trolley made an uncomfortably loud rattling and clattering noise as he pushed it along the block-paved streets. Still disorientated by the darkness, he paused to get his bearings. He pushed the trolley to one side and leaned against a bus shelter to drink from a carton of fruit juice which he'd taken from the store. He opened the carton and drank from it thirstily, the strong citrus flavor suddenly revitalizing him. He'd hardly drunk anything all day and he emptied the carton in a few large gulps. It was when he tipped his head back to drain the last few precious drops of juice that he saw the light.

Christ, he thought. He could see light.

Dropping the empty carton in the gutter, he took a few steps away from the bus shelter to get a better view. At the far end of the road adjacent to the one he'd been following, he could see the outline of a tall office block which, until now, had been obscured from view by other buildings. And there was no mistaking the fact that, almost halfway up the side of the huge tower, in the midst of the darkness everywhere else, he could definitely see light. And where there was light, he quickly decided, there had to be people.

Suddenly filled with renewed energy, he pushed the shopping trolley farther into the shadows (planning to collect it later), then turned and ran toward the office block. A body appeared from out of nowhere, its random path by chance crossing his own. Without thinking he shoved it away to the side, ignoring it as it tripped and crumpled silently to the ground. Paul ran the length of the street in seconds, weaving around more aimless corpses, glancing up at the building ahead of him, shielding his eyes from the spitting rain, making sure he could still see the dull yellow glow coming from the windows high above.

The main revolving door at the bottom of the tower was blocked but a side entrance remained clear and he pushed his way inside. Paul climbed the first three flights of stairs at speed but then slowed dramatically, his adrenaline-fuelled excitement quickly overcome by fatigue. With every step he took, so his unease and anxiety increased. But he couldn't stop. For the first time since all of this had begun there was a very real chance he was about to find someone else alive.

Fourth floor—nothing.

Fifth floor—nothing.

Sixth floor—bodies.

Paul stepped over a corpse which was sprawled on the ground at the bottom of another flight of stairs before reaching out for the handrail and dragging himself up again. His mind was starting to play tricks on him now. Had he actually seen a light at all? Was he going to be able to find the right floor? He forced himself to keep climbing.

Seventh floor.

Eighth floor.

Ninth floor.

Tenth.

This was it. He could see the light even before he'd stepped off the staircase and onto the landing. A warm yellow glow shone through the small windows in the doors which separated the office from the rest of the world. Panting heavily with the effort of the frantic climb, Paul shook and yanked furiously at the door handle but it didn't move.

Inside the office, Donna froze. She was back in the training room again, curled up in a sleeping bag on a comfortable swivel chair in the corner. Every nerve and fiber in her body suddenly tensed. She didn't dare move.

Paul shook the door again, then banged on it with his fist. He couldn't see or hear anyone but that didn't matter, the light was more than enough reason for him to keep trying to force his way inside. He took a couple of steps back and then shoulder-charged the door. It rattled and shook in its frame but still it didn't open.

The landing was almost twenty feet long and five feet wide with access through double doors at either end into open-plan office space. Paul had turned left at the top of the stairs toward the strongest source of light, but the training room where Donna had been sheltering was to the right. She picked up a torch and cautiously tiptoed to the exit nearest to her. She shone the light through the small window and peered into the darkness, sure that she could see some movement at the far end of the landing.

Sensing he was being watched, Paul turned around quickly. Donna quickly pointed the torch down to the ground, trying to stay out of sight, but Paul had seen her. He ran the length of the landing.

"Let me in," he yelled, hammering furiously against the door. "For Christ's sake, let me inside . . ."

He leaned against the door and pressed his face against the glass, breathing hard. For a moment Donna did nothing. Then, slowly, the reality of the situation dawned on her. The bodies

36

that were able to move couldn't speak as far as she was aware. They couldn't make decisions or react with any amount of control either. So the person on the other side of the door had to be a survivor, didn't he? She flicked her pass at the sensor on the wall, and the door immediately unlocked and opened inward. Paul fell into the office and collapsed on his knees in front of her.

"Are you . . . ?" she started to say.

He looked up at her, tears rolling down his face, and then picked himself up and reached out for her. Locked in an awkward, but welcome embrace, Paul and Donna stood together in silence, both reveling in the sudden closeness of another living human being.

5

By the time Clare and Jack reached the center of the city it was almost completely dark. Neither of them wanted to be outside at night. The world had been turned on its head and ripped apart in the last week and nothing could now be taken for granted. In daylight it was difficult enough to try and keep track of what was happening around them. In darkness it would be virtually impossible.

Jack gently pushed Clare toward Bartrams department store. A huge and imposing building that had long been a focal point for city shoppers. Now, drenched in crimson-black gloom and crisscrossed by angular shadows cast by the moon above, its tall, gray walls and many small, square windows made it appear unnervingly gothic, almost prison-like.

"We can stop here tonight," Jack whispered, deliberately keeping his voice low. "There'll be food and stuff inside. We'll be okay here."

Clare didn't reply. Exhausted and dejected, it was all she

could do to put one foot in front of the other and keep moving forward. She hadn't said very much since those few tearful sentences when they'd first met and a few grunted words since then had been all. Jack didn't push her. He understood her pain. He was hurting too, but he'd suffered loss like this before.

"I know it's hard," he'd said foolishly a short time earlier as they'd walked along the remains of the high street. "My missus died last year. I know how you're feeling. You think you're hurting so much that you'll never get over it but you will. Believe me, it will get easier."

"How can it get better?" she'd demanded. "How can it ever get any easier when I've lost my mum and dad and everyone else?"

Jack hadn't tried to respond. She was right. At least he'd known why Denise had died and they'd both known it was coming. Clare's loss had been completely unexpected and without any obvious cause. He'd watched her as they'd walked together. How terrified must she have been? He thought about his nephew Georgie who'd turned five a fortnight ago and wondered whether he was still alive. Maybe he'd survived? Or maybe it was better he hadn't . . . for a second Jack pictured him alone at home. Georgie had done well in reception class at school. He'd learned to read a handful of simple words and he could write his name. He could dress himself, he could count up to twenty and, if he really tried, he could just about tie his shoelace in a proper double-bow. But Georgie couldn't cook. He wouldn't know what was wrong with him or be able to find medicine if he got ill. He couldn't light a fire to keep himself warm. He couldn't defend himself against attack. He simply couldn't survive alone . . .

Their eventual arrival at Bartram's presented Jack with a welcome distraction from his increasingly dark and hopeless thoughts. The large store had just opened for business when the disease, virus, or whatever it was had struck on Tuesday (Jack had decided that some kind of germ was the most likely explanation). A row of large glass doors along the front of the building had remained open, allowing most of the dead shoppers who had subsequently risen inside the shop to stumble back out onto the street.

Jack and Clare wearily worked their way up through the store, floor by floor. From the ground floor they collected food and extra clothing. On the first floor there was a small hardware department where they found torches and lights. Using the motionless escalators running up through the center of the building as a staircase, they climbed up to the second-floor furniture department. The higher they went, the fewer bodies they found. The clumsy figures couldn't climb up stairs but they were obviously prone to tripping and falling down them. The solitary moving body that they did find on the second floor (trapped between a chest of drawers, a wardrobe, and another corpse in a bedroom furniture display) offered no resistance as Jack bundled it into a store cupboard and blocked its way out with a set of bunk beds.

They spent several hours sitting on an expensive leather sofa, picking at the food they'd collected and sharing a few brief, fragmented conversations. Although it was early, the darkness, silence, and never-ending mental strain of the day combined to make it feel much later. Everything suddenly seemed to take a hundred times more effort than it had before. And added to that, everything they did reminded them both of all they had so abruptly lost. By torchlight Jack flicked through a TV listings magazine he'd found in a dead shopper's bag, knowing none of the programs would now ever be shown. Most, probably all, of the celebrities pictured within its glossy pages were dead. In any event none of it really mattered. What good were actors, presenters, and celebrities now? What good had they ever been?

"We'll have more luck tomorrow, I'm sure of it," he whispered hopefully (although not entirely convincingly) to Clare.

"What do you mean?"

"We'll find someone else."

"Where?"

"I don't know. Look, Clare, this is a huge city. There must be more people alive somewhere. You and I can't be the only ones left, can we?"

She shrugged her shoulders.

"Well, we haven't seen anyone else, have we?"

"They must be sheltering. I stayed at home for a while before I came out here; I bet there are hundreds of people sitting in their houses waiting for something to happen. They'll have to come out sooner or later to get food and drink and . . ."

Clare wasn't listening. She was crying again. He knew he couldn't do anything to relieve her pain and fear, but as the only adult around, Jack couldn't help but feel responsible for her. Very cautiously he rested a gentle hand on her shoulder and then, when she didn't shrug him off, he pulled her closer. Half-expecting her to recoil and push him away, he was surprised when she did the opposite and leaned her full weight against him.

41

"When is this going to end?" she sobbed, drawing her knees up and making herself as small as possible.

"Don't know," he answered honestly, wishing he could be more positive and say something that might actually help. "Hey, do you like this sofa?" he asked suddenly, deliberately trying to talk about something trivial and unimportant instead.

"Not bothered, why?"

"You seen the price of it?"

She was leaning on the price label. She sat up and looked at it.

"Is that expensive? I've never bought a sofa."

"Expensive?" he said, shaking his head in mock despair. "It's bloody outrageous. Me and Denise kitted out our whole house for just a little bit more than that a few years back. It's this shop," he continued. "It was always for people that had money or those that wanted to make it look like they had."

"My mum liked this shop," Clare said quietly, still crying faintly. "She used to bring us here when we were little."

"I think everyone's mums used to bring them here."

"What, yours too?"

"Yes, been here for years, this place has. It used to be the only place around that sold school uniforms. I used to get dragged here at the end of the summer holidays to get kitted out for the year. You'd see all your mates here with their mums in the last week before school started back. And shoes too. We used to get our shoes from here."

"Me too."

"Me and my brother both hated it."

"Me too."

"You could see the other kids going through exactly the same thing. There would be loads of us all lined up against the wall to have our feet measured. And we'd all start the next school term with the same shoes . . ."

Clare managed a stifled laugh and sniffed back more tears.

"I'm tired," she said quietly.

"Go to bed, then," he said, shining his torch across the shop floor to a line of double beds. He got up and walked over to the beds, then took a duvet and pillows from a display rack and tore off the plastic packaging. Clare sat down on the bed in the middle of the row of seven.

"You going to be all right here?" he asked as he passed her a pillow.

"I'll be fine," she answered. "Where will you be?"

"Right here," he said as he opened more bedding and threw it onto the bed next to Clare's. He dragged a small bedside table across the room, wedged it between their beds and put a lamp on it. The small circle of yellow-orange light it produced was surprisingly comforting.

6

"So there I am," Paul explained to Donna, "I'm sitting on the train as it's coming into the station and I knew something wasn't right. I remember hearing the first few people starting to panic around me but I wasn't thinking straight. All I could think about was the speed. I mean, we were just minutes away from the station and the driver hadn't started slowing down. I've done that journey five times a week virtually every week for the last year and a half and I know where the train should start slowing down and where the brakes should kick in and . . ."

He stopped talking and turned toward the window to wipe a tear from the corner of his eye, hoping Donna hadn't noticed. They were sitting across from one another in the training room, both still trying to get used to the fact that they were no longer alone.

"So what did you do?"

"By then people were already dying," he continued. "Everywhere I looked they were dropping all around me. But I knew we were going to crash and that was all I could think about. I wasn't thinking about the rest of them, I just got down on the floor and covered my head with my hands and . . ."

"And . . . ?"

"And we hit something, but I was lucky. Nothing seemed to happen for ages and then I felt the impact. It was a real fucking wrench, you know? It threw me right forward and I could hear metal groaning and breaking. I swear I'd have been badly hurt if it wasn't for the bodies. There were so many of them . . . they were like padding all around me. Once the train stopped I managed to smash my way out through a window and climb out onto the track. We'd gone into the back of another train that was still at the platform. Christ knows how we managed to stay on the rails."

"Were you hurt?"

"I did this," Paul replied, lifting up his shirt and turning around to show her his back. Even though the light was poor Donna could clearly see a huge purple welt running diagonally from his right shoulder blade down toward his left kidney.

"Still painful?"

"Guess so. Truth is, I've hardly thought about it since everything happened."

"So where did you go?"

"I went to work. Christ, there's conditioning for you. I just didn't know what else I could do. I couldn't get home and I couldn't think of anywhere else to go. I figured that if I was at work then I'd at least have some shelter and protection. I knew where everything was."

"I know what you mean. That's why I'm still here."

"You worked here?"

She nodded.

"Doing what?"

"Data processing for a bank, not that it matters now."

"Typical, isn't it," Paul sighed. "You spend most of your life trying to get out of work, then you end up stuck here when everything goes tits-up."

"So was there anyone else around when you got there?"

"There were plenty of people around," he replied, "but no one else was alive. Jesus, all the people I'd been working with just the day before were dead. All those people that I'd known for ages just gone . . . You get to know the people you work with, don't you? I had mates there and we'd been out drinking at the weekend and now they're . . ."

He stopped talking and looked up at the ceiling to avoid eye contact, trying not to lose control and start crying again. Donna sat and watched him from the other side of a wide gray desk. She said and felt nothing. Somehow she'd managed so far to distance herself from the pain. Perhaps it was the shock of everything that had happened, she thought. Maybe it would hit her later? Whatever the reason, inside she felt as dead as the thousands of bodies lying rotting on the streets outside, as if every nerve in her body had been cauterized. She didn't seem to feel anything anymore. She knew that was probably a bad thing but she didn't care. For now it was helping.

"Have some food," she said, unable to think of anything more constructive to say. She pushed a packet of biscuits across the desk. Paul shook his head. "You really should eat something."

"No thanks."

"Drink?"

She offered him a half-empty bottle of water. He nodded and wiped his mouth on his sleeve before taking the bottle from her and drinking thirstily.

"So what do we do now?" he asked as he screwed the lid of the bottle back on and passed it back.

"You tell me," Donna replied abruptly.

"I mean, we can't just sit here, can we?"

"What else is there to do?"

"Christ, we should do something. We should get out there and find other people. See if we can actually find someone who knows what's going on . . ."

"Bloody hell, Paul, I haven't seen anyone else alive apart from you. I haven't found anyone else who's still breathing, so what chance have we got of finding someone who knows what's happened?"

"I know, but I—"

"I don't want to go out until I have to," she continued, interrupting. "Right now I just want to stay as far away as I can from those bloody things out there."

Her voice was flat, and tired and her message clear. Paul didn't bother trying to argue. He got up and made himself a makeshift bed in the corner from some of the clothes and blankets Donna had amassed.

He lay there in silence and stared into the darkness for hours. Donna sat back in her chair and did the same.

7

On the outermost edge of the very heart of the city, less than a mile from the office block where Donna and Paul were hiding, was a modern and recently renovated university campus. The campus was vast and sprawling, its most prominent feature a huge, newly built, redbrick accommodation block, the front of which ran parallel to a stretch of the six-lane ring road which encircled the heart of the city. Parts of the university had been absorbed into the local neighborhood. The medical school, for example, was nestled alongside one of the city's main hospitals. With specialist dental, children's, and skin and burns units, the hospital itself had for many years been fundamental to the continuing overall health of the city's population. Tonight, however, only one doctor remained on duty. Tonight, there was only one doctor left alive.

The new accommodation block had enough individual rooms to house several hundred students. In the days since the disaster, somewhere in the region of fifty survivors had gathered there; no one was exactly sure how many. Some had found their way there by chance, a few dull lights and occasional signs of movement revealing the survivors' presence to the otherwise empty world. Others had been in or around the hospital or university when the nightmare had first begun. Dr. Phil Croft, the last remaining medic, had just started his Tuesday morning rounds. An entire ward full of people had died around him, and he'd been unable to help any of them. He'd just discharged a young lad called Ashley with a clean bill of health after his recent appendectomy. Seconds after finishing his examination of the boy and telling his parents they could take him home, the helpless child lay dead at his feet. And it hadn't just been the children. The nurses, parents, cleaners, helpers, orderlies, his fellow doctors and consultants too—everyone else on the ward had been struck down and killed within minutes of the death of the first.

But even now that the population had been slashed from millions to, it appeared, less than hundreds, Croft was still on duty. It was something that came naturally to him; an instinctive, inbuilt response. One of the remaining survivors needed medical attention and he felt duty bound to provide it.

He walked slowly through the uncomfortably quiet building to the room where the woman who needed him laid. The corridor was dark with doors into individual student rooms on either side like a no-frills hotel. Using a torch to guide him, he glanced into a couple of the rooms as he passed, the unexpected light causing mild panic among those people who cowered there in the darkness. Apart from a handful of people who had begun to group together, the majority of survivors chose to remain up here in frightened isolation, almost too afraid to move or even to speak.

The doctor found the room where the woman was resting. She was very attractive—tall, well-toned, strong, and nine months pregnant with her first child. Croft was strangely drawn to Sonya Farley. His girlfriend—Natasha, a nurse in the burns unit—was dead. In those horrific first few minutes on Tuesday morning he had run straight from his building across to where she'd been on duty and had found her lying lifeless on the ground along with everybody else. She'd been eight weeks pregnant. They hadn't had a chance to tell anyone about the baby yet, not even their parents. They'd only just got over the shock of the unexpected pregnancy themselves. Tonight Croft found that focusing his efforts and attention on Sonya helped to slightly ease the constant, gnawing pain he felt inside. It somehow made it easier for him to cope with his loss, knowing that he might still be able to help Sonya bring her baby into the world. And Christ alone knew that Sonya deserved help. When everyone else had died, she'd been sitting in the middle of a huge traffic jam on the main motorway leading out of town. Days overdue, terrified and in agony, she'd walked alone through miles of horror and devastation to get to the hospital.

Croft checked Sonya over and then, satisfied that she was sleeping soundly and all was well, he headed back downstairs to the large assembly hall where several of the survivors had begun to congregate. He found the lack of any noise or conversation in there even harder to handle than the solitude and he kept walking, crossing the room diagonally and leaving through another exit. He couldn't stand the silence, but he completely understood it. What was there to talk about? Did any of the people here have anything in common with each other apart from the fact they were still alive? Even if they did, chances were that whatever interests they may once have shared were redundant now. What was the point of talking to anyone else about your taste in food, film, music, books, or anything anymore? And as every survivor who did speak inevitably found to their cost, it didn't matter who you talked to or what you tried to talk about, every single conversation began and ended with pointless conjecture about what had happened to the rest of the world.

Croft needed nicotine. He walked the length of the next corridor then took a sharp right and sat on a step halfway down a short staircase which led to a glass-fronted entrance door. This small, secluded area had become something of a smokers' corner and two other survivors—Sunita, a student who lived in the building where they were sheltering, and Yvonne, a legal secretary from a firm of solicitors on the other side of the ring road— were already there, smoking their cigarettes and staring out into the darkness. Croft had successfully kicked the habit a couple of years ago but had started again yesterday. It didn't seem to matter anymore. He lit his cigarette and acknowledged the two women, who turned around to see who it was had joined them.

"You all right, Dr. Croft?" Yvonne asked. Perhaps out of respect for his position, few people used his first name. As a result, even fewer people knew it. He didn't much care and responded to Dr. Croft or, more usually, just Croft. After all he'd been through, he didn't feel like Phil any more. That person was long gone. He nodded and blew a cloud of gray-blue smoke out into the still air.

51

"I'm okay," he replied, his voice quiet and tired. "You two?"
Sunita nodded but didn't speak.

"My Jim," Yvonne said softly, looking out of the window again, "he used to love the dark. Sometimes, when he couldn't sleep, he'd get up and sit in the bay window at the back of the house and watch the sun come up. He used to love it when the birds started singing. If he was feeling romantic he'd wake me up and take me downstairs with him. Didn't happen often, mind."

Yvonne smiled fleetingly, then looked down at the ground as the sound of birdsong in her memory was swallowed up by the all-consuming silence again, leaving her feeling empty and alone. She wiped away a tear. She was in her early fifties but the strain of the last few days had left her looking much older. Her usually impeccably styled hair was frayed and untidy, her once smart business suit now crumpled. Sunita sensed her grief and put a hand on her shoulder and pulled her closer. She knew that Yvonne's husband had worked in an office across town and that, on the first morning, she'd gone there and found him dead at his desk, facedown in a pile of papers.

"I can handle the dark as long as I'm not on my own," Sunita said. "When I'm on my own my mind starts to play tricks. I start convincing myself that there's someone else there."

"You'd be lucky to find anyone else these days," the doctor said. "Anyway, sod the dark, I'm having enough trouble trying to deal with what's happening in the light," he admitted.

"You worked out what's going on yet?" Yvonne asked innocently, looking out of the window again. Croft shook his head, and kept his mouth shut to hide his sudden frustration and annoyance. Why did everyone assume that just because he was a doctor he'd somehow be able to explain their impossible situation? Christ, no one had ever come across anything like the virus or disease or whatever it was that had killed so many people in such a short period of time, and to the best of his knowledge no one had ever got up again after lying dead for two days either. He laughed to himself at how stupid that sounded. Nothing had ever happened like this before so of course he didn't know what the hell had caused it. As angry and frustrated as he suddenly felt, he forced himself to bite his tongue and not say anything. He felt like screaming at Yvonne and telling her to go and look for the answers to her stupid fucking questions in a fucking medical encyclopedia, but he knew that wouldn't achieve anything other than make an already impossible situation even more unbearable. Instead he just took a deep breath and sucked in another lungful of smoke. He reminded himself that Yvonne wasn't trying to wind him up. She was just trying to get through this like everyone else.

"You checked on Sonya?" Sunita asked.

"Just now."

"She all right?"

"She's fine. She's sleeping."

"Lucky cow," Yvonne muttered under her breath.

Croft finished his cigarette and dropped the glowing stub onto the floor and ground it out with his foot. Since the power had failed it was as dark inside the building as out. The brightest lights were the glowing ends of Sunita's and Yvonne's cigarettes still waving through the air. Exhausted, the doctor closed his eyes and tried unsuccessfully to clear his mind.

"You see that young lad who came in this morning?"

53

Yvonne asked Sunita. "Poor little bugger. Could only have been six or seven years old. One of the others spotted him running down the ring road. Said his mum had died and he'd come into town to try and find his dad. Wouldn't be told that he was probably dead too. Reckons he's going out to look for him again in the morning . . ."

"How are we supposed to explain this to the children?" Sunita sighed. "If *we* can't make sense of what's happening, how are we supposed to make them understand?"

"Depends how old they are," Croft said, lifting his head.

"Why?"

"Because kids of a certain age will accept anything you tell them," he explained. "I almost envy them. A two-year-old will grow up thinking this is how it's always been, won't they? Bloody hell, imagine how much easier the last few days would have been if you hadn't had to spend hours and hours trying to work everything out?"

"But those poor kids," Yvonne continued, not really listening. "Imagine losing your parents and being on your own like that."

"We've probably all lost our parents," Sunita said.

"I know, but—"

Yvonne was interrupted by a sudden crash as a body smashed into the glass double-doors directly in front of her. Nervously, she stumbled back. Croft jumped to his feet and steadied her. Curious, he took a couple of steps closer to the door and looked at the corpse. Its swollen, parchment-colored face was pressed hard against the glass and it moved slowly along from left to right, leaving behind a long smear of grease and a trail of dark brown, germ-filled drool. When it reached the end of the window it clumsily turned around and began moving back in the opposite direction.

"What the hell is going on here?"

"What's the matter?" Sunita asked. She stared at the creature, her face screwed up with disgust. It didn't look any different from the thousands of other corpses she'd already seen, as grotesque as any of them. She hated the way their faces now appeared swollen, lumpy, and misshapen, how their skin was blistered and discolored, how their mouths all hung open in a chorus of silent moans . . .

"I don't like this," the doctor admitted. He moved closer still and studied the figure's awkward, almost staccato movements. "This one's not like the others."

"Why?"

"Because it isn't going away."

"What?"

"Look at it. By now it should have turned around and fucked off again. It's like it's staying here for a reason. It's almost as if it knows we're in here."

"Like hell," Sunita said quickly. "You've got to be kidding . . ."

"Give me another explanation, then? I tell you, ladies, this body is watching us."

As if to prove his point, he moved even closer to the glass until his face was just inches away from the cadaver. He moved across to his right and then, painfully slowly, the body did the

55

same. He moved back again and, after a few seconds' delay as it shuffled itself around, the corpse copied. Its dark eyes, covered with a milky white film, seemed to be trying to follow him.

"So what does it mean?" Yvonne asked from halfway up the staircase. She was peering down through the railings like a frightened child.

"One of two things," Croft replied, not taking his eyes off the body outside. "Either this one has somehow been less affected than the others, or . . ."

"Or what?" Sunita pressed anxiously.

"They're changing."

8

Paul got up when the rising sun began to shine through the office block windows. He didn't want to move but his bed was less than comfortable and the pressure on his bladder had become too much to stand. Using a security pass which Donna had taken from around the neck of a corpse, he stumbled out onto the landing and went down the single flight of stairs to the nearest toilet. Tripping over a body in the half-light, he crashed noisily through the door into the bathroom which was cold, dark and unpleasant. Another body was slumped on the ground in one of the cubicles, sitting in a dried-up puddle of brown, its trousers down around its bloated ankles. An eye-watering, stagnant smell hung heavy in the air.

Still drugged with sleep and eager to get away from the bodies and back to the relative comfort of the office, Paul tripped again on his way out of the toilet after he'd finished, falling clumsily and knocking a cleaner's bucket up against a radiator. The sound of metal on metal echoed up and down the entire length of the immense staircase, seeming for a few lingering moments to fill the whole building with noise.

When he returned to the tenth floor Donna was awake. More than that, she was up and alert, quickly changing her clothes and tying up her long hair.

"What's the problem?" he asked, immediately concerned. She had no reason to get up so quickly. She had no real reason to get up at all.

"I heard something," she answered breathlessly as she tucked her shirt into her jeans.

"What?"

"Don't know, that's why I'm going to look."

"It was probably me," he said nervously. "It's still dark out there. I fell over a body on my way down the stairs and I almost went right over on the way back up. I bet that's all it was . . ." He stopped talking. Donna was still shaking her head.

"It wasn't you. It was upstairs. Right above us."

"But you said you'd already been upstairs. You said there was nothing up there."

"Apart from a couple of bodies."

"So was that what you heard?"

"I don't know. It was probably nothing. I'm just going to go and have a look around. I'll only be a couple of minutes."

"It must have been me," Paul continued to babble, desperately searching for an explanation which didn't involve anyone or anything else. "Like I said, I kicked a bucket into a radiator. It made a hell of a noise."

Tired of listening to him talking, Donna turned around, reached out for the door handle, and froze. Through the small glass panel in the door she could see a face staring back at her. Even though the light was poor she could tell immediately that it was an emotionless, dead face. The bloody thing was just standing there, staring straight at her.

"Christ," she cursed as she stumbled back in surprise.

"What is it?"

"One of those bodies," she whispered, rooted to the spot.

"So?"

"So the damn thing's watching me!"

"What are you talking about?"

He began to walk toward her, but stopped short when he saw the corpse on the other side of the door. Completely silent and largely still but for an occasional unsteady swaying, its eyes moved from side to side, looking from Donna to Paul and back again. It didn't look any different from the others they'd seen: it was male, slouched forward with rounded shoulders, discolored skin with occasional ruptures, glistening with the seeping signs of early stage decay . . . It hadn't been there when he'd returned from the toilet minutes earlier, so could it have followed him back?

"Why doesn't he go?" Donna asked. "He should just go away like the rest of them. Why's he staying here?"

Paul crept forward again to get a better view. He waved his hand in front of the glass but there was no immediate response.

"Think it's watching us?" he asked. "Maybe it's—" The creature outside threw itself against the door, immediately silencing him. Paul and Donna both instinctively moved back and watched as it did it again and again—shuffling backward a step, then staggering forward and slamming up against the door.

"I'm going to let him in," Donna said, her mouth dry and her pulse racing.

"What? Are you out of your bloody mind? You don't know what it'll do if you—"

"And you don't know either. For God's sake, he's trying to get to us. He wants help, he must. He's different from the others . . ."

"But you can't just assume . . ."

Paul's words were wasted; Donna had already made up her mind. The man's body standing in front of her looked as diseased as all the others, its movements as slow and labored as the rest, but it appeared to have retained a basic level of control, and that separated it from every other corpse she'd so far seen. The body in the corridor continued to thump against the door then stagger back. Donna flicked her pass at the sensor beside the door and pulled it open. The body stopped.

"See," she said, relieved. "I told you—"

The creature lunged toward her, knocking her off balance and sending her thudding back into the wall. With sudden energy—uncoordinated but unmistakably savage in intent—the remains of the rotting fifty-two-year-old man clawed at Donna. Paul ran toward the obnoxious cadaver and grabbed it from behind, wincing with disgust as he tightened his grip, feeling its cold, leathery flesh give way under the increasing pressure of his fingers. With surprisingly little effort he yanked the body away and threw it to the ground. Regardless of what it had just done, it was still little more than a shell: an empty human husk.

"Bloody thing," Donna spat. She pushed Paul out of the way and stood over the corpse, which was already struggling to pick itself back up again. It leaned over to one side and with clumsy, swollen hands, lunged for her again.

"We've got to kill it."

"How do we do that, then?" Donna yelled, shoving it back down with her foot. "Fucking thing's been dead since Tuesday."

"I don't know!" Paul screamed back at her. Mounted low on the wall just to the side of the entrance door was a fire extinguisher. He grabbed it quickly, lifted it from its bracket, and held it over the creature's head. Donna pushed down harder on its bony chest, pinning it to the floor. It didn't have the strength to fight her off.

"Do it. For God's sake, just do it!"

Paul held the extinguisher high above the corpse but didn't strike. With a mix of disgust and fascination, he watched its head thrashing tirelessly from side to side. Its yellow-green, pockmarked skin seemed saggy and ill-fitting and its black, gaping mouth opened and closed continually, making only the faintest rattling, rasping sound.

"Do it!" Donna yelled again.

Paul didn't move. Frozen. Terrified. Again the body tried to lunge and its sudden movement finally forced him into action. With his eyes screwed shut, he slammed the base of the metal cylinder down onto its head. It hit the side of its face with a dull thud and a faint cracking sound as the cheekbone fractured. With the sickening taste of bile rising in his throat, he lifted the fire extinguisher again and hammered it down, this time completely caving in the back of its skull. The body finally lay still.

"Let's get it out of here," he said, dropping the bloodied

extinguisher and letting it roll away. Donna held the door open as he dragged the creature out by its feet, leaving behind a thick trail of dark red, almost black blood on the pale purple carpet. He pulled it out through the landing door and dumped it on the staircase, too afraid to go any farther. He noticed there were more bodies on the stairs now. Jesus Christ, he could see another three of the damn things—one tripping down toward him from the floor above, two more dragging themselves up from the floor below. He sprinted back to the office. The farthest forward of the dead managed to stumble through the landing door after him before it swung completely shut.

For more than an hour they were too afraid to move or even make a sound. Hiding behind a hastily built barricade of desks in the training room, Donna and Paul sat close together. Occasionally one of them would pluck up enough courage to peer out into the main office again. They could just about see out onto the landing through the locked doors which separated them from the rest of the world. Although indistinct and unclear, they could see constant movement outside.

Donna sat upright and stared out of the window into the swirling gray skies around the office block, trying to make some sense of their impossible situation. Paul lay on the carpet beside her, curled up in a ball.

"Why did it attack you?" he mumbled, forcing himself to speak about what he'd seen.

"I don't know if it did."

"What are you talking about? Of course it attacked you!"

"Are you sure? It might have been trying to get us to help. How do you know if . . . ?"

"Okay, okay," he whined, covering his head with his hands. "The one thing I do know is that you should never have opened the bloody door in the first place."

There was another crash and a muffled thud outside. It sounded like something falling down the stairs—the cleaner's bucket Paul had kicked earlier, perhaps? He decided that one of the bodies must have tripped over it.

"It's like they're coming back to life," Donna said quietly.

"What?"

"They died last Tuesday. I know that's true because I watched it happen and I checked the bodies of enough of my friends in here to know that they were all dead. And then they started to move. It's like they're beginning to function again. They walked on Thursday, and now . . ."

"Now what?"

"How did they know we were here?"

"Maybe that one saw me?"

"I think you disturbed them when you went to the toilet."

"But we've been off this floor before now, haven't we? How come they didn't react to us then? I walked past a hundred of those damn things outside on the streets and not one of them reacted like that—"

"I know," she interrupted quickly, increasingly aware of Paul's obvious nervousness, "and that's exactly what I'm saying. They couldn't move; now they can walk. They didn't have any control and coordination; now that seems to have improved.

They couldn't hear us and I don't know if they could see us before, but now it seems that they can."

"So why did it attack you?" he asked again, repeating his earlier question.

"If their control is that limited, what else could it have done? It couldn't ask me for help, could it? Christ, Paul, look at what's happening to them. Their bodies are beginning to rot and decay. Imagine the pain they must be feeling."

"Can they feel anything?"

"I don't know. If they can move, my guess is that they must be able to feel something."

Paul sat up and drew his knees tight to his chest.

"So what happens next? What do we do?"

Donna's head was spinning. She didn't want to think about it until she absolutely had to.

"For now all we can do is keep our heads down and stay out of sight. Don't let them know we're in here."

9

Music woke Jack from his light, fitful sleep. He thought he was imagining it at first but no, there it was again: faint and tinny, but for the first time in days he could definitely hear music. Once he was fully awake it took him a couple of seconds to get his bearings. He looked around and let his eyes slowly become accustomed to the low morning light. The department store looked very different in daylight—completely different, in fact, from how he'd pictured it last night when they'd first arrived. He remembered being with Clare and he quickly sat up and looked around for her.

"Over here," she shouted from the other side of the floor. Jack swung his legs out over the side of the bed, got up, and slowly shuffled over to the dining room furniture display where Clare was sitting. He sat down at the opposite end of a long, mahogany table, instinctively checking the price label as he did. Clare was playing the music. He didn't say anything to her but he wished she'd turn it down. It wasn't that it was particularly loud, he just decided it seemed that way because everything else was so quiet.

"How you feeling this morning?"

"I'm okay," she replied. "I didn't mean to wake you up. I hope you don't mind the noise, I just couldn't stand the quiet. I got the music from the electrical department just past the beds."

Jack looked back over his shoulder and saw a huge bank of lifeless television screens behind the row of beds where they'd just spent the night. Still sleepy, he stood up again and walked back over to where he'd left his belongings. After searching through his rucksack he found a little of the food he'd brought with him from home. He took it back to Clare and sat down again. He opened a plastic tub and took out some chocolate and fruit, which he laid out on the table between them.

"Hungry?" he asked. She shook her head and laughed at him. "What's funny?"

"You brought a packed lunch to the end of the world!"

He scowled at her. "It's not a packed lunch, and it's not the end of the world."

"Isn't it?"

He ignored her. "You really should try and eat something. We both should."

Clare took a chocolate bar and bit into it. It was surprisingly good. Its taste and smell were familiar and comforting. She'd hardly eaten anything since Tuesday. After days of feeling nothing more than emptiness, hurt, and constant disorientation, the food was a welcome distraction.

"I love this song," Clare said as another track began to play. She chewed thoughtfully on her chocolate and turned up the volume. She closed her eyes and, for a few blissful seconds, she tried to imagine she was somewhere else. Jack wasn't impressed. To him, this song sounded no different and no less processed and manufactured than the last bland track she'd played. He remembered the good old days when music was played by real musicians using real instruments, and when talent mattered more than appearance and . . . and he could hear something else. He switched the music off.

"Hey . . ."

"Shh . . ."

Jack pushed his chair back then got up and walked toward the escalators, which snaked up through the center of the department store, sure that he could hear movement on the floor below them. Cautiously he peered over the top of the handrail and saw that a large crowd of bodies had gathered there. The light was poor but he could see more than a dozen of them, all grouped together, and that, incredibly, several of the corpses were trying to climb up the stationary escalator toward him. They tripped over fallen displays, dead shoppers and other obstructions as they tried to move forward. Clare appeared at his side, startling him.

"What's going on?"

"Look," he answered, gesturing down toward the figures below. He concentrated his attention on the diseased body which had made the farthest progress up toward the second floor. It was now almost halfway up the escalator but had been forced to stop, its way ahead blocked by an upturned baby's pushchair. Although it had been considerably darker last night, it had been fairly easy for Jack and Clare to negotiate their way around such obstacles. The stilted, ungainly movements of the creatures below were nowhere near as controlled and precise as their own. They crouched down together and watched as the crowd below them gradually began to dissipate. Those bodies on the outside of the group were beginning to stumble away. The corpse halfway up the escalator overbalanced and fell back down again, then picked itself back up and walked away in another direction.

"Was it the music?" Clare asked.

"Must have been."

"But why?"

"What d'you mean?"

"Well yesterday and the day before I spent ages shouting for help and none of them reacted. I didn't think they could hear us."

Jack realized she was right. He remembered the first moving body that he himself had come across—that ghoulish woman in the street outside his home. The rest of the world had been quiet and there had been no other distractions at the time, but she hadn't heard him, nor had she reacted when he'd spoken to her.

Clare moved around Jack and took a couple of steps down the escalator.

"Don't go down there . . ."

She stopped when she got to the upside-down pushchair and picked up a baby's rattle. She shook it, and the entire building rapidly filled with its ugly clacking sound. Down below, the bodies slowly turned and began moving back toward the foot of the escalator again. She watched a little longer and then, hoping to distract them, she threw the rattle away. The slothful figures followed its noise.

Clare ran back to Jack but he wasn't there. She found him back at the beds, frantically packing everything away into his rucksack.

"What are you doing?" she asked, starting to gather up her own things.

"Getting out," he replied, his voice a hushed, frightened whisper. "I'm getting away from those things."

"But they're everywhere. Where are we going to go?"

He didn't answer. Clare stopped what she was doing and sat down at the table again and watched him.

"But they can't get up here, Jack. You saw them."

"Give them enough time and they might. Who knows what they might be able do."

"But we can block the escalators off, can't we? We can use some of this furniture. They're never going to be strong enough to get through, are they?"

Her simple logic floored him. He stopped packing and just stared at her. His throat was dry and he could feel beads of nervous sweat running down his back.

"You might be right, but—"

"But what?"

"But we don't know for sure, do we?"

"I'm scared, Jack," she admitted. "I don't want to go anywhere."

Jack threw down his rucksack and sat down heavily on the end of his bed. She was right. Would anywhere be any safer than here?

* * *

A while later Jack had calmed down enough to be able to creep quietly across the shop floor to the top of the escalator and peer down again. He couldn't see any bodies. In the silence of the morning they had drifted away.

10

Just before noon, the unexpected roar of an engine outside disturbed the silence. Clare and Jack jumped out of their seats and ran over to the huge display windows at the front of the department store which looked out over the city's main shopping street. They watched as a single car forced its way down the middle of the crowded road, plowing into random staggering bodies and smashing them to the side or simply crushing them beneath its wheels.

"Get your stuff together," Jack said in a surprisingly calm and collected voice before turning and sprinting frantically across the room, desperate to get out of the building before the car disappeared.

Inside the car, Bernard Heath and Nathan Holmes looked anxiously from side to side, trying desperately to see something through the rotting crowds which converged on them from all directions. From their low vantage point there seemed no end to the hundreds of bodies surrounding them.

"Where the fuck are we going?" cursed Nathan, a stocky security guard with a face full of piercings, from behind the wheel.

"I don't know," Bernard replied. He was educated and well-spoken and completely out of his depth. Until the world had been turned on its head last week, he had been a university lecturer. More than twenty years spent almost exclusively in the company of students and other academics had left him dangerously underprepared for the sudden physical danger he now found himself facing.

"There are a couple of restaurants just up here," Nathan said. "They'll have food."

Bernard didn't say anything. He was transfixed by the absolute horror he saw all around the car. On every side he saw nothing but blood, death, and decay. Spending the last few days sitting in the isolation and relative safety of the university accommodation block with the rest of the survivors hadn't prepared him for any of this. He knew that he had to keep calm and not panic or lose his nerve. All they had to do was fill the back of the car with food and whatever other useful supplies they could find, then get back to the others. He had to remember that as foul and grotesque as these creatures were, individually they were weak and could easily be brushed aside. But there were thousands upon thousands of them, and more seemed to be arriving with each passing second.

"How the hell did this happen?" Nathan asked as he struggled to keep the car moving forward. Bernard lifted himself up in his seat to try and see over the heads of the mass of bodies.

"I don't think this is going to work," he said nervously. "What in God's name were we thinking coming out here? Christ, at this rate we won't even be able to get out of the bloody car."

Nathan didn't respond. Instead, as they approached the unlit traffic lights at what had once been one of the busiest junctions in the city, he wrenched the steering wheel hard left and turned the car, knocking down another swathe of figures with the back end as it swung out. He slammed his foot down on the accelerator and winced in disgust as they collided with body after body after body. Physically weak, it didn't take much to clear them out of the way. But the constant thud, thud, thud of lifeless flesh and bone thumping against the sides of the car was sickening. Bernard tried breathing in deeply to calm his nerves, but that just filled his lungs with the steadily increasing stench of rot even faster.

"Where are we going now? I thought you said we were heading for a restaurant?"

"I've had a better idea," Nathan said, grunting as he forced the car over another motionless body in the road and up the steep ramped entrance into a multistory car park built over a shopping mall. "I used to come here a lot," he explained as he steered around the tight climbing curve of the spiraling entrance road. "We'll get what we need here."

Bernard relaxed back in his seat momentarily. Now that they had left the main road, the number of bodies had reduced substantially and, by the time they reached the top, only a handful of figures remained close. The relief he felt was immense.

Nathan stopped the car directly in front of the door which

opened out onto the staircase leading down into the mall. Climbing out into the open, Bernard allowed himself to briefly look down over the side of the car park into the chaos which filled the streets below. An enormous dark mass of featureless figures had slowly begun to drag themselves up the steep access road, following the car. Although he had spent long hours watching the remains of the world through the windows of the university, seeing the destruction from this new perspective shocked Bernard even more. It looked like nothing had escaped unscathed.

"Come on," Nathan shouted. He was already on his way down to the shopping area. Bernard followed close behind, not wanting to be left alone.

"We should try and find food first," he said, already panting with effort as he ran down the dark steps, trying not to lose sight of the younger and much fitter man in front. "Concentrate on essentials."

Nathan wasn't listening. He crashed through a swinging pair of heavy double-doors at the bottom of the staircase and ran the length of a short, marble-floored access corridor to get to the shops. He paused at a second set of doors to let Bernard catch up slightly before going through.

The mall was silent. In the near distance he could see a few shuffling bodies, but other than that there was nothing—no movement and no sound. It was surprisingly dark. Being in the center of a once busy and vibrant city, prior to the disaster the mall had been brightly illuminated at all times. This was the first time that either of them had set foot in such a place without it being filled with crowds of shoppers and without the benefit of artificial light, air-conditioning, and constant, annoying background music and PA announcements. It felt unnatural and unnerving.

"There's a supermarket over in the far corner," Bernard gasped, still struggling to get his breath back after the sudden physical exertion of the run downstairs. From the shadows of an open-fronted jeweler's shop behind them, a clumsy body lurched toward him and knocked him off balance. He yelped with surprise and disgust and struggled to push the obnoxious figure away. It clung onto him, numb fingers snagging his clothes and pulling him down. Nathan wrenched the body away from him and threw it down to the ground. He kicked it in the side of the head and then stamped on its face, feeling a degree of satisfaction as it lay bloodied and battered, twitching at his feet.

The two men ran toward the supermarket. Behind them the broken body tried to pick itself up off the ground and follow.

"They've got to be in there somewhere," Jack whispered as he crept toward the mall with Clare at his side. They'd lost sight of the car as soon as they'd left Bartram's. Fortunately, the trail of bloody devastation and the huge mass of desperate bodies staggering away in the same general direction made it easy to deduce the route it had taken. They could see that an enormous number of the diseased figures were gathering close to the entrance of a multistory car park.

"They must have gone into the shopping center," Clare said quietly.

In silence the two survivors made their way toward the immense and still growing crowd of bodies, doing all they could to look and act like them and not arouse suspicion. The events of the morning had allowed them to quickly deduce that it was primarily sound that the creatures were reacting to. Having braced themselves for some kind of bloody struggle once they were back out on the street, they discovered that as long as they remained silent and matched the painfully slow pace of the dead, they didn't attract any unwanted attention. Weaving slowly around the corpses and stepping over and through the remains of those which had been wiped out by the car took more self-control and determination than either Jack or Clare had bargained on. The tortuous pace left them feeling constantly exposed and vulnerable. One false move, Jack kept thinking, just one false move . . .

A journey which should have taken thirty seconds took more than fifteen minutes. Still silent, and now daring only to communicate with subtle nods of the head and momentary glances, they finally reached the shopping mall. With their disgust and trepidation increasing as the crowds around them became more tightly packed, they worked their way through the bulk of them and began to climb the entrance road which led up into the car park.

"What color was it?" Jack asked, allowing himself the luxury of a whisper now they were away from the majority of the dead.

"What?"

"The car? What color was the car we saw?"

"Dark red, I think," Clare replied quietly. "Couldn't see much."

They had only managed to glimpse the vehicle for a few

seconds, and they'd only really seen its roof at that. It had been surrounded by a constant shroud of bodies, making it almost impossible to see anything clearly. They didn't know what size, shape, make, model, or style it was, and there were hundreds of cars in this car park.

"This is pointless," Clare whined. "They'll be long gone."

Jack shook his head. "No, we'd have heard them."

"I don't like being out here, Jack. What if those things on the street start to . . ."

"Shh . . ." he interrupted, turning around and lifting a finger to his lips. "They're here somewhere, they must be."

He kept moving forward. The same logic which had guided him to the top floor of the department store last night was now making him gravitate toward the top story of the car park. It seemed sensible to presume that a survivor would have gone up as far as they could, knowing that the lethargic bodies below would struggle to follow.

"That's it," he said suddenly as they rounded a corner and reached the top level of the car park. He walked toward a single car parked next to the staircase. It was obvious that it was the one they'd seen driving. Apart from the fact that the engine was still warm and it had been parked close to the door, its battered bodywork was covered in small dents and was dripping with blood and gore.

"So what do we do now?"

"Wait for them to come back."

They crouched down in the shadows together, hidden from view by a large 4×4.

"That's enough," Bernard protested. "Come on, Nathan, we're never going to get that much stuff up those stairs."

Nathan wasn't listening. He was busy loading more food and drink into boxes and bags which he then wedged into several shopping trolleys. Shaking his head with despair, Bernard finished emptying a shelf of dehydrated snack meals into a cardboard box, carried the load over to Nathan, and then stopped to complain again when he realized that the other man had filled most of his boxes with cans of beer.

"Now come on, we're here to collect food. We can take some drink back with us if we've got enough space, but . . ."

Nathan leaned forward until his face was only inches from Bernard's, immediately intimidating and silencing him. "Shut up," he hissed. "I'm the one who's out here putting my neck on the line to get this stuff. If I want beer, I'll take beer. And if I've forgotten anything that any other fucker wants, well, they can just get in the car and come get it for themselves, can't they?"

He turned his back on Bernard and began pushing the first trolley out of the supermarket and back toward the stairs. Bernard followed, pushing one trolley ahead of him and dragging another behind. He stared at the huge pile of supplies they'd gathered and tried to work out how much of it they'd actually be able to get into the car and how they were going to get any of it upstairs.

"Come on," Nathan shouted at him as he picked up several badly packed carrier bags in each hand and began to climb the gray concrete stairs back up to the top level of the car park. "Get a bloody move on, will you?"

With his legs and arms already aching with effort, Bernard struggled to carry half as much up the stairs in twice the time. He finally pushed through the door into the car park and dropped his bags on the ground by the car. Nathan did the same and they began to cram their supplies into the boot and back seat. Hiding behind the 4×4, Clare started to get up.

"Wait," Jack warned, watching the two men intently.

"Come on, Jack," Clare whispered, shoving him forward. He nervously stood up and stepped into the open.

"Hey," he said, clearing his throat. "Are you—"

Nathan instantly reacted to the presence of an unexpected body, moving even before Jack could finish his sentence. The fact that this particular body was speaking didn't register. He dropped his shoulder and charged into him, sending him flying across the grubby floor of the car park.

"You idiot!" Clare screamed, jumping up, running over and forcing herself between Jack and his attacker. "What did you do that for?"

Realization dawned. Nathan stared at the other man as he rolled around on the ground, groaning and doubled up with pain. Bernard pushed past and helped him to his feet.

"Get in the car," he said. Clare did as she was told. Still in considerable pain but too relieved to care, Jack collapsed heavily into the seat next to her, clutching his chest.

Bernard paced up and down anxiously in front of the car. Nathan had disappeared again. He soon re-emerged from the stairs, carrying yet more provisions including, Bernard noticed, his precious beer. They loaded the boot until it was filled to capacity, then Nathan passed more bags to Clare, who crammed as many of them around her as she could. He slid two crates of lager onto her lap, the weight crushing her legs.

Bernard sat down in the front passenger seat and packed more supplies in the footwell, bracing himself as Nathan slammed his door and started the engine. As he turned the car around in a quick, tight arc and drove back down the ramp, Bernard struggled to look over his shoulder and speak to Jack and Clare.

"I'm Bernard Heath," he said. "This is Nathan."

"Jack Baxter," Jack replied, still wheezing. "This is Clare. Thanks for . . ."

"Just the two of you?" Nathan interrupted.

"Just us. What about you?"

"There are about forty of us," Bernard answered quickly.

"Does anyone know what's happened?" Jack asked hopefully.

"Haven't got a clue," he replied, abruptly ending the brief conversation. He gripped the sides of his seat as Nathan accelerated down the last part of the entrance ramp and hit the road at speed, driving deep into the crowd of bodies and obliterating as many of them as he could.

11

Nathan drove the car the wrong way down the ring road, swerving around more meandering bodies and the abandoned wrecks of countless crashed vehicles. He slammed on the brakes suddenly, took a sharp right turn and followed a narrow service road down between two imposing university buildings, driving around the back of the redbrick accommodation block. They noticed that the number of bodies here was considerably fewer. Clare looked up and saw people watching their arrival from the first-floor windows of the large building.

Nathan stopped the car on a churned-up grass verge a short distance away from the building, alongside an enclosed artificial turf football pitch. In silence and moving fast, the four survivors climbed out and grabbed as many bags and boxes as they each could carry from the boot of the blood-soaked vehicle. Struggling with their individual loads, they followed Bernard toward an inconspicuous blue door which was being held open by another man. Nathan ran back to the car after dumping his first load of supplies indoors, not about to leave his precious beer behind after he'd risked so much to get it. He slammed the car door shut and scrambled back toward the building, pulling the door closed just seconds before the first of five approaching bodies could reach him.

"We'll come back for this lot later," said Bernard. He led Jack and Clare deeper into the bowels of the building. It was dark, cold, and quiet but it still felt safe and strangely welcoming in comparison to anywhere else they'd been recently. Their surroundings didn't matter, Jack decided—all he cared about was being with other people again.

"How many people did you say are here?" Jack asked. He'd already been told once but so much had happened so quickly that he hadn't been able to take everything in. Less than an hour ago he'd been sitting in the department store with Clare, too afraid to move. Until then she'd been the only other living person he'd seen.

"Forty or so, I think," Bernard replied. "I'm not really sure. This part of the campus was mainly student accommodation. There are a few hundred individual rooms here and so far most people have kept themselves to themselves. Lots of them just found a room and shut the door behind them and no one's seen them since. There are a few of us who've started to work together to try and get things sorted out, but we're in the minority."

"We're all in the minority now," Jack said.

Leading the group through the building was a tall, lean man named Keith Peterson. With his long hair tied in a loose, untidy ponytail, and wearing several layers of baggy clothing, he looked as scruffy and disheveled as any of the corpses roaming the streets outside. His face was pale and drained of emotion. He hadn't shown any interest or surprise when the car had returned with two additional passengers. Jack tried to catch his eye in an attempt to make contact but it was obvious that Peterson wasn't interested. Like everyone else here, he was preoccupied with trying to make sense of the illogical hell that his previously normal, structured life had suddenly become.

They climbed a short staircase to the main part of the ground floor. Jack and Clare looked anxiously from side to side as they were led across a wide, glass-fronted reception area. Tightly packed bodies were pressed against every available square inch of glass. They were trapped, being rammed forward by more and more of the sickly creatures which continued to slowly drag themselves away from the center of the city to the university. The rest of the world had become almost totally silent and the noise the group of survivors made—no matter how slight and insignificant it might have sounded to them—was enough to attract the unwanted attention of the dead hordes. Over the course of the last twenty-four hours or so, Bernard had observed a worrying new development, almost a chain reaction. As the nearest bodies had reacted to the survivors, so more bodies had subsequently reacted to their reaction, and so on and so on. The implications were terrifying. They had become a magnet for the dead.

"See that lot?" Bernard said quietly, gesturing toward the bodies behind the glass. "They started gathering here late last night. There's got to be more than a hundred of them already. I think the damn things can hear us."

"I know," Jack replied, suddenly feeling like he was in a zoo and the corpses were watching him. "We found that out this morning."

"God alone knows what's going on, but if they can hear us and see us today, what are they going to be able to do tomorrow? That's why we were out fetching supplies. We're going to batten down the hatches for a while. Good job we found you two when we did."

Clare was relieved when they began to walk down another darker, windowless corridor, away from the inimical gaze of dead eyes, to a large assembly hall. Her eyes widened as they entered and as she saw that there were people scattered all around the edge of the room—living, breathing people, not empty husks like those damn things outside. The hall itself was quiet. The only noise came from a couple of very young children playing together in the farthest corner, blissfully ignorant to the pain and fear eating away at everyone else.

No one seemed interested in their arrival. Most of the survivors sat silently and stared into space. One man was lying on his side on the floor, covered by a thin gray blanket, rocking continually. His dark eyes were wide open, as big as saucers. Clare thought to herself that he looked too afraid to shut them.

They crossed the room, then went outside through an open fire escape door which led to a small concrete courtyard. There were a few more people outside. An older woman wrapped in a thick overcoat, sitting on a wooden bench, nodded and managed half a smile at Clare as she followed the others through.

"These are the rooms we're using," Bernard explained as they entered another part of the building which looked and smelled much newer than the rest of the site. Up several short, steep flights of stairs and they then followed a long and narrow corridor with small bedrooms on either side. "Those of us who were here on the first day cleared this whole place out," he continued, slightly breathless again. "You won't find any bodies in here. Fortunately, term hadn't started so there weren't many people around, just a few of the overseas students who'd come back early."

Still at the front of the group, Keith Peterson suddenly stopped walking. He turned around to face Clare and Jack and, for the first time, he spoke.

"Most of us are on this floor," he mumbled, his voice flat and monotone, "so find yourselves an empty room. I suggest you stay on this side of the building," he added, nodding his head to the left.

Jack nodded in appreciation as the thin man walked on and disappeared into a room at the far end of the corridor. Bernard watched him go before speaking again.

"Get yourself settled," he said. "I'm going back to the hall. Come down when you're ready and we'll get you something to eat if you're hungry."

"We really appreciate this," Jack said, his voice suddenly filling with obvious and yet wholly unexpected emotion. "I was starting to think we weren't going to find anyone else . . ."

Bernard smiled and rested a reassuring hand on the other man's shoulder. "It's not a problem. I know exactly how you're feeling." He sighed. "As does every other poor bastard who's unfortunate enough to be stuck in here with us."

The lecturer paused for a moment and thought carefully, as

if he was poised to say something of great significance. But the words wouldn't come and instead he turned and began to walk back down the corridor.

"Thanks, Jack," Clare said. "I don't know what I'd have done if we hadn't—"

Her words were abruptly truncated by a sudden scream of pain from somewhere else in the building. It seemed to be coming from the floor above them.

"Bloody hell," cursed Jack. "What was that?"

"Nothing to worry about," Bernard explained, stopping and turning back around. "We've got a lady upstairs who's about to have a baby. The doctor reckons it might even be born before today's out."

Another scream. Jack looked down at Clare, concerned that the woman's noise might upset her.

"Poor cow," he said quietly. "What a time to have to be going through that. I mean, it's enough of an ordeal at the best of times, but now . . . ?" He let his words trail quietly away.

"Look, I'm going to leave you to it," said Bernard. "I'll catch up with you later, okay?"

With that he was gone and Jack and Clare were left alone. They stood together in the middle of the corridor and for a few seconds neither moved.

"You okay?" Jack eventually asked.

"I'm all right," she replied. "What about you?"

He managed a faint smile. "I'm fine. We should get these rooms sorted out."

The rooms were small, compact and functional units containing just a narrow bed, a wardrobe, a couple of small cabinets, a desk, two chairs and a sink. They managed to find adjacent rooms two-thirds of the way down the corridor. Jack left his rucksack on the end of the bed, but he didn't bother to empty its contents. There didn't seem to be much point. Although the accommodation block looked like a safe and sensible place for them to shelter in, he didn't imagine they'd be staying for any length of time. The world was full of so much uncertainty and fear that nothing could be taken for granted anymore.

As the pregnant woman's screams echoed through the building again, Clare sat down on a hard chair by the window in her room and gazed into space. She wanted to cry but she couldn't. The relentless pressure of their bizarre situation seemed to be acting as a kind of stopper, suppressing her emotions. The room was cold and clinical and her sense of bewilderment was overpowering. She pulled up her legs, made herself as small as possible, and stared at the wall.

After he'd been alone in his room for little over ten minutes, Jack got up and walked across the corridor to the empty room directly opposite. The panoramic view over the city from the window was, for a few seconds at least, impressive and for a moment he was distracted, trying to find where he used to live on the skyline. But then he allowed his eyes to drop down to street level, and he immediately wished he hadn't. An immense crowd of diseased corpses surrounded the front of the building, far bigger than any other crowd he'd so far seen. He tried to estimate how many of them there were but it was impossible. They were hard to distinguish from one another, and they moved continuously.

The rest of the city was completely lifeless and still, and he could see more and more of the damn things dragging themselves out of the shadows, constantly moving closer.

12

"I can't do this," Paul said suddenly. It was the first time that either of them had spoken for more than an hour.

"Can't do what?"

"Stay here like this. I can't handle it. I can't just sit here knowing they're out there waiting for us . . ."

"Well you're going to have to handle it, aren't you? You don't have any choice."

They were still hiding in the training room where they'd been since the attack hours earlier, but they knew that there were many more bodies out on the landing now. They could hear them shuffling and bumping about. Donna couldn't understand why they were still there. Had they been trapped on the landing by the heavy doors swinging shut, or had they made a conscious decision to wait there for her or Paul to emerge from hiding again? Were they even capable of conscious decision making? It was impossible to tell.

Assuming that it had been sound that first attracted them,

Donna had come to the conclusion that it had been a domino effect of sorts which had caused so many of them to converge on the tenth floor. It seemed logical to assume that the noise made by the first body trying to force its way inside had attracted another, which in turn had attracted another and another until a steady stream had become an unwanted wave of rot which threatened to fill the entire landing, if not the whole building.

"So what are we going to do?" Paul moaned. Christ, he really was beginning to irritate Donna now.

"Jesus, Paul," she sighed. "I don't know."

"We can't sit here forever, can we?"

"What else are we going to do?"

"We're ten floors up! The only way out is to go down the staircase and if any more of those things appear then we're going to have a hell of a job getting through them if we need to get out, aren't we?"

He was right. She didn't bother to acknowledge it but she had to admit that he did have a point. The easiest option was to stay hidden in the office, but she knew that if she followed through with her earlier line of thought, more and more of the bodies could drag themselves upstairs until it became impossible for the two of them to get through the corpses and away. Her options were beginning to look increasingly bleak: take her chances up here with the diseased population, or sit and wait with this whinging mouse of a man for them to disappear. It didn't take long to reach a decision.

"You're right," she said. "We should do it. We'll get out of here and try and find somewhere safer—if anywhere's any safer, that is."

The expression on Paul's face immediately changed. He looked terrified. Although he'd been the one who had suggested they should go, he clearly hadn't thought through the implications.

"But how?" he stammered nervously. "How are we going to get past them? We don't know how many of them there are and . . ."

"We distract them," she interrupted. "There are doors at either end of the landing, aren't there? We'll draw them toward one end of the office, then get out through the other."

"Okay," he said, still sounding far from convinced. "So where do we go once we're outside?"

"Don't know. From what I've seen we can pretty much take our pick of the entire city, maybe even the country."

"We could find ourselves a car and try and get away . . ."

"Might not be a good idea. If those things outside are reacting to noise, all we'd be doing is drawing more attention to ourselves. What we need is to find somewhere secure like this place, but with more than one way out."

"There must be hundreds of places like that around here. This is the city center, for God's sake."

"There's the main police station around the corner, for a start. Then there's the hospital, the university, shops, pubs . . ."

"We need somewhere we can get food and drink . . ."

"Christ, I could murder a drink . . ."

"And a bed? What about finding somewhere with real beds? Bloody hell, a decent-sized house would do, wouldn't it?"

"There aren't that many houses around here," Donna said, beginning to feel slightly more positive about their situation.

"But you're right—when we're ready we could head out into the suburbs. Maybe even farther?"

Paul stopped to think again.

"There's one thing that we're not taking into consideration here."

"What's that?"

"The bodies. We both saw what that one tried to do to you. We'll be sitting ducks as soon as we go outside . . ."

"They don't seem to be attacking each other, do they?"

"So?"

"So how would they know that we're not like them if we played dead? We're stronger and we look in better condition than they do, but after everything that's happened to them are they really going to be able to tell the difference?"

"I'm not sure. Can we afford to take a chance like that?"

"Can we afford not to? You're right, Paul, we could end up trapped in here if we don't do something. There might be thousands of those things here in just a few hours; there might even be that many out there now. We don't have a lot of choice."

"When then? Now?"

"Tonight."

"Why wait?"

"If we're relying on the fact that their senses are poor, then we should wait until it's dark outside. If they can't see us properly in daylight, what chance will they have at night?"

13

By the time the city was bathed in darkness again, Donna and Paul had settled on a plan: they were going to distract the bodies on the landing as they'd discussed, then make a break for it. They hoped that their strength and control would give them enough of an advantage to get them through the crowd outside the office doors. As the afternoon and early evening had worn on, their simple plan had slowly gained more purpose and direction, but they knew they had to act quickly.

In the oppressive gloom of the dying day, Donna gathered up her things and put on as much of the clothing she'd collected as was comfortable. The lamps around the office floor remained unlit, both of them electing to remain in darkness until the time was right and they were ready to make their move. The night was unseasonably cold and even though they were indoors, Donna's breath condensed in billowing clouds around her mouth and nose.

"We need to stir them up at the other end of the office,"

she said quietly. "We need to make enough of a disturbance so that they try and get in through the far doors."

"And then we come back to this end?" Paul asked anxiously. He knew full well what they were planning to do, but he needed reassurance.

"We'll prop the doors open up there and let them get inside. We'll get ourselves back down here and wait for a couple of minutes until the bulk of them are in. Then we'll get out. They'll follow each other like sheep."

"You certain?"

"As I can be. Anyway, there's only one way of finding out for sure, isn't there? Now make yourself useful and start getting the lamps together."

She turned and walked out of the training room, leaving Paul sitting alone in the darkness. For a few seconds he stayed exactly where he was, suddenly too afraid to move. It didn't matter how long they'd talked about it, now that it was time to act he just wanted to curl up again and hide. Hearing no movement, Donna turned back.

"Problem?"

His mouth was dry and he couldn't answer. "I . . ." he began, not knowing what he was trying to say.

"Get off your fucking backside and move!" Donna cried. She waited for a second but he still didn't react. "Now!" she yelled.

Paul scrambled to his feet as the volume of Donna's voice resulted in an outburst of frenetic activity on the landing as the bodies again began to shove themselves up against the doors, trying ceaselessly to force their way inside.

They set off around the perimeter of the office, collecting up the torches and lamps which Donna had placed there previously. They then assembled them on a single desk in the farthest corner of the room, in full sight of the bodies behind the door.

"We ready?" she asked when the final lamps were in place. Paul swallowed hard.

"Think so."

"Good," she replied and she started to light the lamps and torches. She stopped after she'd only lit four. The creatures out on the landing were already becoming agitated, the sudden bright light in the corner of the room whipping them into a frenzy.

"Bloody hell," Paul moaned. "All you've done is light a few bloody lamps and just look at them! What the hell are we doing?"

"What we have to do," Donna said, returning her attention to the task at hand. "Now shut up and get on with it."

Shaking with nerves, Paul lit a match and began to light the gas lamps. The room was quickly filled with even more light and with the faintly acidic smell and dull roar of burning jets of gas. The noise out on the landing continued to increase.

"Shit," Paul said, "listen to them. Bloody things are going mad out there."

"Good, that's what we want. The more fired up they are, the better a distraction this will be, and the easier it'll be for us to get out."

Paul wasn't convinced. The far right corner of the office was filled with bright light and a strangely comforting warmth, making him want to stay put.

"Okay," Donna whispered, stepping back into the shadows again, "let's go."

Paul began to backtrack. "Are you completely sure about this? What happens if we get out there and . . . ?"

She turned and stared at him, her face harshly illuminated from the right. Her anger was blindingly apparent.

"Just stop your damn whining and move. It's too late to back out now, in case you hadn't noticed. Now get back to the other end and get the bags ready."

He obediently scuttled away to the far end of the office.

"And keep out of sight," she shouted after him. "Don't let them see you. You screw this up and we've both had it."

Breathing deeply, trying to calm her own frayed nerves, Donna walked away from the light and moved toward the doors. Through the small glass panels she could see the creatures outside continuing to react to her presence, the nearest of them thrashing around to get closer to her. The ferocity of their movements increased as she approached, and she could see the reaction spreading back through the crowd. The landing was filled with movement and she wondered what, if anything, was going through their decaying minds. Were they frightened of her? Did they want to harm her? Or did they want her to help end their suffering? Whatever the reason she knew that ultimately it wasn't important. Self-preservation was all that mattered now. She took a deep breath and opened the door, using the blood-splattered fire extinguisher to prop it open.

For a split second there was nothing. Then the force of the mass of bodies on the landing and stairs caused the crowd to surge forward, spilling into the office and sending countless corpses stumbling and tripping in front of her. She jumped to the side to get out of the way of the sudden tidal wave of foul-smelling rot. The brightness of the light in the corner of the room was thankfully much more of a distraction than she was, and in the relative darkness she was able to turn and run back to the training room.

"Okay?" Paul whispered. "Is it working?"

"Keep quiet," she snapped at him angrily. "If they hear us they'll start coming up this way."

She pushed him forward and they crept quietly out of the training room, toward the doors at the other end of the landing. Down at the far end of the office they could see a huge mass of bodies still flooding into the room, all of them heading for the light. The farthest forward few reached out and grabbed inquisitively at the lamps. Unable to grip with their unresponsive fingers and thumbs, one of them knocked a lamp to the ground, shattering its protective glass cover and exposing the burning mantle. Within seconds the carpet and a pile of papers were alight.

"Bloody hell," Donna said under her breath as she watched the fire spread quickly.

"Let's go," Paul whispered

"No, wait. This is better than we planned. We should give it a little longer."

The light at the other end of the floor had now changed from a steady white-yellow to a flickering orange-red as the fire spread and took hold. Some of the pitiful creatures staggered into the flames, ignorant to the heat and danger. Their ragged clothes were tinder dry and quickly began to smolder and burn.

"We've got to go," Paul insisted. "Christ, that fire's going to spread through the whole building. And when the gas bottles on the lamps start to go—"

"I know," Donna interrupted, picking up her stuff. Several bodies were burning now (and yet were somehow still managing to move), and a desk and chair and a window blind had also caught light. Thick smoke was billowing up and was beginning to roll back along the low ceiling toward them.

Donna flicked her security pass at the control panel at the side of the door and then quietly pushed it open. Even now after the bodies had been flooding into the room for several minutes there were still more of them on the landing, tripping desperately toward the open office doors opposite. She glanced back momentarily to check that Paul was with her and then led him out toward the staircase. Silently they crept along the landing with their backs pressed against the wall, terrified that they would be seen by the desperate hordes which continued to surge toward the heat and light. Donna stopped just short of the open door which led out onto the staircase.

"Ready?" she mouthed silently. Paul nodded. "Just keep moving until we get outside. I'll meet you in the car park."

Donna waited for yet another cumbersome corpse to haul itself through the door, then turned and forced her way out onto the stairs. She pushed random bodies out of her way as she started down toward ground level, batting away countless grabbing hands which reached out for her. The heavy footsteps of the survivors echoed throughout the dead building as they ran down and down, turning one hundred and eighty degrees at the foot of each short flight to get to the start of the next. Numerous bodies emerged from the darkness around them, some trapped on the lower landings and bathrooms and unable to climb up, but the sheer strength, speed, and fear of both Donna and Paul was too much for any of the cadavers to withstand. They were pushed out of the way, falling to the ground like discarded rag dolls.

They reached the reception area, where yet more bodies crowded toward them. Donna led Paul down a final flight of stairs and out into the office car park through a basement entrance. The car park was virtually clear of corpses. In the safety of the shadows and the darkness they finally allowed themselves to stop.

"You all right?" Paul asked, panting, bending over to catch his breath.

"I'm okay," she replied.

Donna took a few steps out toward the center of the car park and looked up. She could see the floor from which they had just escaped, the windows along two-thirds of its length now illuminated by the fierce flames. Even from where they stood, many meters below, they could hear the crackle and pop of the fire as it consumed the office and the hundreds of bodies still continuing to cram themselves through its doors. The sudden muffled bang of an exploding gas cylinder and the cracking of glass made them both catch their breath.

Without saying another word, Paul and Donna left the car park and began to head toward the center of the city.

14

The atmosphere in the university accommodation block was tense and expectant. Those survivors who had chosen to emerge from their individual rooms had gathered together in the assembly hall, where they sat in silence and waited. It was impossible for any of them to rest or sleep at the best of times, but tonight it was particularly difficult. Deep in the bowels of the building, Sonya Farley was reaching the final stages of a long and difficult labor. Her pain could be heard and felt in every corner of every otherwise silent room.

The makeshift delivery room upstairs was brightly lit in comparison with the rest of the dark building. Several survivors had willingly given up torches and other battery-powered lights to allow Phil Croft—the only person with any relevant medical experience—to deliver Sonya's baby. He was apprehensive: this was only the third delivery that he'd been actively involved in. Paulette, the large and remarkably bright and enthusiastic lady standing at his side, had been involved in three times as many births, five of them her own children. Croft was pleased to have her around; she was essential to the first-time mother-to-be's well-being tonight. Although Croft knew all the technical terms and he could monitor and react to mother's and baby's vital signs, Paulette was able to do something far more important. She could reassure Sonya. She could talk to her and tell her when to push and when to relax, when to breathe in and when to breathe out. She understood what Sonya was going through. Croft admired her ability to shut out her own personal fears and loss while she concentrated fully on the young woman lying in nervous agony on the sweat-soaked bed.

"Come on, lover," she said softly, gently stroking Sonya's forehead and at the same time gripping her hand tight. "Not long now. We'll have this baby born within the hour."

Sonya's face screwed up in pain as another contraction peaked. Croft crouched at the end of the bed, feeling momentarily redundant, wishing he could have used some of the monitoring equipment from the hospital. Since the power had failed the machines were useless. Sonya was fully dilated. He could see the first wisps of greasy dark hair on top of the baby's head.

"Nearly there," he said quietly.

Sonya relaxed momentarily as the pain faded away. Apart from the expected agony and emotion of childbirth, she felt surprisingly calm. This was just how the midwife had said it would be during the prenatal classes she'd attended. Even though it hurt more than any pain she'd ever felt before, it somehow felt good. It was positive pain. Nothing in what remained of her life made sense anymore except this. Her husband was gone. Her friends and family were almost certainly dead. She had lost her home and possessions, and she had nothing left now except the precious little person inside her who was about to be born. And it felt so right. For the first time since this nightmare had begun, something was happening as it was supposed to.

Another sharp contraction. They were becoming unbearable. Sonya screamed out in agony and squeezed Paulette's hand so tightly that the other woman winced in pain.

"Come on," she soothed, her voice calm, crouching low so that her face was close to Sonya's. "Baby's ready to come now."

Thirty-five minutes later and Sonya's pain again built to an almost unbearable crescendo before being dramatically relieved as her baby was delivered in a sudden release of pressure and a rush of activity and emotion. Croft guided the child safely down onto the bed between its mother's legs and gently wiped blood and other bodily fluids from its face. He clamped and cut the cord and then quickly whisked the baby away to the makeshift crib they'd prepared. His face was a picture of intense concentration as he checked the child's vital signs and waited anxiously for it to respond.

The silence was deafening.

"You did it, lover," whispered Paulette, kissing the top of Sonya's sweat-soaked head.

Sonya watched with overwhelming nervousness as Croft worked on her child. When she'd first fallen pregnant she remembered her mother telling her that this was the worst part— the wait for the baby to realize it had been born and to start to breathe and react for itself. She'd tried to prepare herself but it was impossible. Every long second of silence felt like hours. And then it finally happened: a sudden shrill, piercing cry of surprise and realization from the child in the crib. Croft glanced across at Sonya and smiled.

"Perfect little baby girl," he said. "Well done."

For a few blissful moments nothing else mattered. With huge, saucer eyes filled with tears of joy and relief, Sonya watched as the doctor wrapped her little baby in a soft blanket and carried her across the room. Ignoring the pain and discomfort she felt, she sat up and took the little bundle from him. Shutting out the rest of the world, she stared down into a beautiful, wrinkled, blotchy blue-pink face. She stroked the baby's cheek with a single gentle finger and reveled in the warmth, movement, and noise that the little girl had innocently brought to her otherwise lifeless world.

"What are you going to call her?" asked Paulette, peering over the mother's shoulder.

"Don't know," Sonya replied quietly. "We had a few ideas for names but we hadn't settled on anything for definite."

"Take your time and get it right. I always said it was easier to give them a name once you knew what they looked like and you'd got to know them. Until then you . . ."

Paulette suddenly stopped talking. The baby had stopped crying. The room was quiet. The three adults in the room exchanged nervous glances. Both women looked to Croft for an explanation, and when he remained silent, Sonya looked down and gave her little girl's hand a gentle squeeze. And then the baby opened her mouth wide and let out a sudden, rasping cry. The cry turned into a helpless splutter, then a high-pitched cough. Then another cough, and another and another until the noise had become a virtually constant scream of helpless agony. Sonya held her daughter close to her breast, desperate to help but knowing that there was nothing she could do. Croft tried to take the baby from her but she wouldn't let go. They all knew what was happening.

The deadly contagion still hung heavy in the air.

Just minutes after being born, Sonya's baby was dead.

15

Croft broke the news to the survivors in the assembly hall before heading back upstairs to look after his heavily sedated patient. The range of drugs available to him was desperately limited but he'd pumped the devastated girl full of whatever he could find until she'd finally stopped screaming and slipped into unconsciousness.

Jack Baxter sat with Bernard Heath in a corner of the hall. Clare was lying on a thin foam mattress next to them. They had been talking intermittently for a few hours with neither man able to contemplate sleep. In that time Jack had been given the opportunity to finally ask some of the questions which had weighed heavy on his mind since last Tuesday morning. Bernard, of course, had been unable to answer any of them, but the conversation had still helped.

When they heard that the baby had died, Bernard began to cry. He seemed ashamed by his public show of emotion and tried unsuccessfully to hide his tears.

"You know what this means, don't you?" he said after a few minutes of awkward silence, his voice unsteady.

"What?" Jack replied.

"It means this is definitely the end."

"Why do you say that?"

"Stands to reason. It's got to be over now, hasn't it? There are only a handful of us left, Jack, and if we can't reproduce then as far as I can see, that's the end of the human race."

Jack stared into the darkness. "You can't be sure," he said quietly.

"We can't be sure about anything, but you've got to admit, it doesn't look good, does it? I'd started to think that there might have been some hope. I'd been thinking that whatever makes people like you and me immune might make our children immune or our brothers or . . ."

Tears continued to roll freely down his tired face.

"You might still be right."

Bernard shook his head sadly. "I've got a son," he said, wiping his eyes again. "I *had* a son," he corrected himself. "He lived in Australia. My wife went over there to be with them. She flew over three weeks ago to see the grandchildren. I know she's—"

"She's probably with them all right now," Jack interrupted, anticipating what he was about to say and instinctively saying the opposite. "For all you know they could all be safe. It might only be this country that's affected. We might—"

"I know they're dead," Bernard interrupted sadly. "Doesn't matter what you say, I know they're dead."

Jack rubbed his eyes and looked up at the ceiling. It was pointless trying to argue but he tried anyway.

"Until we know for certain . . ." he began.

"Don't waste your time, Jack," Bernard interrupted, sitting upright and staring into the other man's face. "There's no point holding on to hopes or dreams or half-baked ideas or . . ."

"But you can't just dismiss everything—"

"I can. Listen, do you realize how insignificant you and I really are now?"

Jack looked at him, puzzled and indignant. "No, but I—"

"Can you really say you've stopped and tried to appreciate the scale of what's happened here?" He paused for an answer that didn't come. "I hadn't. But something struck me a couple of days ago that put all of this into perspective. Did you own a car?"

"Never learned to drive," Jack answered, surprised by the question. "Why?"

"I remember when I brought my first car home. My mother thought it was a death trap and my old dad spent the day outside with me trying to get the engine tuned. I'll never forget it . . ."

"What point are you making?"

"How many crashed cars have you seen since it happened? How many abandoned cars have you seen 'round here?"

"Hundreds. Probably thousands. Why?"

"Because somebody owned every single one of those cars. Every single one of them was someone's pride and joy."

"I'm not sure I understand what you're saying . . ."

"What about your home? Did you own your house?"

"Yes."

"Remember the feeling when you picked up the key and walked inside? Remember your first night there when it was your house and you could shut the front door and forget about everyone else?"

A faint smile flickered across Jack's face as he remembered setting up home with his dear Denise. "God, yes," he said quietly. "We had such a laugh. We hardly had anything. We sat on packing boxes and ate chips out of the paper with our fingers and . . ."

"Just think about the fact that someone had memories like that about every single house you've passed, and chances are they're all dead now. Hundreds of them. Millions of them."

"It doesn't bear thinking about."

"But we need to think about it. And what about children? Did you have children, Jack?"

He shook his head sadly. "No, we wanted to . . ."

"Every single corpse that's still lying and rotting on the streets and every one of those bloody things walking around outside this building, they were all somebody once. They were all someone's son or daughter or brother or sister or mum or dad . . ." Bernard stopped talking again. More tears ran down his tired face. "This is the end," he said. "There's no doubt about it, Jack, this is the end."

16

Physical and emotional exhaustion had drained Sonya almost to the point of collapse. The cocktail of drugs hurriedly prescribed by Dr. Croft had knocked her out for the best part of four hours, giving her body time to regain a little strength. When she next woke it was shortly after five in the morning and it was dark, save for the first few rays of morning light which were beginning to edge cautiously into the room. She was still lying on the bed where she'd delivered her daughter, the linen beneath her soiled with blood. The body of her baby lay in the crib at her side, wrapped in a pure white blanket. As soon as she'd regained consciousness she reached out and picked the little girl up and held her tightly, keeping her safe. Instinctively but pointlessly she still wanted to protect her lifeless child.

Whenever Sonya moved it hurt, but the physical pain and the other aftereffects of childbirth were nothing compared to the anguish she felt inside. She was hollow, as if everything of value inside her had been scraped out and thrown away. She felt detached from her surroundings, almost as if she was looking down on herself. She didn't know if she was warm or cold. She didn't know if she was tired or wide-awake. She felt as if everything—her ability to communicate, to make decisions, to laugh or cry, to react or to withdraw—had gone. Her aching body was filled with nothing but relentless pain, tinged with anger and bitterness. Why did this have to happen?

Croft was asleep on a chair in the corridor outside the room. She could see his feet through the half-open door.

The pain she felt inside was increasing with each passing second. Groaning with discomfort, she sat upright and swung her legs out over the side of the bed. She was bleeding heavily and waited for the blood to stop before lowering herself down. The floor beneath her feet was hard and cold. She grabbed a toweling dressing gown from a hook on the back of the door and struggled to put it on while still cradling her lifeless child, and then she wrapped the thick material around both herself and the baby.

The corridor was even colder.

Dragging her feet, Sonya slowly walked past Dr. Croft. She could hear Paulette stirring in the next room. Apart from the woman's muffled movements and the sound of another solitary soul sobbing on a different floor, the building was silent. What do you know about pain, Sonya silently asked whoever it was who was crying. If only they knew how she felt.

The staircase was colder still.

Sonya found it difficult to climb the stairs. She was tired and she hurt and she felt nauseous. The doctor had given her every drug he'd been able to find to help her cope. That, combined with the blood loss, and exhaustion, left her feeling bilious and faint. But somehow she managed to ignore everything and keep moving.

The fifth floor, then the sixth, then the seventh. She wasn't sure how tall the building was, but she was certain that she had to be somewhere near the top floor now. Anyway, this would do. She walked down another corridor, still leaving a dripping trail of splashes of blood behind her, and tried a few doors until one opened. It led into a small, square room, a mirror image of the one she'd just left. In one corner there was a single bed with a suitcase on top, next to that a cheap Formica desk. On the desk was a collection of letters and a couple of photographs of a group of happy, smiling people standing in a sun-drenched garden somewhere. Presumably the pictures were of the room's now deceased occupant and his or her dead family.

Sonya tenderly cradled her baby close to her chest and looked down into her gray but still beautiful face. She stood in the center of the room, rocking gently, instinctively soothing her dead child. Slowly she opened up her dressing gown and lifted the little girl up to her face. She kissed the top of her cold head, stroked her wispy hair, and then carefully laid her down on the bed next to the suitcase. Before moving she folded back the blankets to keep her warm.

She picked up a metal-framed chair and threw it through the window.

The silent world was suddenly filled with noise as the glass shattered and the chair dropped into the rotting crowds below. Their unwanted interest immediately aroused, thousands upon thousands of creatures surged toward the building again. Sonya didn't look at them, didn't even think about them. She could hear other survivors down on the lower floors now, running around frantically, trying to find where the sound had come from, terrified that the safety of their shelter had been compromised.

Ignorant to the sudden panic she had caused both inside and outside the building, Sonya dragged another chair over to the broken window. She carefully picked her daughter up off the bed again and then, holding her close to her chest, climbed up onto the chair, then sat down on the windowsill and shuffled around. With her bare legs hanging out of the building and dangling in the cold morning air, she sat in silence and surveyed what remained of the world and its devastated population. There was a massive crowd of bodies below her—the vacant shells of ordinary people like her, people who had died last week before somehow dragging themselves back up from their undignified resting places—and she looked at them and wondered if they felt like she did. And beyond them were millions more corpses, lying and rotting where they'd dropped on that first morning. But none of them mattered. Even the bodies of the people that Sonya had known and loved and who were out there somewhere didn't matter anymore. Nothing mattered.

Sonya pressed her feet hard against the outside wall, leaned forward, and pushed herself out of the window. She fell headfirst, falling through three-quarters of a turn as she dropped heavily through the germ-filled air, crashing down on her back onto the roof of a parked car and killing herself instantly.

The nearest of the cadavers took slow, lumbering steps toward Sonya's body. With dull, clouded eyes they stared at her battered and smashed remains, then staggered away, disinterested. In spite of the force of the impact, Sonya still held her baby tightly.

The sound of the window shattering echoed for miles around the empty city. Paul and Donna heard it, and it prompted them to move. They'd spent the last three and a half hours sitting in a third-floor, glass-fronted pizza restaurant, having only traveled a short distance from the office block. Their earlier supposition that slow movements and silence would be enough to avoid attracting the attention of the wandering bodies had thankfully proved to be correct, but what they hadn't bargained on was the relentless mental effort required to maintain that slow and tedious pace in close proximity to such unpredictable danger. They instinctively wanted to either hide away from the bodies or destroy them, but they could do neither. The creatures were unnatural, obnoxious, and repellent and, for all Paul and Donna knew, potentially lethal, but they couldn't afford to let their emotions give them away. To Paul, walking through the crowds was like being forced to hold his hand in a bowl of boiling water and having to ignore the pain. After spending several hours outside, exposed and vulnerable, he and Donna had taken shelter in the restaurant to calm themselves and rest for a while.

Half of the restaurant had been destroyed by fire, and the flames had left plastic tables and chairs mangled and misshapen. An explosion in the kitchens had blown a hole in the wall of the building the size of a small car, and it was through that hole that they heard the sound of the window being smashed. Holding onto the blackened remains of a large oven for support, Paul leaned out of the building and looked up and down the deserted street below. The early morning light was low and a single figure moving farther away was all that he could see at first. Gradually his eyes became used to the light and he was able to focus in the gloom. And then he saw the crowd. Hundreds, possibly thousands of bodies, gathered together in an area of town no more than half a mile away. It took a few seconds for the importance of his discovery to fully register.

"Christ," he said as he quickly pulled himself back inside.

"What?"

"There's a crowd down there," he explained. "Hundreds of the damn things."

"Where?"

"At the edge of the ring road. Down by the university, I think."

"So in the morning we'll go the other way."

Tired, Donna shuffled in her seat, trying to get comfortable. She needed sleep.

"We should go toward it," Paul said with surprising certainty in his voice. He knew that what he was saying was right, but he also knew that they would be taking an immense risk. Replace putting a hand into a bowl of boiling water, he thought—thinking back to his earlier analogy—with diving headfirst into a swimming pool full.

"Why?" Donna asked.

"Because if these things are attracted by sound and movement," he explained, "then there's something over there that's got them interested."

17

Stay calm, keep steady and keep moving. Donna repeated the silent mantra to herself over and over again as she and Paul walked into the huge mass of bodies. With each step forward they took, so the nervousness and apprehension increased. They were walking into the lion's den. Surrounded by decaying corpses on all sides, they knew that a single unexpected movement or ill-judged sound might be enough to start a chain reaction within the crowd which could engulf them and cut them off, leaving them with no means of escape. On their own the bodies were weak and until now had been more of an inconvenience than a threat. In a crowd of this size, however, the danger was undeniable and there was no obvious way out.

The stench was appalling. Since they'd been out in the open they'd been aware of a suffocating, noxious taste in the air which had steadily increased as they'd approached the mass of decaying bodies. A combination of disease and decay, the rancid odor seemed to coat and tarnish everything. Struggling to keep her nerve, Donna watched the corpse nearest to her out of the corner of her eye. It had once been a girl—about her height and age, perhaps—but now it was barely recognizable. She might even have known the pathetic creature before it had been struck down by whatever it was that had laid waste to the world less than a week ago. The early light was still dim but there was enough illumination for Donna to be able to make out what remained of the girl's features. Her once smooth skin was being steadily eaten away, giving her flesh an unnatural, mottled blue-green tinge. Weeping sores had erupted around her mouth and nose. Her mouth hung open and a thick string of bloody, germ-filled saliva trickled constantly down the side of her face. Her once smart, well-fitting clothes were heavily stained, and were stretched tight where her rotting body had become swollen and distended. Donna forced herself to turn away and look down at the pavement. She had to hold her nerve and ignore the grotesque sights all around her. To react now would be suicidal.

Paul had gradually moved farther ahead, the uneven flow of the dead carrying him forward slightly faster. He was a couple of meters in front of Donna now and there were several bodies between them. The size of the crowd they had become part of was extraordinary, its vastness only fully apparent now that they were on the inside. There had to be a reason for them being here, Paul thought, and, with no other indication of where they might find help or safety, all they could do was go along with the movement of the mass of corpses. The sun was beginning to rise over the skyline and, as the brilliant orange light spilled silently over the city, he looked up ahead and thought he glimpsed movement in the windows of a large, modern building on the other side of

116

the ring road. He wanted to tell Donna but he forced himself not to react.

A few steps behind, Donna let her head hang heavily on her shoulders, mimicking the listless creatures around her. To look up and move with control would mark her out as different. She tried to keep her eyes focused on the back of Paul's legs, desperately trying to keep track of his movements. The longer they walked, the more tightly packed the crowd became and her nervousness made matching the slow and awkward pace of the shuffling cadavers increasingly difficult. Although they were all moving in the same general direction, the creatures' poor motor control meant they frequently lurched, tripped, or staggered to one side or the other, colliding randomly with others or with her.

Paul allowed himself to look ahead again. Bright orange sunlight reflected back at him from the windows on the far side of the building, hurting his eyes. Maybe that was all he'd seen? Perhaps there hadn't been any movement at all, just the morning sun glinting off the bronze-tinted windows. But wait . . . yes, there it was again. Knowing that he was taking a risk by continuing to hold his head high, he stared at the building until he saw movement again. Christ, there were people in the windows. He was still a couple of hundred meters away, but he could definitely make them out now. Unlike the thousands of sickly bodies that surrounded him and Donna, he knew instantly that the people up there were different. They were grouped together in several rooms and they were largely still. They had control over their movements. They were communicating with one another. They were looking down at the bodies and surveying the remains of the city, and they were thinking and talking and pointing and planning and . . . and it seemed impossible. Paul wasn't fully able to accept what he was seeing until he was close enough for it to be undeniable. These people were alive! Without thinking, he reacted. Unable to contain himself, he stopped and spun around to look for Donna. He stood still like a rock in a stream, the bodies stumbling past on either side. When she was close enough to reach, he grabbed her arm.

"Up there," he said, pointing up at the people in the windows. "Look!"

She glared at him in disbelief, not listening to what he was saying, stunned that he had been stupid enough to blow the cover they'd managed to maintain for so long. Aware that the bodies nearest to her were already beginning to react, albeit slowly, she dropped her head again and kept walking.

"Keep moving," she hissed, her voice just loud enough for him to hear.

"But Donna . . ." he started to say. He stopped speaking when he realized that several of the corpses surrounding them had stopped moving also. Now he and Donna stood alone in the middle of a sudden unexpected pocket of space. The dead dragged their clumsy feet to turn around and face them. He tried shuffling forward again but it was too late.

"Run for it, you fucking idiot!" she yelled at him as the first body lunged at her. Without waiting for him to react, she dropped her shoulder and began sprinting toward the building ahead. She collided with body after body, each impact sending the weak figures tumbling to the ground like skittles, causing more and more of them to react.

The sheer mass of bodies crammed hard against the front of the building ahead made the main entrance appear impassable. Already gasping for breath, Donna looked around anxiously for another option as she ran. She was surrounded on all sides by hideous corpses, either lurching toward her or obliviously blocking her way. She just kept moving, hoping that her comparative strength would get her through the bulk of the crowd. She sensed that Paul was close behind but she didn't bother to check. He'd have to look after himself now. Stupid fucking moron.

She had reached the ring road. She tripped down the high curb and began to run across the wide stretch of tarmac, managing to push bodies away while avoiding the wreckage of cars and rotting corpses strewn haphazardly across her path. The crowd surged around her relentlessly, moving slowly, almost as a single mass like a thick and viscous liquid. Up and over the low central reservation barrier and she knew she was almost there. She could hear Paul closing on her now, grunting with effort as he too forced his way forward through the seemingly endless tide of dead flesh.

"Go right!" she heard him shout, and she immediately changed direction. The building in front of them was long and narrow and they were considerably closer to the right end than the left. It was logical to try and get around the back, but who was to say there wasn't a crowd twice as big behind the building? As she rounded the corner she saw, to her relief, that there were fewer bodies here. She ducked down under a red-and-white-striped entry barrier, took a deep breath, shoved another two corpses out of the way, and continued to run.

"Climb up!" she heard Paul yell from somewhere close behind. "Get up off the ground."

Donna looked around helplessly, not sure what he was expecting her to do. He sprinted past her and ran toward a large delivery truck which had crashed into the side of the building. He hauled himself up the front of the vehicle, using the mirrors, then clambered onto the roof of the cab, away from the grabbing hands below. Clinging onto the roof, he reached back down for Donna.

"Come on," he screamed at her. Exhausted, she fought her way over to the truck, caught his outstretched hand, and climbed up. By the time she'd made it onto the top of the cab, Paul was already working his way along the length of the vehicle's trailer. Donna followed a few steps farther, but then stopped and dropped to her knees.

"Help!" she yelled desperately, praying that someone would hear her. Paul kept moving. The back end of the truck was less than a meter from the outside wall of the building. Just above his head was a small enclosed balcony. Without stopping to consider the risks he leapt up and grabbed hold of the metal railings which surrounded the balcony area. He grimaced with pain as the sudden weight of his body threatened to wrench his shoulders from their joints. Slowly, and with much effort, he hauled himself higher and swung his legs up and over. Donna watched from the roof of the truck as he began to smash his fists furiously against a double-glazed window.

Donna lay down and rolled over onto her back, and looked up into the gray morning sky above. The noise that Paul was making faded away, as did the constant shuffling of the bodies swarming around the front of the building and now surrounding the truck upon which she lay. She stared up into the clouds moving over her head and watched as they blew across from left to right, trying desperately to shut everything else out. *If I look up and I keep looking up,* she told herself, *then everything will seem normal. If I don't look down then I can pretend that none of this is real. Just for a few seconds I can pretend none of this is happening.*

After locating the room where the noise was coming from, Keith Peterson forced it open and helped Paul inside. Using a metal stepladder to bridge the gap between the building and the top of the truck, he cautiously ventured out into the cold and inhospitable morning to bring Donna into the shelter.

18

Midday.

Donna had managed to sleep for a couple of hours. It was the first time in almost a week that she'd had a proper bed and even though it was in a cold and unfamiliar place, it still felt reassuringly comfortable and safe. A man she hadn't seen before walked past the open door of the room she'd been sleeping in and, seeing that she was awake, stopped to talk to her.

"How you feeling?" he asked.

"Crap," she replied with brutal honesty.

"I'm Bernard Heath," he said, taking a couple of hesitant steps into the room.

"Donna."

"Are you hungry? We've got food downstairs and . . ."

Donna was up and on her feet before he'd even finished his sentence. She was starving. Bernard led her along the corridor and down the stairs.

"Bloody hell," she said under her breath as she walked into

the assembly hall. She began to cry and self-consciously wiped the tears away. She couldn't help herself. They'd brought her through here earlier when she and Paul had first arrived, but she'd been tired and terrified and hadn't appreciated what she'd seen. She'd almost given up hope of ever seeing this many people together again. She counted at least seventeen of them. In one corner a handful of subdued children played quietly. Elsewhere people sat around the edges of the room, generally keeping themselves to themselves.

Bernard fetched Donna some food. Standing alone in the middle of the hall with a tray in her hands, she suddenly felt exposed and vulnerable. She looked around for somewhere less conspicuous to sit and saw Paul sitting, talking to another man. Despite the fact that she still wanted to punch him in the face for the stupid stunt he'd pulled this morning, he was the only other person she knew. Wearily she sat down next to him.

"You okay?" he asked. She grunted but didn't answer properly. She began to eat the crackers and cheese spread that she'd been given. Her hands shook as she tried to spread the cheese with a flimsy plastic knife.

"This is Richard Stephens," Paul continued, introducing the man sitting next to him. "Rich, this is Donna."

"How you doing," Richard said wearily, managing half a smile. Donna managed another grunt.

"Rich says there's almost fifty people here, you know," Paul whispered. "Thank God we found this place. He says that most of them don't come out of their rooms and . . ."

"Finding it wasn't difficult," Donna said, swallowing a mouthful of dry food and summoning up enough energy to bring herself to speak. "It was getting in here that was the hard part. It wouldn't have been so much of a problem if it hadn't been for you, you stupid bloody idiot."

"What was I supposed to do?"

"You could have tried staying quiet and kept walking, like we agreed."

"We got here, didn't we?"

"No thanks to you."

Paul turned back to face Richard, trying to ignore her anger. "So what's the plan?" he asked. "What happens next? Are we staying here or . . . ?"

"As far as I know there is no plan, mate," Richard replied, his voice sounding as tired and flat as he looked.

"Even if there was you'd only go and screw it up," Donna snapped. Paul ignored her again.

"Don't think anyone knows what to do next," Richard continued. "Doesn't seem to be a lot of point, does there? Seems like it's going to be as bad wherever you go so you might as well stay put. A couple of us have got some ideas, though, haven't we, Nathan?"

Nathan Holmes was walking across the hall on his way back to his room. At the mention of his name he stopped and turned around. Glad of the distraction, he pulled up a chair and sat down in front of Richard and Paul.

"I was just telling Paul that we'd been assessing our priorities."

Nathan cracked a broad, knowing grin. "Too right," he said.

"So what are you going to do?" Paul asked.

"When those things outside start to drift away," he explained, "we're going out on the town."

"What do you mean?"

"I mean we're going to shut ourselves in one of the clubs 'round here and we're going to have the biggest fucking party you've ever seen. We're going to blow all the drinks and drugs we can find in the place. And when they start to wear off and we start to come back down, we're going on to the next club and we're going to do it all over again. The biggest bloody pub crawl in history!"

"Sounds good," Paul said, far from convinced.

"You've watched too many movies," Donna said. "That's the kind of thing people *think* they're going to do when the world ends. You'll probably just spend your time shut in here with everybody else." Nathan ignored her and continued.

"We're going to hit this town and—"

"You been outside recently?" she interrupted again. Nathan leaned back on his chair to get a proper look at her. He hadn't seen her around before.

"Yeah, I was out there yesterday. Why?"

"Because the world's dead, that's why." She sighed.

"Exactly. That's why we're going to do it. Nothing matters when you've had a few drinks."

She looked at him sadly and returned her attention to her food. Nathan leaned across and helped himself to a cracker.

"Do you mind?"

"Not at all," he replied in a smug, self-assured voice. "Don't remember seeing your face," he said, chewing noisily. "When did you get here?"

"This morning."

"You been out there all this time?"

"Yes."

"You're right. It's grim, ain't it?"

Donna nodded. She didn't want to talk to Nathan. She didn't really want to talk to anyone, least of all this brash and irritating little man. Much as she'd craved company and conversation recently, now all she wanted was some space and time alone. Now that she'd found a relatively safe place to shelter, the full enormity of what had happened to the rest of the world was beginning to hit her hard. She didn't want to discuss it yet, or talk endlessly and pointlessly about the whys and wherefores. Having other people close by was comfort enough.

"I tell you," Nathan continued, completely oblivious to Donna's lack of interest in him, "there's no way I'm sitting in here with this lot much longer. Soon as I'm ready I'm getting out. We've got the whole bloody country out there just waiting for us, isn't that right, Rich?"

Richard nodded. "Damn right."

Donna looked at the two men in disbelief. Was getting drunk really all that was left for them to do? With the world lying in tatters at their feet, did they not have any higher priorities? Maybe it was a sensible way to try and forget all that had happened and enjoy what time remained, but could their suggestion really be the only alternative? Looking into Nathan's gormless, grinning face, she knew that there had to be a better option than the seedy, selfish, and dangerous escape he was planning.

"You can finish this," she said as she stood up and dropped

the tray of food onto his lap. He watched her as she walked away.

"Where are you going?" he asked, getting up and following her.

"Somewhere else."

"Where's somewhere else?"

"Somewhere away from blokes like you."

"I've got some bad news for you, sweetheart," he said, walking alongside her. "Blokes like me are all that's left."

Donna stopped walking and turned to face him.

"If that's true, then we really are fucked."

"Come on, darling—"

"Listen," she said quietly, not wanting everyone to hear, but not really caring if they did, "I'm twenty-four years old, I'm female, and I'm blonde. I've had to deal with fucking idiots like you for as long as I can remember. I've seen hundreds of your type—you're all mouth but you've got no balls. If you're really all that's left then I'll be spending the rest of my time on my own. Now piss off!"

"I'll see you around, then." Nathan smirked as she stormed away.

Donna got lost in the accommodation block. The different floors, corridors, staircases, and rooms all looked the same. She remembered that her room was the third or fourth along from the stairs, but she couldn't remember whether it was on the second or third floor. She opened a third-floor door which looked vaguely familiar. It was immediately obvious that she was wrong—a young Asian man was sitting on the bed, staring into space.

"Sorry," she mumbled instinctively, "wrong room . . ."

He looked up at her and smiled. He looked lost, and terrified.

"You okay?" she asked. He nodded. "I'm in the room next door, I think," she said slowly, pointing down the corridor and hoping that she was right. "Give me a shout if you need anything, okay?"

He continued to look at her blankly. "No English," he said simply. Another smile and Donna left the man alone and returned to her room. She lay down on the bed and closed her eyes. For a while she couldn't get his face out of her head. As if everything that had happened wasn't hard enough already, that poor sod was having to cope with it all without being able to understand a word the other survivors said. If she felt detached and alone, she thought, how the hell must he be feeling?

Dark thoughts filled Donna's mind, and the longer the silence in her room continued, the darker her thoughts became.

19

Jack Baxter left his room and walked to the end of the corridor. He wasn't going anywhere in particular, he just needed a change of surroundings. Like most of the other individuals sheltering in the university, the oppressive quiet and lack of distractions in the building left him with nothing to do but dwell on the empty hell which his life had become. He'd spent most of the day sitting on the end of his bed just thinking. He couldn't even remember what he'd been thinking about.

At the far end of the corridor was a narrow rectangular landing which led out onto the staircase. Floor-to-ceiling windows let the gray, autumnal light seep inside. Jack stood a short distance away from the nearest window and peered down into the swarming mass of dark, decaying bodies still being drawn toward the university and, in particular, to the accommodation block. Why did they stay? he wondered. He took a single cautious step forward. He was too far away and too high to be seen by any of the bodies, but he still instinctively tried to keep out of sight. He was terrified that one of them might see him and start to react, and that that might cause others to do the same. He imagined the effect of that single reaction rippling uncontrollably through the entire crowd. He'd seen it happen several times already today—a slight disturbance in one part of the crowd would spread across the immense gathering like a shock wave. It had happened when the woman had jumped to her death from the window earlier. He could just about see her broken body from where he was standing. Poor cow, he thought. He couldn't help thinking that she was better off where she was now.

"Bloody mess, isn't it?" an unexpected voice said from close behind him. Jack spun around. It was Bernard. Jack had noticed that he seemed to have a real problem with being on his own. He could often be seen walking around the building in search of someone to talk to. Jack found his conversations a little overpowering, but he knew it was just his way of trying to cope. "Sorry, Jack," Bernard continued, "I didn't mean to disturb you. It's just that I saw you standing here and I thought I'd check that you were okay . . ."

"I'm fine," Jack said quickly. Bernard took a few steps forward and peered down into the rotting crowd.

"I reckon this lot will start to disappear sooner or later," he said with a tone of unexpected optimism in his voice. "As soon as something happens somewhere else to attract their attention, they'll be off."

"Like what?" Jack asked. "That's the problem, isn't it? Nothing else *is* happening out there."

"I'll tell you what's starting getting to me," Bernard said, that faint trace of optimism gone, his voice now sounding tired and candid instead. "It's how slowly everything seems to happen around here. I mean, I've been sitting downstairs with the rest of them and no one says a word. Every time I look up at the clock it feels like hours have gone by, but only a couple of minutes have passed . . ."

"That's why I'm here," Jack said, not taking his eyes off the crowd below. "I was just sitting in my room staring at the walls, going out of my bloody mind."

"Have you tried reading?"

"No, have you?"

"I did," he said, scratching the side of his ragged beard. "I used to lecture here. I went back to my office a couple of days ago and picked up a few books. Brought them back with me and sat down to read one, but . . ."

"But what?"

"Couldn't do it."

"Why not?"

Bernard didn't immediately answer. Jack looked up from the bodies and stared into his weary face.

"Don't know," he finally admitted. "I started to read a novel but I only managed a few pages before I had to stop. All it did was remind me of what's happened and what's gone and . . ."

He stopped talking, feeling suddenly awkward and somewhat embarrassed that he was letting his feelings show so readily again.

"So what happens next, then?" wondered Jack, making a conscious effort to change the focus of their conversation to trying to look forward, not back. Bernard appeared to go through the motions of thinking carefully for a few moments but it was pointless, really—he'd spent most of the last week pondering endless variations on the question he'd just been asked and in all that time he hadn't yet managed to find a single answer.

"We sit and wait," he said eventually.

"And is that it?"

"What else can we do?"

The two men stood side by side in silence and looked out over the desolate world. Both wanted to talk, but neither could think of anything to say. Several minutes later Bernard walked away, soon followed by Jack, who went dejectedly back to his room. He wasn't tired but he lay down on the bed and tried to sleep, because sleep was just about the only way he had left to try and block out the nightmare for a while.

PART II

20

In the desolate shell of the city, very little changed from day to day. Thousands of corpses continued to shuffle endlessly through the streets, their bodies gradually decaying, but with a degree of mental strength and control somehow continuing to slowly return. Although the survivors remained quiet and largely out of sight, the almost total absence of any other sounds or distractions through- out the surrounding area continued to draw vast and unwanted crowds of stumbling figures toward the university campus. Inside their shelter the frightened people sat and watched and waited. For two painfully slow and drawn-out weeks, nothing changed.

Without warning, on a cold, wet Sunday some nineteen days after everything had changed, the precarious equilibrium was disturbed again.

Thirty miles west of the city where the survivors sheltered, in a bleak and nondescript field miles from anywhere of any impor- tance, was the concealed entrance to a military bunker. Waiting underground inside the vast concrete complex, shielded and protected from the dead world outside by thick walls, numerous layers of different insulations, and industrial-strength air purification systems, were almost three hundred soldiers. They were as tired, frightened, and disorientated as the bewildered survivors left out in the open, and they too had struggled to cope with the constant uncertainty of their situation. Inside the bunker no one knew what had happened. From the most senior officer in the base down to the lowest recruit in the ranks, no one had anything more than a few scraps of unconfirmed information to go on. They had been acting on hurriedly given orders when they'd been scrambled on that first morning and had heard nothing from anywhere else since the bunker had been locked down and sealed. Communications had either failed or simply stopped, no one knew which. Countless rumors sprung up to explain the soldiers' incarceration—a terrorist attack, a mutated disease, an industrial accident, a new strain of superbug, and a hundred variations on a hundred other ideas—but there were no concrete facts available to substantiate any of them or to confirm or deny the hearsay. In reality, the men and women in the bunker didn't need to know the details of what had happened and neither, for that matter, did the officers in charge of the base. All any of them knew was that sooner or later they'd have no option but to send troops up to the surface to try and take control of whatever was left.

Those orders had finally been given by the base commander. Today was the day the first troops would go outside.

21

Despite years of dedicated service and postings in some of the most dangerous, godforsaken places imaginable, when Cooper heard he was going above ground he was terrified.

The soldiers had been underground for nineteen days, their time routinely filled with pointless exercises, unnecessary maintenance chores, regular domestic duties, and redundant training. The officers did all they could to keep the troops busy and occupied, but they had still been left with far too much time to sit and think and wonder about what was happening to the outside world and the people they'd left behind. In the absence of any reliable explanations, a thousand and one unchallenged rumors had swept through the base, massively increasing the tension and unease. Cooper usually managed to rise above rumor and ignore baseless speculation, but in the absence of any genuine explanation for what had undoubtedly been an unparalleled event on an unprecedented scale, it was impossible.

A rudimentary briefing took place before the bunker doors

were opened. The most senior officers told the soldiers who were about to go outside everything they knew about conditions on the surface, but that amounted to next to nothing. Cooper found what they didn't say more disturbing than what they did. They talked in vague, generic terms about some kind of disease or virus, but they didn't know anything about the symptoms or the effects. The only facts which could be reported with any certainty were that the base had been unable to make contact with anyone else—civilian or military—and that it was to be assumed that the germ was still in the air outside, waiting like a deadly predator poised to strike. Full protective gear was to be worn at all times. Hours, maybe even days of decontamination would follow the reconnaissance mission, if and when they returned.

Feeling less like a soldier and more a sacrificial lamb, Cooper collected his gear from the stores, put on his kit, checked and rechecked his weapons, then sat and waited for the call. Sometimes, at moments like this, he questioned why he continually put his life on the line. Although always remaining unfailingly loyal and professional, the temptation to throw down his arms and desert the force was stronger than ever. Today, however, he had no option. By all accounts there was nowhere left to run to. He could die fighting, or die running.

The quiet of the countryside was shattered as the bunker doors opened and an armored transport emerged at speed into the dull light of a cold, wet autumn afternoon. The powerful machine roared up the access ramp, climbed the steep incline, and followed the track away from the hidden base.

It took the troops more than an hour to travel the thirty or so miles to the city. They followed a direct route along major roads that were littered with the wreckage of crashed vehicles and the decaying remains of countless bodies. Occasionally other figures appeared in the near distance and at the sides of the road but they were lethargic and painfully slow, seeming to drag themselves along with considerable effort. The soldiers didn't stop to offer assistance or investigate. The driver of the transport had his orders, and those orders were to go directly to the heart of the nearest city. It didn't matter anyway. What could they do for these first few poor people? What could just fifteen soldiers possibly do to help millions of plague victims?

Cooper turned to look at Mark Thompson, who was sitting next to him. Even through the tinted visors on their cumbersome, full-face breathing masks, Cooper could see that Thompson was scared. He could see it in his expression—the way that, although his head remained perfectly still and fixed forward, his eyes darted frantically around the inside of the transport, never daring to settle on any one thing for fear of catching sight of whatever it was that was terrifying him. And that was still the problem, Cooper decided, the not knowing. They'd been trained to deal with the aftermath of nuclear war, conventional war, terrorism, and many other types of conflict, threat, or attack, but this was different. The details of cause and effect were sparse, but it was already clear that no one could have been trained to deal with anything on this massive scale.

It was uncomfortably hot in the protective suit. Cooper knew that his life depended on the protection, of course, but the oppressive atmosphere beneath the layers of rubberized material did nothing to calm his nerves. The initial burst of adrenaline he'd felt on leaving the bunker had gone and he now felt claustrophobic, desperate to get back to the base, the place he'd wanted so badly to escape from for every minute of the last two and a half weeks. His mouth was dry and he needed to drink, but he wouldn't risk compromising his suit. Eating, drinking, going to the toilet, and many other simple and ordinary tasks would be risky until they were back. To remove any part of the suit for even a second might be enough to let in the invisible virus, which, if the information his officers had was correct, would quickly end his life. Judging by the number of bodies lying on the ground as they drove through the suburbs and into the city, this was a disease that had killed many, many thousands more than it had spared.

Heavy rain clattered down constantly on the metal roof above the soldiers' heads, echoing around the inside of the transport. There was no conversation, only sudden, brief explosions of static and voices from the radio, followed by equally brief reports back to base.

The soldiers were seated in two rows along either side of the transport, all of them facing into the middle. Thompson suddenly got up out of his seat, hung onto a handrail, and leaned across the inside of the machine to look out through a small square window between the heads of the two troopers sitting directly opposite.

"Bloody hell," he said, loud enough for the rest of them to hear. There was sudden movement throughout the vehicle as the others immediately crowded around to see what it was that their colleague had spotted deep in the murky grayness of the afternoon. All around them they could see movement. It was slow and labored but it was very definitely movement.

They had reached what Cooper thought of as the inner suburbs of the city—a ring of small shopping areas and high streets which had once been villages in their own right but which, over the years, had gradually been swallowed up and consumed by the ever-expanding city center. These areas were the first real pockets of civilization that the soldiers had seen since leaving the base. There were many more bodies on the ground here, and there were many more people moving through the streets too.

"Why ain't they done anything with any of the bodies yet?" asked another one of the soldiers, his voice muffled by his face mask.

"And what the hell are they doing outside?" said another, watching through a back window as a fast growing crowd of moving figures dragged themselves pointlessly along the road after the transport, even though they had no hope of catching it. "If these people are sick, then what are they doing out here in the open? It's pissing down, for Christ's sake."

"Who says they're sick?" asked Thompson. "These are supposed to be the survivors, aren't they?"

"Have you seen the state of them?" the other soldier replied nervously, his mouth dry. "Jesus, look at them. They've got fucking scraps of clothes on and they don't look like they've eaten for weeks. Bloody hell, they look as bad as the dead ones on the ground."

Cooper shuffled around to look out of the window nearest to him. The temperature outside was unseasonably low and the thick glass was smeared with condensation. He wiped it clear with the back of one gloved hand and peered out into the afternoon gloom.

"Christ . . ." he muttered under his breath.

The world outside the window looked as if it had been bleached, almost totally drained of all color. Perhaps naively he had expected to find a disorganized but otherwise relatively normal city scene—after all, he thought, there hadn't been any fighting on the streets, had there? This didn't sound like it had been a battle which would cause damage to buildings and property. But where he had expected to see a thousand familiar colors, he instead saw just a thousand different dull shades of gray, black, and brown. And the same was true of the people he could see too. Devoid of all energy, they were dragging themselves along with painful effort and a lack of any real speed or coordination. They looked like they had given up all hope.

In a few more minutes they had reached the city center and their target coordinates. The driver slammed on the brakes and for a second the only sound inside the transport was the rain hammering down on the metal roof. The troops sank back into their seats and waited for orders.

"Okay," Captain Williams, the officer in charge, yelled from his position near the front of the powerful machine, "I want all of you outside now. Get a perimeter formed around the transport. Move!"

The nearest soldier pushed open the heavy, armor-plated door at the back of the vehicle and led the others out. In a well-rehearsed maneuver they fanned out and formed a loose circle around the machine, equidistant to each other. The driver remained behind the wheel—ready to get them away quickly—

while Williams stood shoulder to shoulder with the men and women under his command.

Cooper stood motionless and stared into the city. Torrential rain drenched the grim scene like a mist. He watched the water run down a gutter toward him. A short distance from his feet lay several decomposing bodies. The world looked completely alien and unfamiliar. He had been to this city several times before, he'd even driven along this very road, but today it was unrecognizable.

Some of the people were approaching, emerging slowly through the gloom. They were difficult to see at first as they moved silently and awkwardly toward the soldiers. Christ, Cooper thought, they could hardly even walk in a straight line.

"So what are we supposed to do now?" Lance Jackson— a twenty-two-year-old soldier who looked no older than seventeen—nervously asked. He anxiously shifted his weight from foot to foot, holding his automatic rifle tight against his chest. Williams forgave his lack of discipline. He was scared too, although he didn't allow himself to show it.

"Keep your nerve, son," he said from close behind, resting a reassuring hand on Jackson's shoulder. "Just remember that these people are going to want help and answers from us, and we're in no position to provide either. Stay calm and stay alert and we'll . . ."

His words trailed away as he watched the first bodies stagger ever closer. They were near enough for the soldiers to be able to see into their disfigured faces now, their features ravaged by disease and decay. Each one of the troops seemed to focus on whichever one of the pitiful creatures was nearest. Williams watched a dead office worker lurch toward him unsteadily. What remained of the once smartly-suited woman lifted its weary head to look in his direction. It seemed to fix him with a cold, emotionless stare from its dark, sunken eyes.

"Fuck," he cursed, letting his guard and his nerve slip for the first time in seventeen years of active service. The bodies continued to shuffle forward toward the increasingly anxious soldiers. Amanda Brice, standing four men around to Cooper's right, lifted her rifle and took aim. Others did the same. Cooper cleared his throat and readied his own weapon.

"Stop moving," Williams shouted through a loud-hailer to the advancing people. "Stay where you are. We're here to help, but you need to do exactly as I tell you."

The figures continued to move closer. He wondered if they could even hear Williams.

"I repeat," the Captain bellowed again, "stay where you are and no harm will come to you . . ."

Still no response.

The nearest body was now just a couple of meters away from Brice. Terrified by the unnatural, emotionless expression on its pallid face, she aimed her rifle into the air just inches above the man's head and pulled the trigger. Ignorant to any danger, it continued to stagger forward. *Fucker didn't even flinch,* she thought.

"Jesus Christ," she cursed under her breath. "What the hell's the matter with them?"

The figures closed in on the circle of soldiers. Bewildered, and trying not to panic, Brice aimed at the body in front of her and fired, sending a single bullet thudding into the dead flesh just above the creature's right knee. It crumbled and fell to the ground, but immediately began to pick itself back up again, seemingly oblivious to its injury. Brice stared into its face. There was no expression of pain, no display of any emotion whatsoever, but it was hard to see anything through the discoloration and disfigurement. She looked down at its wounded leg and saw congealed blood dribbling in clots—not pouring—from the bullet hole. She fired at it again and again and again, the body jerking backward with each individual impact, but between shots it continued to approach.

"Get back inside," Williams ordered, already on his way back. "There's nothing we can do. Let's get out of here."

The troops turned and ran. Thompson was caught by the arm as several of the creatures reached out and grabbed hold of him. He began to beat at them, battering them away with his fists and the butt of his rifle. As quickly as he could break their hold, however, more gripped onto his suit.

Finding himself suddenly the only other soldier left outside, Cooper tried to help his colleague and wrestle him free. Out of the corner of his eye he saw that the others had disappeared into the back of the transport, crowds of gray figures following close behind. Billowing black fumes belched from the vehicle's exhaust as the driver prepared to leave.

"Come on," he yelled at Thompson. "Move!"

Disorientated by the foul mass of rotting faces around him, Thompson panicked and tried to force his way farther forward through the ever-increasing crowd, moving away from the transport. Cooper again tried to drag him back. Still swinging his fists furiously, Thompson battered a swathe through the decaying hordes, his comparative strength meeting with little resistance. He quickly beat his way through the main mass of cadavers and reached an area where they were considerably fewer in number. Still surrounded, Cooper glanced back over his shoulder and saw that the transport had now been almost completely swallowed up by even more of the abhorrent figures. Suddenly aware that his path back to their armored vehicle had been cut off, Thompson swung out with the butt of his rifle, then pushed his way through the remainder of the crowd, running toward the dark shadows of the city center buildings.

"Shit," Cooper snapped. The transport was beginning to push through the swelling crowds, moving away from them, the roar of its powerful engine filling the afternoon air with noise. More and more of the bodies dragged themselves after it as it began to accelerate away. The situation was dangerously unpredictable. Cooper knew that the others wouldn't wait and that, if it came down to it, both he and Thompson were expendable. Williams's priority would be to return to the base and report back as ordered and it didn't matter how many of them returned with him. As long as someone made it back the mission objectives would have been achieved. He started to run back toward the vehicle as it began to speed away, but he was too late. He stopped running before he hit the outermost edge of the mass of diseased civilians, not wanting to get any closer, and all he could do was watch as the transport disappeared into the driving rain.

Behind him, Thompson yelled out with anger and rage. Cooper spun around and watched as the soldier clubbed another body to the ground, then turned and ran again. *Bloody idiot,* he thought as he wrestled himself free from two more bodies which grabbed at him incessantly. With their transport gone he knew he had little choice but to follow Thompson into the center of town, then hope they could find somewhere safe to shelter and plot their way back. He ran after Thompson, smashing still more weak and clumsy figures away, trying to make silent escape plans. He knew the way out of the city and the route to the base. It would just be a question of finding a car or some other form of transport and . . . and what the hell was Thompson doing now? He'd been running up the middle of a sloping street lined with dilapidated shops and cafés, but he'd suddenly slowed down. There were several grotesque figures advancing toward him from different directions. He knew they were there, but he didn't seem to care.

"For God's sake," Cooper yelled at him, his voice muffled by his breathing apparatus but still loud enough for the other man to clearly hear, "what the fuck are you doing?"

Thompson ripped off his mask.

"I'm not going back," he shouted, his terrified face flushed red. "Look at this bloody place, Cooper, it's a fucking nightmare. I'm not going back there to bury myself underground. I'm going to try and get home and—"

He stopped speaking abruptly and lifted a gloved hand to his throat.

"Thompson?" Cooper shouted at him but he didn't respond. He stood and swayed for a moment, surrounded by advancing corpses but paying them no attention, then he dropped to his knees as if someone had kicked his legs from under him and began to cough and spasm violently. Doubled over with sudden, searing agony, he clutched at his neck as the lining of his throat began to swell and split, cutting off his air supply. By the time Cooper had reached him he was already choking on the blood running down his windpipe and draining into his lungs. He lay on the dirty ground and shook and convulsed next to Cooper's feet, spitting crimson blood out over the wet tarmac. He looked up at him with bulging, helpless eyes and then lay still, his limbs twitching occasionally.

Cooper looked up and saw that he was already surrounded, bodies dragging themselves toward him from every conceivable angle. He nudged Thompson with his boot and then, sure that his colleague was dead and he could do nothing for him, he ran deeper into town.

The torrential rain was falling harder than ever, bouncing back up off the pavement. Cooper ran up a steady incline toward a small precinct filled with sad-looking shops and rotting human remains. There were even more of the staggering survivors here (if that was what they really were), but their reactions were uniformly slow: dulled by whatever it was that had happened to them weeks ago. As Cooper pushed his way through them it was all they could do to turn around and stumble after him, grabbing at the air where he'd just been. As a soldier it was his duty to defend and protect these people, but it was clear that they were already beyond hope. Forget about the uniform, he told himself as he ran. As a human being, his priorities had just become infinitely simpler and more selfish. Fuck everything and everybody else, he needed to get away from the unrecognizable hell that this city had become and look after himself. His own safety was his only remaining concern.

A sharp right took him down a narrow passageway between a tall office building and an equally high development of luxury city center flats. In the confined space the driving rain seemed to echo louder than ever before. There were people up ahead now, moving toward him. The passageway was tight and he knew it would be difficult to get through the crowd, their sudden numbers alone presenting him with a major problem. A quick glance over his shoulder revealed that even more of them had followed him from the other direction. He was boxed in, and although these pitiful creatures were individually unimportant, there were far too many of them to simply dismiss as not being a threat. By the same token, however, he had no desire to cause them any harm. They had clearly already suffered enough. They were weak and malnourished, innocent victims who hadn't done anything wrong. He'd spent enough time in war zones around the world to appreciate the damage caused to indigenous populations whenever the military got involved.

Halfway down the passageway in an alcove was a large cylindrical metal waste bin which Cooper scrambled up onto. From there he was able to haul himself up onto a metal fire escape ladder. He climbed to a first-floor window which he kicked in with one of his heavily booted feet. Carefully clambering through the broken glass (*Watch the damn suit,* he screamed to himself) he found himself in a large, open-plan office. There were more of the silent people inside, all in a similar condition to those walking the rain-soaked streets. They immediately turned and began to move toward him, their dark, clouded eyes following his every move. Why were these people still at work? Why hadn't they gone home to be with their friends and families? Had they really been here for almost three weeks . . . ?

"Look," he began to say, struggling to know what to tell them, "please don't be afraid. I'm not going to . . ."

It was pointless. The people in the building were as catatonic as those he'd seen outside. Cooper stared with mounting horror into the face of the nearest one of them. Once an attractive graduate trainee, this woman's blistered, weeping, peeling skin was now tinged with an unnatural blue-green hue. Clumps of long hair were missing from the side of her scalp. He glanced down at one of the lifeless cadavers slumped across a desk next to him. Even though he was looking through a tinted visor, it occurred to him that those bodies which were still moving and those which weren't all appeared to be in the same appalling physical condition. He'd seen it before when he'd been out in the field on active duty. This was the unmistakeable look of death. Jesus, these people were rotting . . .

With increasing panic and the taste of bile rising in his throat, Cooper ran across the room, climbing up onto the furniture and leaping from desk to desk to avoid making contact with the shadowy figures now clamoring around him. He jumped down to the floor and crashed through a heavy fire door into a dark corridor. Pushing his way past another wandering body he reached a staircase and instinctively began to climb. He moved as quickly as he could until he'd reached the top floor and could go no farther. After trying three locked office doors he forced his way into a small storeroom. He slammed the door shut behind him and pulled a metal storage rack across to block it and prevent the people outside from getting in.

Twenty minutes later, when Cooper had caught his breath and managed to calm himself down slightly, he walked across the room to the single window and peered out over the world outside. He could see huge numbers of bodies drifting about aimlessly. He could hear them moving around in other parts of this building too.

These grim surroundings weren't Cooper's prime concern. There was an invisible killer hanging in the air, a germ which would get him one way or another—either by poisoning him, or forcing him to suffocate and starve in this damn protective suit and mask. He'd witnessed for himself the speed with which it had destroyed Thompson. Cooper knew that while he was out here, his life depended on this suit. And it would stay that way until he made it back to the bunker.

22

The dead world had been silent for what felt like forever. Even the slightest noise traveled huge distances, carried for miles on the wind. The movement of the soldiers in their powerful transport had caused the dead population to react along the entire length of their journey—from the rolling hills around the bunker itself right through to the desolate heart of the city. In a frighteningly short space of time, the crowd around the university had become a seething mass of movement and hostility. Random waves of bodies tried to move away from the buildings in search of the source of the disturbance while others continued to move toward it, still hunting for the sheltering survivors they knew were close.

In the university accommodation block, every single survivor had been stirred and encouraged by the sounds outside. More than just another random crash or unexplained disturbance, the noises they heard through the rain today were different. These were purposeful, intentional, mechanical noises. These were sounds which could only have been made by others like them. And the gunshots and shouting which followed had confirmed beyond doubt that, today, there really had been other living people in the city.

The people living in the complex had cocooned themselves within the walls of their hideaway. Surrounded by the dead and too afraid to leave the relative safety of the building, the bravest of them had climbed up onto the roof, battling against the appalling weather conditions to look out over the town. Even from their precarious vantage point they had been unable to see the other people, but they had watched as huge numbers of rotting bodies had begun to drift deeper into the city, reacting to the presence of the new arrivals. Although thousands seemed to have moved away, many thousands more remained behind.

Some of the living were encouraged by the ease with which the bodies had been distracted. Others saw it as a temporary victory, and surmised that those same corpses would inevitably drag themselves back again before long. People began to realize that if they wanted to let others know where they were sheltering, then they had to be prepared to risk attracting even more of the dead to the area around the university too. That was the quandary which suddenly threatened to split the group in two.

"I'm not going to agree to anything that's going to bring those bloody things back here again," snapped Bernard Heath. The sudden force and volume of his voice belied the fact that fear was the only reason he was opposed to the idea which had been proposed.

"For God's sake, Bernard," Donna sighed, frustrated by his belligerence, "can't you see what we're saying here? We know that whatever we do will bring the bodies back, but chances are it'll bring whoever else is out there to us as well. Do you really think we can afford to stay out here on our own for very much longer?"

"But we're not on our own, are we?" he argued. "There are more than forty of us here."

"That may be, but how many of them are in this room with us now? How many people do you actually see each day?"

Bernard looked around the largely empty assembly hall. She was right, less than half of the total number of people in the building were in the room with them. It was rare to see more than ten of them together at any one time, and it was only the activity in the city center which had brought most of them out of their rooms today. Most continued to cower in silence in their individual spaces, only emerging when they needed food or water.

"But did you see how many of them left when they heard the noises?"

"And did you see how many stayed?" Donna responded quickly. "So what if the size of the crowd reduced by half, Bernard? That'd still leave far too many for us to deal with. We'd still be in the same position. The number of those fuckers out there is academic now."

"Whatever happens we're going to end up stuck here," Dr. Croft interjected from across the hall. "I can see what Bernard's saying—give it a few more weeks and a few thousand more bodies and this shelter of ours will become a prison."

"No matter what we do those bodies will keep returning here," Donna continued. "The rest of the city is a tomb. We can't help but draw attention to ourselves, can we?"

"We can try," Bernard protested. "We could—"

"We could what? Shut ourselves away in a single room up high and hold our breath so they don't hear us?"

"No, I just think—"

"You've seen how those things are beginning to behave, haven't you?" she asked, her voice weary. "They're becoming more active and more violent every day. I know they're not particularly strong on their own, but look at the numbers we're dealing with."

"And like it or not, we're going to need to go out for supplies again soon," Croft interrupted. "I'm down to my last few packs of fags."

"Then quit," Bernard said angrily. Croft shook his head.

"I'm taking the piss, Bernard. The point I'm making is that as time goes on, we'll need to go further and further afield to get the supplies to keep everyone alive. We're going to have to spend longer out in the open and that means taking more risks unless we do something about it now. Donna's right. We need to let whoever it was that was out there know that we're here."

"We need to start getting ourselves organized," Donna continued. "Get some kind of routine and order to what we're doing. We need to find a way of letting those people know we're here without stirring up the bodies again."

"You're contradicting yourselves," Bernard said. "How are you going to attract anyone's attention without bringing even more bodies here?"

Nathan Holmes had been sitting in the corner of the room. He stood up and walked straight through the middle of the group to get to the exit.

"You're a bunch of fucking idiots," he said. The rest of the people in the hall turned and stared at him. "Just look at you. What are you trying to do here? Think you're going to build some brave new fucking world, or—"

"We're not trying to do anything except survive and—" Donna started to say before Nathan interrupted her.

"This is pointless. It's all pointless. You shouldn't even be wasting your time talking about it. As soon as I can I'm getting out of here and I'm going to . . ."

"We all know exactly what you're going to do," Donna said, annoyed. "You keep telling us. You're going to drink yourself stupid so that you can forget everything. We've all heard you say it a thousand times. I wish you'd just go and do it instead of hanging around here, getting in the way. You don't give a damn about anyone but yourself."

"Too right I don't. Why should I?"

"Can't you see how our chances will improve if we work together?" Croft asked him. Nathan looked up to the ceiling in despair.

"But that's my point, what chance have we got? Everybody in this damn building has lost everything. If there are other people out there, the last thing they need to do is lock themselves away in here with you lot. Getting out of here and trying to forget the fucking mess we're all in is the best option for anyone who's got any degree of sense left."

"You're confusing sense and selfishness," Donna told him.

"Look," Croft said, his patience wearing thin, "all we're talking about doing is setting up some kind of beacon temporarily so that if and when those others come back, they'll know

156

we're here. We're not trying to make great plans for the future because, Nathan, I happen to think you're right. We don't know if any of us have got a fucking future!"

"But your beacon will attract the bodies," protested Bernard.

"For Christ's sake, man, change the record," Croft seethed. "Can't you see that's a short-term risk we're going to have to take?"

Jack Baxter had been watching the increasingly tense conversation develop. "What if we put a beacon on the roof?" he suggested. "Think about it—if we put some kind of beacon up high, then it's not going to be immediately obvious to the bodies, but a survivor—"

"A survivor would know that anything up on the roof would probably have been put there intentionally," said Donna, realizing what he was saying. "If we're talking about lighting a fire, then a survivor would know that any blaze would most probably start somewhere inside a building and work its way up—it wouldn't start on top, would it?"

"I understand that," said Bernard, "but if and when those other people get here, they're going to bring the bodies with them, aren't they? It's not going to matter how careful you are with your bloody beacon, is it?"

Donna stared at the frightened lecturer in despair. She understood what he was saying, she just couldn't understand why it was such an issue for him. To her, the solution to their problem and the potential side effects were both obvious and unavoidable. They had a real chance of making contact with more survivors—people who had transport and weapons and who, it

157

seemed, were capable of moving out in the open, not just hiding away like they were. And if making contact with them meant temporarily increasing the number of bodies around the university, then that was a small price to pay.

23

Just over thirty miles from the city, and several miles from the entrance to the underground bunker, two survivors sat together in silence. Hiding in a relatively well-appointed motor home they had taken from outside another dead town just a few days earlier, the couple had driven out to the most isolated and exposed area of land they'd been able to find.

Since being forced to leave the farmhouse where they'd previously sheltered together, Michael Collins and Emma Mitchell had lived from hand to mouth like scavenging animals, moving from place to place and hiding in the shadows until the number of bodies surrounding them had reached critical mass. Five days ago the building where they'd holed-up in relative safety for more than a week had finally been overrun by hundreds of wandering corpses, attracted to their remote and otherwise inconspicuous location by the noise the survivors made simply by existing. They had taken many precautions to separate themselves from the rotting remains of the dead population, but all their efforts had ultimately been in vain. Michael and Emma had learned to their bitter cost that there was no way of escaping the unwanted attentions of millions upon millions of desperate, diseased, and increasingly vicious corpses.

The couple had heard the engine in the distance when the soldiers had emerged from their hidden base earlier in the day. At first it had seemed impossible to believe—since leaving the farmhouse neither of them had seen any indication that any other people were still alive; not a single sound or movement that might have pointed to the existence of other survivors. But the noise of the engine had been definite and unmistakable, and it had filled them both with sudden unexpected hope where before they had felt only emptiness and fear.

By the time they'd emerged from the motor home, the sound had faded away and the world was quiet again. They did, however, stumble upon a straight gravel track at the bottom of a hill near to where they had been parked. The track served no obvious purpose and, in the absence of any other roads or pathways for miles around, it seemed a logical starting point for their search. Michael had supposed that anyone else attempting to survive in this brutal, inhospitable world might have found themselves a base similar to the farmhouse where he and Emma had originally hidden. It followed that if these people were heading out from their base, looking for supplies, there was a fairly good chance they would be back again before long.

He was right.

The darkness of early evening had all but swallowed up the last light of the gloomy afternoon when they heard engine noise again. Distant and faint at first, it had quickly increased in volume. Ignorant to the dangers of being outside and exposed, Michael threw open the motor home door and jumped down the steps. He sprinted through the long, rain-soaked grass and crouched down on a small rocky outcrop from where he was able to get a relatively clear view of a long stretch of the track below. And then he saw it: a huge military transporter, roaring defiantly along the track. He couldn't see the driver of the vehicle or make out how many people were inside, but it didn't matter. More important than just finding other survivors, he now knew that these people were strong and well-organized. And if they really were the military, what did that mean? How many hundreds more of them could there be nearby?

The transport disappeared into the darkness, followed by a stream of slow-moving cadavers. He stood up and ran along the exposed brow of the hill, following the transport until it was completely out of view. Where did the track lead? He stared into the distance and contemplated what he had seen for a moment longer, before remembering the danger of being alone outside and running back to the motor home.

"Well?" Emma asked as he let himself back in.

"Bloody big army machine. Don't know exactly what it was for, but—"

"The army?"

"Looked like it," Michael said breathlessly as he locked and bolted the door behind him and drew the thick blackout curtains they used to stop any light from spilling out into the night and revealing their location to the rest of the world.

"Where did it go?"

He scowled at her. Emma had an infuriating habit of asking questions which she knew he couldn't answer.

"It was following the track we found earlier, so I guess it was going wherever the track leads."

"And where's that?"

"Bloody hell, Emma, how am I supposed to know? We should try and find out tomorrow."

"Not tonight?"

"Too dangerous. The light's almost gone. We'll have more chance of finding them in the morning."

24

Cooper was becoming increasingly claustrophobic in his suit. Made from layers of rubberized nylon and other, less easily identifiable materials, as well as preventing any contamination from getting inside it also stopped everything from getting out—and he was uncomfortably hot. He decided he'd make a move in a short while but, for now, he wanted to rest up and fully prepare for the journey back to the base. He didn't relish the thought of having to fight his way back out of the city. And what if he couldn't get access to the base when he finally made it back there? What if they wouldn't let him inside because the decontamination process had already started for the others? What if they hadn't even made it back themselves? What if the decontamination process didn't work? His imagination working overtime now, he envisaged having to wait outside on his own for days—unable to eat or drink or even to breathe freely.

Christ, what exactly *had* happened to the world?

He had been so preoccupied with his own situation since

becoming stranded, that the fate of the rest of the world had temporarily passed him by. The effects of the virus had been devastating beyond compare, that much was clear, but what had the deadly disease actually done? Why had some people survived when so many others had died? Had those people actually survived at all? Their skin bore the same telltale signs of decomposition and decay as the corpses on the ground and their movements and reactions were unnaturally slow. He checked himself. What was he actually saying here? Cooper laughed and leaned his head back against the wall. Were those people that had followed him dead? That was impossible. Maybe the air had been filled not with disease, but with some particularly effective hallucinogenic drug that had somehow breached the protection of his suit? Perhaps nothing that he thought he'd seen had actually happened. That was a marginally more plausible explanation of the bizarre events of the day so far.

The world outside was suffocatingly black now and he wondered whether he might be better making his move now under cover of darkness. Whatever the people he'd come across were—contaminated survivors or reanimated corpses, he wasn't sure which—he was clearly stronger and quicker than any of them. He also had the advantage of having been trained to fight and survive in the most extreme conditions. He was confident that getting out of the city wouldn't be a problem.

His stomach growled angrily with pangs of hunger. To add to the discomfort, his bladder was full to capacity, despite the fact that his throat was dry and he hadn't drunk anything for hours. He needed a distraction, and short of leaving the storeroom and taking his chances with the diseased population outside, he couldn't immediately think of one.

In a desperate attempt to keep his mind occupied for a while, Cooper began to look around the metal racking which surrounded him. Even a pen and paper would be sufficient—he could prepare his last will and testament, write a final letter to the people who mattered, compose a list of all the things he'd always wanted to do but hadn't, scribble pictures, play noughts and crosses, or do any number of things that might distract himself until the time was right to leave. Using the light from the Mag-light strapped to his belt, he peered dejectedly around the room.

Up high on the opposite side of the room he could see several dusty cardboard boxes. Most of the rest of the racking was loaded up with paperwork, files, basic office supplies, and stationery, but from where he stood he couldn't make out what these other boxes might contain. A mixture of inquisitiveness and sheer boredom drove him to climb up and look. Disappointingly they contained nothing more exciting than used printer cartridges and a spaghettilike mess of discarded computer cables.

Cooper lowered his foot to get back down but lost his balance when the racking (which was not attached to the wall as he'd assumed) tipped forward slightly. He dropped down heavily and landed hard on his back on top of a photocopier with a crash which sounded disproportionately loud. Winded and wincing with pain, he rolled off the top of the machine and hit the floor in an uncoordinated heap, smashing his face against more racking on the way down. Numb with shock and breathing heavily, he lay where he had fallen for a moment and listened to other sounds which had suddenly begun to echo around the building. The unexpected racket he'd made had caused the office's other occupants to stir again. With effort he slowly dragged himself back onto his feet and brushed himself down, cursing his stupidity.

He could feel air on his face.

Thrown into a desperate panic, Cooper scrambled around in the darkness for his torch. Switching it on again, he shone it across the room and in the light which came from it, he saw that the visor of his face mask was damaged. With his heart pounding in his chest, his eyes followed the route of a snaking crack across the visor from bottom left to top right, where he saw that the protective glass—Perspex, or whatever it was the mask was made of—had chipped.

An ice-cold wave of terror washed over the soldier as he realized the implications. His suit had been compromised. He had seen how quickly Thompson had been infected. He panicked, covering the crack in the visor with his hand, hoping to prevent the disease from getting inside, checking his belt for gum or tape or anything with which he could try and repair the damage. With each second that passed, so his fear increased. He knew full well that, in all probability, his lungs were already full of the deadly germ. All he could do now was wait for the inevitable to happen.

Cooper screwed his eyes shut.

He held his breath for as long as he could, knowing that the next time he breathed in might be the last.

A few seconds longer still and he ripped off the face mask.

He was already contaminated, that much was clear. He might as well breathe his final breath freely and not through the sterilizing filters of his army-issue breathing apparatus.

He opened the window and leaned at, sucking in deep lungfuls of cool but polluted autumn air, and waited.

And he waited.

After five minutes had passed he began to wonder why he wasn't dead. Or was he? Was this how the people who were still able to move had been affected? He didn't feel any different. It didn't hurt. He wasn't suffocating or choking or spitting out blood like Thompson had earlier.

It was several hours before Cooper finally allowed himself to accept the fact that he had somehow been left untouched by whatever it was that had torn apart the rest of the world.

25

"They must be somewhere down that track," Michael said, knocking back the last dregs of lukewarm black coffee. "They might be a mile from here or ten, but they're going to be down there somewhere."

"So what do we do?" Emma asked, leaning across the melamine-covered table and watching the shadows dance across his face in the dull light of a flickering gas lamp. She was tired. They'd been talking about this for hours, going around in circles.

"Find them," he said simply.

"But is that wise?"

"Why wouldn't it be?"

"If this really is the army or the air force or whatever, do we really want to get involved with them?"

"Do we have a choice? Whoever they are, they're obviously well-organized. There could be hundreds of them. You never know, they might have an antidote or something."

"But we don't need an antidote."

"I know that, all I'm trying to say is that things might not be as hopeless as we've been thinking . . ."

"And anyway," she continued, ignoring everything he'd just said, "everybody's already dead. It'd need to be a bloody good antidote to help those poor buggers out there."

"Okay," Michael sighed, annoyed by her reluctance to find any good in the day's events, "you've made your point."

In the silence which followed, Emma looked around the cramped motor home where she'd spent virtually every minute of the last few days. She hoped with all her heart that Michael's optimism was justified. After weeks of desperately running and hiding, every hour filled with confusion and fear, the possibility that some semblance of normality might somehow be about to return to their lives was welcome and unexpected. But it was so unexpected that she wasn't going to allow herself to believe it was true until she'd seen some concrete evidence.

"You okay?" Michael asked, concerned by how quiet she had suddenly become.

"I'm all right."

"Sure?"

She shook her head and looked down at the table. "No," she mumbled. Feeling self-conscious, Michael shuffled awkwardly in his seat. He'd spent weeks alone with Emma but there was still a frequent distance between them. Moments like this felt uncomfortable. When all was said and done, they were two strangers, thrown together by disaster and chance. Neither knew much about the other's history except for what had happened since the world had fallen apart. He didn't know what to say. He didn't know how to make her pain go away.

"What's wrong?"

She wiped her eyes and looked up at him.

"Sorry," she whispered, "I can't help it. Most of the time I'm okay, but then sometimes I . . ."

"What?"

Emma looked around the caravan, searching for the words to express how she felt.

"I just want this to stop," she explained. "I want to go to sleep tonight and wake up in the morning and find everything back how it used to be. And if that's not going to happen, then I want to wake up and find the bodies gone and the uncertainty gone and the fear gone and . . ."

"Shh . . ." he said. Her voice was increasing in volume and he was worried that she'd be heard from outside. "Listen, you know as well as I do that the only certainty around here is that things are never going to get back to normal, don't you?"

"Yes, but . . ."

"This is our new normal, and if this is all we've got left then we've got to make the most of it. We'll get used to living like this and—"

"But this isn't living. This is barely existing, for Christ's sake. Look at us, Mike. Look at what's happening to us. We smell. We're dirty. Neither of us has washed properly in weeks. Our clothes are filthy. We both need to cut our hair and you need to shave. We're not eating properly or drinking enough or exercising or—"

"We're making do and we're getting by," he interrupted. "And it'll get better. When we can we'll find somewhere to live where we can relax and grow our own food. We'll get new clothes, have a bath, and we'll build ourselves a bloody palace somewhere, okay?"

She sniffed back more tears and almost laughed. "Okay."

"Believe me?"

"I believe you."

Michael stared into her tear-streaked face. She was right, of course, but what could they do? As far as he could see there was no immediate way out of the situation they found themselves in. They had to remain mobile and that meant going without some basic necessities in order to survive. He truly believed that things would change eventually. They had to. The bodies would decay away to nothing in time.

"You hungry?" he asked, trying to find a way of distracting her. She sank back into her seat.

"A little."

"I'll get you something."

She watched him as he stood up and walked the short length of the motor home to the cramped kitchen area. This vehicle was safe but stifling. She might have been able to cope with the confined space had she been able to venture outside occasionally. As it was she was trapped, and she was feeling increasingly claustrophobic.

Michael returned to the table with more coffee and two plastic pots of dehydrated snack food. Steam snaked up into the air from the top of each pot.

"Beef and tomato or sweet and sour?" he asked. They'd found a job-lot of these snacks in the storeroom of a small shop they'd looted earlier in the week. The food tasted awful but it was hot, easy to prepare, and reasonably nutritious.

"Can't stand sweet and sour," she answered, "but it's better than beef and tomato."

He passed her the tub and a fork. Still sniffing back tears she began to eat hungrily and without further complaint.

"I think they'll be back," Michael said between tasteless mouthfuls.

"Who will?" asked Emma.

"Whoever it was I saw today," he sighed.

"Not again . . ."

"We have to talk about this."

"We've done nothing *but* talk about it. Listen, I'm sorry," she said quietly, "I'm tired. I know how important this is, but I—"

"Do you?"

"Yes, of course I do."

"Have you stopped to think where these people might be from, or how many of them there might be? This might not be as widespread as we'd thought. Maybe it's only this country that's been affected."

He stopped talking, aware that Emma had put down her fork and that she was staring at him.

"Don't do this," she said softly, reaching her hand out across the table and gently squeezing his. "Please don't let your imagination run away with you. Until we know more let's just keep our feet on the ground and take every day as it comes. I don't want to start thinking things are going to change only to find that we're back in the same damn mess again and nothing's happened. Do you know what I'm trying to say?"

"No, not really."

She sighed and squeezed his hand again.

"As far as I'm concerned you're all I've got left. You're the only thing that I can rely on. My family and friends are gone. I don't have a home and I don't own anything other than what's in this van. You're the only thing I seem to be able to hold onto and I don't want to do anything to risk losing you."

26

Sunita had run out of cigarettes. It was one thing having to spend all her time imprisoned in the bloody university where she'd studied for the last two years, but being stuck here without cigarettes was another matter altogether. Wrapped up against the cold, she shoved her hands in her pockets and crept out through the back of the accommodation block. Get it done quick before the light's completely gone, she told herself.

There were no bodies here, and it was safe to be out in the open. During their last couple of weeks of confinement, the group had managed to close off a few exits and block off a couple of pathways to make slightly more of the campus accessible. This part of the grounds, being completely enclosed with buildings on all sides, had been officially designated as "corpse free." As it was, few people actually bothered to come out here. Most of them, Sunita included, chose either to remain in their individual rooms or instead loitered around the assembly hall where other survivors were always close at hand.

Sunita felt uneasy being out here alone, but her craving for nicotine was too strong to ignore. Part of her felt bad that she'd kept this secret supply to herself; part of her couldn't give a damn. All the smokers had had enough cigarettes up until now and if it came down to it, she'd tell them about the machine if she had to. It was only Dr. Croft and Yvonne and maybe one or two others anyway. She wouldn't begrudge them a few smokes.

She approached the outside of the student guild building and felt her legs weaken with sudden emotion. The contrast between what she saw today and what she remembered from before was stark. This part of the campus had always been a hive of activity—a social hub which was full of light and noise and students, twenty-four hours a day, seven days a week during term-time. Now it was as cold, quiet, and empty as everywhere else. She climbed the steps, slid the clattering metal security grill across, and disappeared inside. She walked through the large, high-ceilinged atrium, and passed the on-site supermarket, its shelves stripped of anything useful by the others during the first few days of the disaster. She continued past the careers advice office, past the stationery shop and reprographics unit, past the Gay and Lesbian Society office where she'd volunteered from time to time, past the coffee shop and into the bar. Christ, the time (and money) she'd spent in here over the last couple of years. It looked so different today, illuminated only by the little light which trickled in through the door she'd just come through. She looked around the large, sparsely decorated space . . . the bar she'd been propped up against on many occasions, the mirror tiles which decorated the walls, florescent posters advertising events which were either long gone or which were never going to

175

happen, the quiet alcove in the far corner where she'd first sat with Monique that night and talked and talked and talked . . .

And there it was at the end of the bar. The cigarette machine. Nathan Holmes and his mate Richard had cleared out all the liquor from here shortly after they'd arrived at the university, but they'd somehow managed to miss the machine. She only knew it was there because she'd been a regular here and had bought late-night cigarettes on more than one occasion. Despite all that had happened over the last few weeks, and no matter how much the world, her priorities, and her morals had changed, she still felt uneasy as she pried the front of the machine open with a long screwdriver and fished out a packet of fags. It wasn't stealing, she told herself, shoving a couple more packets into her coat pockets to save her coming back again for a while. In fact, she decided, as possibly the last remaining student here, she was entitled to them.

Sunita couldn't face returning to the others just yet. She'd had to pluck up courage to come out here but now that she had, she didn't want to immediately go back. Instead she sat down in her and Monique's alcove, and remembered the brief time they'd had together. She lit a cigarette, took a long, slow draw, then breathed out steadily and tried to relax. She remembered how much she'd been looking forward to seeing Monique again. When she thought about what had probably happened to her, she felt unbearably empty inside. She had to stop and snap herself out of this depression. It wasn't helping. Still not ready to return to the others and lock herself away again, she looked around for a distraction.

There was a door behind the bar she'd never noticed before. In the dull light she could only just make out its outline and handle. She got up and walked toward it, wondering if she might find a previously undiscovered stash of booze on the other side, or some food perhaps. The door was stiff. She yanked and tugged at it several times before it finally opened.

She waited and listened. Absolute silence. A single window in one wall allowed a little more early evening light into the room and she took a couple of steps inside. On her left was a desk with a lifeless computer, its keyboard buried under a pile of papers. On the other side of the small room was a tall pile of cardboard boxes and some cleaning supplies which she moved toward quickly, hoping she'd maybe find a forgotten bottle of lager or wine. It was immediately apparent that this was just the discarded remains of Nathan Holmes's last visit here and that there was nothing left worth taking. Thinking for a second that she'd just seen a single bottle of something (Christ, she'd drink *anything* right now), she bent down and tried to move one of the bottom boxes out of the way. She tugged at a cardboard flap which came off in her hands, sending her stumbling backwards. She trod on something and when she looked down and saw it was someone's upturned palm, she yelped with disgust and surprise and jumped away. She tripped over the handle of a discarded broom and fell against a crate of empty beer bottles, filling the room with unexpected noise.

Nothing to worry about, she told herself, struggling to stay calm. *Just a body. It's nothing to worry about . . .*

Sunita breathed in deeply again, trying to compose herself. She'd managed to keep hold of her cigarette and she drew on it again as she peered across the room to get a better look at the corpse on the floor. She couldn't see much from where she was standing, just the outstretched fingers of a single clawed, male hand, barely even visible in the shadows. Was that someone she'd known? Was it Sam, the guy who worked behind the bar who'd had a room a few doors down from hers? Or was it that Australian bloke who used to make her laugh every time he got her order wrong, or . . . ?

She could hear something else now. Had one of the others come out here looking for her? Figuring she should start heading back, she closed the door (to give Sam, or the Australian guy, or whoever it was a little unnecessary privacy), picked up a couple more packets of cigarettes and the screwdriver, then made her way back through the guild toward the atrium.

What was that?

Sunita could hear a strange scurrying, scratching noise. She turned around and saw that the floor behind her seemed to be moving. As the dark wave of sudden movement came closer she saw it was a pack of rats and, as the vile, disease-ridden rodents scuttled over and around her feet, she screamed and tried to kick them away. Her heart racing, she ran through to the atrium and pressed herself back against the nearest wall, watching the wretched vermin disappear down the steps like a brief waterfall of mangy fur.

But she could still hear something. She gripped the screwdriver tight. *If that fucker Nathan Holmes has followed me here,* she decided, *I'll shove this damn thing up his arse.*

"Anyone there?" she shouted, her voice echoing around the empty space. She stood in the middle of the atrium as a dark shape lumbered toward her. She could tell from its unsteady

178

movements and the shuffling, squelching sounds it made that it was a body. Its speed surprised her and she began to back away. How had it got inside? The front of the guild building was secure, so had this one found another way in? There were other entrances around the far side of the building, and a corridor which connected the guild to other parts of the campus, but it wasn't a direct route and the dead had never come this way before. How had this corpse managed to get here and, more importantly, why? Had it stumbled here by chance or . . . ?

Christ. More of them. Loads more.

A sudden mass of bodies swarmed toward her, moving with unexpected speed and intent. She turned and ran, pausing only to slide the security grill back across the guild entrance. She forced the latch back into place, snatching her fingers back quickly as the first of the corpses clattered against the metal. Seconds later there were bodies pressed across the full width of the barrier, stretching their diseased arms through gaps in the metalwork, reaching out for her. It had been over a week since she'd been this close to any of the corpses and the dramatic change in their behavior was terrifying. Last time they'd barely even seen her, now it was almost as if they'd sought her out. Dumb and lethargic no more, the creatures were becoming increasingly fast and dangerous.

Sunita ran back to the accommodation block, slipped back inside, and headed straight for the others. Damn the secret stash of smokes, she needed to tell then what she'd seen.

27

Cooper woke up.

He couldn't remember falling asleep. He remembered sitting by the window last night, staring out into the darkness and enjoying listening to the rain hitting the glass but other than that nothing. His foot nudged his discarded face mask on the floor and recollections of what had happened came flooding back again. He instinctively checked himself over, and had to admit he felt okay. He was still breathing and he still had a pulse. As far as he could tell he was still fit and healthy and alive. Surely the disease would have affected him by now if it was going to affect him at all?

The morning outside was now dry and, despite the sky being dull and overcast, relatively bright. The heavy smell of death and decay hung over the city like a dense cloud of polluting fog, tainting everything with its abhorrent scent. Now that he had discarded his breathing apparatus the stench was inescapable. Regardless, he quickly decided it was preferable to the recycled air that he'd been forced to breathe for most of the last two and a half weeks. He reminded himself that he was in the middle of a large city which had had a densely packed population, and that the air would surely be cleaner and more palatable elsewhere where there were fewer bodies. There would undoubtedly be better places than this.

For a short time he allowed his mind to wander. Instinctively he thought again about making the return trip to the base. He'd already made basic mental plans and preparations before the realization dawned on him that he didn't actually have to go back at all. Was there any point? What difference would three hundred soldiers make to the world now? The military was as useless and defunct as everything else now.

For a while Cooper alternated between feeling free and then feeling compelled to return to his duties. He looked down into the alley below the window and watched as a single bedraggled figure tripped along like a half-speed drunk, bouncing off the walls. Shouldn't he do something to try and help here? Could he really disappear selfishly into the distance and leave everyone and everything else to rot? It was the immense scale of the disaster that ultimately convinced him there was nothing he could do.

Feeling more confident now that he wasn't reliant on his suit, Cooper decided to move. He didn't know where he was going or what he was going to do, he just knew that he wasn't going to spend any more time imprisoned in this cramped and cluttered storeroom. Still sweating profusely in his heavy suit, he peeled it off and dropped it to the ground, stripping it of any useful equipment. He felt cold and the effect of the sudden drop in temperature was sobering. For a moment he considered going home and trying to find his friends and family. Much as it hurt him, he knew it was better to believe they were already lost. If he did try and find them, chances were they'd be dead or dying and there would be nothing he'd be able to do for them. But then again, he thought, he appeared to have survived the disease, so why shouldn't they have also? What if his immunity was linked to his genetic make up? Strange to think that his survival this morning might have only been as the result of some combination of DNA unknowingly handed down to him by his parents.

He cautiously moved the metal racking which blocked the way out and, with his rifle held in front of him, gently pushed the door open and peered out into the corridor. He checked left and right and, once he was sure the way was clear, stepped out of the shadows. His footsteps echoed loudly on the linoleum floor and he soon heard muffled sounds nearby. Somewhere in the building something was already reacting to his movements.

Cooper crept down the stairs, taking care to avoid making even a single unnecessary noise. Years of training enabled him to move through the building with relative stealth. He passed close to several of the decaying figures trapped inside the office, freezing still and pressing himself back against a wall as one of them brushed past him unaware. He eventually pushed open a heavy glass entrance door and stepped out onto the street.

The morning was blustery and cool, although the gray cloud, so prevalent earlier, was now beginning to break up, allowing occasional patches of blue sky to appear above him. It was an exhilarating feeling seeing daylight and feeling the wind on his face again. It had been good to get out of the bunker yesterday, but this was a thousand times better. For the first time in weeks he was free. Cooper was almost beginning to feel human again.

He turned toward the heart of the city, continuing to move in the same general direction in which he had run yesterday. Another listless, bedraggled figure traipsed toward him awkwardly, its face and features made indistinct by bright autumn sunlight which had suddenly spilled across the scene. Cooper thought carefully for a moment and considered his options, not sure how he should react. Should he attack it before it attacked him? The pathetic creature looked so weak and weary that he couldn't imagine it could pose a serious threat to him. Keeping his guard up, he stood still and watched intently as it moved closer and closer toward him. He remained rooted to the spot, standing in the shadows, moving only his eyes. The figure stumbled past, apparently oblivious to his presence. The sun disappeared behind another cloud when the pitiful body was level with him. Despite the sudden gloom he was still able to clearly see the full extent of the of the creature's deterioration. Its discolored skin looked to have been stretched across its skull in places, but it was loose and baggy elsewhere. Across one of its cheeks was a deep, dark gouge which, Cooper noticed, didn't appear to have bled.

Once the way ahead was clear he began to move forward again. He followed a long, gently curved stretch of road around and eventually found himself at the stepped entrance to a large public square. He'd last been to this city on a warm summer's day a couple of years ago, but it hadn't looked anything like this. The tiered square had been a popular public meeting place and a well-known city landmark. He remembered sitting with friends outside a bar here while on leave, drinking, laughing, and generally wasting the day. Today the bar was silent and tomb-like, its windows obscured by a layer of dust and grime. He remembered kids playing around a huge, modern-looking fountain at the top of the square, water cascading down a series of steps into a large, shallow, circular pool. Today those same steps were dry and the waterfall and fountain eerily silent. Last time he'd been here the water had been clear and bright; today the remaining dregs were green-gray and stagnant. There was a bloated body floating facedown in the pool.

He noticed there were several figures nearby and he started to move again. It appeared that as long as he matched their slothful speed and didn't get too close he didn't seem to attract any unwanted attention to himself. These people were catatonic: somehow still moving but not thinking or reacting to anything but the most obvious stimulation. Occasionally pigeons would land in the square with a sudden unexpected burst of flapping and noise. The arrival of the scavenging birds caused the bodies to turn awkwardly and to lurch and stagger pointlessly toward them, managing only a couple of steps forward each time before the pigeons disappeared again. It might have been comical if it wasn't so damn frightening.

Cooper began to feel strangely invincible. His apparent immunity to the disease or virus or whatever it was seemed to set him apart from every other person he had so far seen, and his comparative strength and speed massively compounded his advantage. Allowing himself to become dangerously distracted, he tripped on one of the large concrete steps and dropped his rifle.

It landed on the paving stones with a loud clatter that shattered the silence.

"Shit," he cursed as he stooped to pick up the weapon. Before he had even lifted his head again he was aware of them all around him. Pouring out of the shadows from every direction were hordes of the sickly, diseased figures. For a second he stood still and looked around in disbelief at the sudden numbers swarming around the edges of the square, stumbling closer toward him. There seemed to be slightly fewer bodies over to his right and so that was the way he ran, brutally shoving his way past the nearest few. He glanced back over his shoulder and saw that more and more of the bloody things were coming after him now. Their speed was not a problem, but their huge numbers and apparently relentless determination clearly were. He struggled to contain his mounting panic as he barged another clump of them away. Instinctively he ran, even though he knew that did nothing to help him hide. There were buildings on either side of him but more emerging bodies prevented him from getting to them easily. In desperation he jumped up into the back of a delivery truck, yanking the roller-door down behind him and shutting out the crowds. After quickly scanning the space around him with his torch and confirming that he was alone, he sank down amidst bales of out of date newspapers and magazines and closed his eyes. Corpses continued to thump against the sides of the truck as they lumbered after him. He covered his ears and waited for them to disappear.

28

Michael woke up with a start. "Listen."

Still half asleep, Emma propped herself up on her elbows. "What?"

"Listen," he said again. In the distance, and disappearing quickly, was the sound of an engine. "Same as yesterday," he said, jumping out of bed and struggling in the gloom to find his trousers, jacket, and boots and put them on. "I've got to get out there and see where they're going."

"Why?"

"Stupid bloody question," he snapped at her. "You know why. These are survivors. These people could—"

"These people are leaving here," she said, her voice still tired and heavy with sleep. "There's no point going running out there now. All you're going to be able to do is watch them disappear."

"That's got to be better than just sitting here."

"Why not wait? They came back yesterday, didn't they? Surely they'll come back again today."

186

"Not necessarily," he said as he pulled on his jeans and fastened his belt.

"No, not necessarily, but probably."

"Yes, but—"

"But what?"

Michael stopped what he was doing. Dejected, he threw his jacket down onto the bed in front of her and sat down next to her feet. He knew she was right. In the time it had taken him to put on his jeans and socks the noise outside had already gone.

"Come here," Emma said quietly. She could see that Michael was struggling. As strong and brave as they both constantly tried to be for each other, it was becoming harder and harder just to get through each day. The lack of any news, direction, or purpose was slowly killing them, and that was why Michael had reacted to the sound of the engine in the way he just had. Every last fiber of his body wanted to believe that the survivors they had heard would bring an end to the relentless nightmare that their once ordinary lives had become.

Michael lay down on the bed next to Emma and rested his head on the pillow close to hers. She rolled over onto her side and looked deep into his tired face. He stared up at the motor home roof, excited by the sound but frustrated that he was still no closer to finding out who these people were and where they'd come from. He knew he'd probably get the answers to his questions soon enough but he wanted to know now.

Emma wrapped her arm around him and pulled him closer. He could feel her breath on the side of his face. It relaxed him. For a moment it made the importance of what was happening outside fade away.

"They will be back, you know," she whispered again with real conviction in her voice. Michael knew she was probably right. "I'm sure of it. You've just got to have a little faith. It's too much of a coincidence for us to hear them traveling past here two days running. They must be based nearby."

"I know," he admitted.

"We should move the van. Try and get it so we're overlooking the track."

"Suppose."

"Look, that's what we'll do," she said gently, trying to keep him positive and focused. "We'll drive across the hills until we find somewhere we'll get a clear view of the track, then we'll wait. We can sit in the front and watch and as soon as we see them we'll follow them back to wherever it is they've come from."

Her well-meaning words, although perhaps spoken more out of duty than any genuine belief, were appreciated. Michael knew he was lucky to have Emma. He lifted his hand and brushed a fallen curl of hair away from her face. She smiled and pulled herself even closer so that their faces were almost touching. He kissed her lightly on the cheek and then kissed her again before pulling back slightly and staring into her eyes. Much as they both craved warmth, comfort, protection, and countless other things, to be safe and to be this close to each other was enough for now.

29

Exhausted by the mental effort of moving silently through the city and avoiding the diseased crowds, Cooper dragged himself on. Despite all of his training and preparation for dealing with nightmare scenarios, he was finding it increasingly difficult to keep moving forward. Every single step took more concentrated effort than it ever should have. Every time he turned his head he saw something else which shocked, repulsed, disgusted, or terrified him. The gray streets were littered with the remains of decaying bodies—the residue of thousands of innocent, unsuspecting plague victims. If he half-closed his eyes and tried to ignore the vile, shuffling bodies that milled hopelessly around him, then it felt like he was walking through a bizarre still photograph. It was almost as if the world had been frozen in an instant of time, and that every part of it was now dying the slowest and most painful death imaginable. He could no longer see any goodness around him, nothing positive. Death, decay, and destruction were everywhere he looked.

He had reached the ring road which ran around the perimeter of the city center. His local geography was far from comprehensive. He looked hopefully at every road sign he passed, trying to find the name of a suburb or nearby village that he recognized. It made sense for him to head for somewhere beyond the city, somewhere where the buildings were spread out over a wider area rather than packed tightly together as they were in the inner-city districts. He'd had plenty of time to think about what he was going to do, but the constant distractions around him had prevented him from coming up with anything which resembled a coherent plan of action. All he really wanted was to find somewhere relatively safe and comfortable where he could stop and rest for a few days and take stock of everything that had happened. He didn't expect to be able to make sense of any of it, but for the sake of his sanity he needed the opportunity to take a deep breath and at least try to understand why he suddenly found himself the last man alive.

On Cooper's left as he trudged slowly down the middle of the ring road was the city center proper and, just ahead to the right, the first few buildings of the hospital and university complex. The road slowly dropped down and wound lazily around to the left, and as he followed it he became aware of something bizarre which made his blood run cold. Up ahead, little more than a quarter of a mile away by his estimations, was an immense crowd of bodies, the largest he'd seen. Instinct urged him to turn and head in the opposite direction but he didn't dare make any obvious movements.

He neared the bodies with the initial intent of shuffling around the farthest edge of the massive gathering and carrying on out of the city. As he approached, however, he began to ask himself why so many of them might have gathered there in the first place. The answer, it occurred to him, was simple. He'd seen how the dead had reacted to him when he'd dropped his guard. The creatures seemed to be devoid of virtually all decision making capabilities and they only reacted to the most basic of stimuli. So that meant there was something happening here, there had to be. Something was drawing them to this place.

The wide road was littered with the remnants of the city's final rush hour grind, and that made it difficult for Cooper to accurately estimate the number of bodies ahead of him. They appeared to be gravitating toward a large, modern-looking building on the other side of the road, each one of them advancing forward step by slow, dragging step, until the number of tightly packed creatures ahead prevented them from getting any closer. Cooper made a subtle alteration to his course so that he continued to drift over toward the far side of the road where there were fewer figures. He glanced back and noticed that behind him, more and more of them were continuing to appear almost constantly, emerging from the shadows of the city center.

The vast crowd was silent, save for the incessant slow shuffling of rotting feet being dragged along the ground. Over this low background noise, however, Cooper thought for a moment that he could hear something else. Wary of drawing any more attention to himself by lifting his head and looking around, he continued to stare at the ground in front of him and concentrated so that he could try and distinguish and identify this new noise. It sounded like the cracking and popping of burning wood. Was that all, he wondered? Just another burning building? He'd already seen several places which had been gutted by fire as the result, perhaps, of a fractured gas main, food which had been left cooking in an unattended oven, heaters left alight or lights left switched on or any one of a thousand other reasons. Such accidents were inevitable, given the sudden demise of so many people so quickly when whatever happened here had happened. And was that all this was? With resignation he planned how he should best change direction again and where he should go.

Then he heard something else. Was that someone shouting? It only lasted for a second or two and was completely unintelligible. Had he imagined it? He'd convinced himself he was the only one left, so was this his mind playing tricks? Unable to contain his curiosity or his desire to see other living, breathing people like himself, he cautiously lifted his head and looked up. He saw that a pall of dirty gray smoke was drifting lazily away from the top of one of the large buildings beside the wide road. He squinted and saw movement on the roof. People! Although he only dared look for a few seconds, he was sure he'd seen several of them and, despite having seen them for only a moment, he knew they were like him.

Against his better judgment, Cooper allowed himself to drift deeper into the crowd. He didn't dare shout to the people on the roof to try and make them aware of his presence, knowing instead that his only option was to slowly edge closer to the building until he could work out how he could gain access. Just a few steps farther forward, however, and he suddenly found himself swallowed up by the rotting crowd. Random decaying figures collided with him constantly and more closed in from behind and it was all he could do to keep his nerve and keep moving. The smell of putrefaction was appalling. He'd been around death many times before during his years of service, but never anything like this. The cloying, relentless smell hung over everything like a suffocating blanket. Keeping control of his stomach was beginning to take almost as much effort and concentration as keeping control of his speed and holding his nerve.

There were shuffling bodies all around him now. Although the creatures were withered and relatively slight, there were so many of them and they were packed so tightly together that it was impossible to see clearly in any direction. He knew he had to keep moving along with the slow flow and hope that luck would eventually carry him in the right direction. Unlike his earlier uncomfortable encounters with the dead, this time they paid him little attention. And the reason for that, he realized, was there was something far more interesting up ahead—a much bigger distraction than one tired, confused solider wearily traipsing through town.

Cooper tried for a while to convince himself otherwise, but there was no escaping the fact that, after a few minutes, he'd made hardly any real progress forward. There was very little that he could immediately do about it. He felt himself being pushed away from the front of the building and back out to his right, along the ring road in the general direction from which he had just come. All he could do was keep moving and hope that he'd eventually drift back the other way. He stumbled, tripping over a mangled body on the ground. Even as his boot crunched bones and he skidded through greasy, decayed flesh he forced himself to remain steady and emotionless and not react.

A subway.

Out of the corner of his eye he saw it: the entrance to a pedestrian connection between the rest of the city and the buildings on the other side of the once-busy ring road. It was proving difficult enough to negotiate today but, before everyone had fallen and died, this road would have been impossible to cross on foot. Still going nowhere fast, Cooper decided to take a chance and head underground. Although there would surely be even more bodies trapped down there, it would be darker and, he presumed, safer. He cautiously veered off toward the sloping concrete entrance, his nervousness and apprehension increasing as he stared into the darkness and began to walk down the ramp. As the light faded, so the smell intensified. Unnerved, he broke out in a sickly sweat, the sudden close confines reminding him of the moment he'd entered the bunker on that first morning almost three weeks ago.

Inside the subway it was virtually pitch-black, much darker than he had expected. He was aware of some degree of movement all around him but most of the bodies had by now dragged themselves up above ground, attracted, no doubt, by the light and sound up there, and by glimpses of the the movement of the rest of the vast crowds.

No more than twenty meters down, Cooper suddenly came upon an unexpected T-junction where a second tunnel crossed the path of the one he'd been following. His eyes were slowly becoming accustomed to the low gloom, but as he followed the second tunnel (still moving, he hoped, toward the building with the fire on the roof) the light continued to fade. The smell outside had been bad enough but down here it was appalling: the sharp, musty stench of festering flesh which had been trapped underground, unable to easily escape out into the comparatively fresh air on the surface. He could see slight shadows and movements all around him, and at times it looked like the dark walls of the subway tunnel themselves were shifting. He shuffled forward a step at a time, dragging his feet along the ground and clearing a path through the endless debris with his heavy boots. He was positive the tunnel he now followed was leading him along the length of the road, closer toward the front of the building he was aiming for.

An unexpected collision sent Cooper tumbling heavily to the ground. He had walked into one of the stumbling bodies and, although there had been virtually no force in the impact, the surprise had sent him reeling. He fell awkwardly, crushing the chest of another indistinguishable corpse which completely collapsed under his sudden weight, his gloved right hand sinking into its innards.

"Shit!" he cursed as he struggled to pick himself back up. His clumsy boots slipped in sticky gore and he lost his balance again before finding the wall with an outstretched hand and steadying himself. Breathing heavily, he stood completely still in the middle of the subway. He didn't need to be able to see to know that no matter how still he was now, it didn't matter. The damage had already been done. His fall and sudden outburst had attracted the unwanted attention of every one of the bodies down here in the subway. He could already hear them moving awkwardly in the darkness, scrambling forward, clambering over each other to get closer to him.

The first vicious grabbing hands reached out for him. He brushed them off easily and instinctively primed the rifle which he'd carried slung over his shoulder. He didn't know if bullets would have any effect on the creatures—it was just a gut reaction. In another equally instinctive move he dropped his shoulder and ran forward. Half-blind and panic-stricken, he hurled himself farther down the tunnel at speed, smashing body after body away on either side. He tried to feel his way ahead with the end of the rifle, frightened that in the blackness he might be about to run headfirst into a wall or some other obstruction, but he knew he had no alternative other than to keep moving. It was that or risk being trapped underground in almost total darkness, buried under the weight of the ever-increasing numbers of rotting bodies now swarming all around him.

The barrel of his rifle effortlessly pierced the torso of another corpse like a bayonet, then it hit a wall, sending a sudden jolt through his body. Cooper had reached another T-junction. He had to make an immediate decision—right or left? Both were equally dark. Although disorientated, his instinct suggested right and, as he had no other information on which to base his decision, that was what he did, shaking the cadaver off the end of his rifle and forcing his way through yet more insipid figures toward where he believed he'd find the building and the survivors.

Another body crashed into him, then another and another. With his shoulder still dropped and his head down he charged forward, sliding in the mire but determined to keep moving at all costs through the sea of rotting flesh, terrified at the thought of what might happen if he dared stop or even slow down. He glanced up and saw a chink of light ahead through a gap between the lurching creatures.

Visible only for fleeting moments between shifting shad-

196

ows and gangling, staggering shapes, the light was all that Cooper had to focus on. He squeezed the trigger of his rifle and fired off a short round of shots, just enough to blast some of the bodies out of the way. With his path marginally clearer he sprinted forward with renewed speed, the light around him increasing steadily until he finally burst out into the open again. Relieved, he stopped for a fraction of a second. He shielded his eyes from the sudden brightness and looked anxiously from side to side. There were hordes of decaying shells advancing toward him already, their interest aroused by the noise of the shots echoing along the subway passages beneath their feet. His mouth was dry, his heart was pounding and his legs were heavy but he knew that he had to keep moving. The building was just ahead of him now.

More bodies spilled out of the subway after him and grabbing hands reached for him from behind. He raised the barrel of the weapon and fired off another volley of shots. After spending hours trying desperately to remain silent and anonymous he was now ready to do all he could to make his presence known.

"Over here," he yelled, looking up at the side of the tall redbrick building just ahead of him. "Can anyone hear me?"

Down at ground level it was impossible for the lone soldier to know if his cries or shots had been enough to illicit any response. On the roof of the building, however, the second round of gunshots had triggered a sudden flurry of anxious activity. Several people inched cautiously toward the edge of the roof and peered over, hoping to catch sight of whoever had fired the rifle. Far below them, Cooper moved closer to the building, constantly looking for a way to get inside. He could see plenty of doors but

197

there was a deep wedge of bodies rammed hard against each of them. There were plenty of windows too, but he knew that smashing any of them would do more harm than good. He'd be letting himself into the building but, at the same time, he'd also be paving the way for a flood of corpses to follow him through.

"'Round the back," a hoarse voice yelled at him. Cooper didn't waste time trying to locate the source of the sound; instead he sprinted away from the front of the building as instructed, swinging the butt of his rifle around now like a club.

Inside the accommodation block the frenzied activity continued as those survivors who had been up on the roof bolted down the nearest staircase to get to the ground floor. A handful of them, Donna Yorke and Phil Croft included, continued around to the back of the building, where they threw open an innocuous-looking door and burst out into the daylight. Using sticks and other basic weapons, they began to batter the bodies away.

Slipping and tripping up a steep and soggy grassy bank a short distance from the door, Cooper heard them before he saw them.

"Over here!"

"There he is," shouted Richard Stephens, who'd been in the wrong place at the wrong time and had been swept up with the others. He swung a snooker cue around his head like a samurai sword, thudding it into the neck of another cadaver and knocking it clean off its already unsteady feet. Phil Croft edged farther forward, trying to clear a path for the soldier with a garden fork, wincing with disgust as he skewered a dead woman's chest. Cooper smashed the butt of his rifle into the jaw of a corpse which stumbled into his way before pushing past the doctor and disappearing inside. Richards was right behind him.

"He's in," Donna shouted, trying to drag Croft (who was still trying to shake the thrashing corpse off his fork) back inside. "Shut the bloody door!"

Croft dumped both the fork and the corpse and ran back toward the door, slowed down by two of the dead which doggedly clung onto him with their clawlike hands. He dragged them inside, hauling them farther along the narrow gray corridor before even trying to release their relentless grip. As Donna slammed the door shut and bolted it, Richard Stephens grabbed the nearest of the two corpses and pulled it away.

"Shit," he said as he held the creature tightly by its spindly wrists and stared into its blank, expressionless face. Its empty gaze chilled him to the bone. The decaying flesh around its wrists felt like wet putty under his grip, which he instinctively and nervously increased.

"Just get rid of it," Croft said. Before anyone else could react, Cooper yanked the body away from Richard and pushed it back against the wall. He lifted his rifle and put a single bullet through its head, right between the eyes. As the corpse slid down the wall (leaving a trail of black-red blood and shards of splintered bone behind it) the soldier turned and did the same to the second body. The remains of a dead vicar dropped at his feet.

The sound of the final gunshot echoed along the corridor and faded away, only to be replaced by a relentless thudding noise as a horde of bodies hurled themselves against the other side of the door, trying desperately to reach the survivors inside.

30

"So where the fuck did you come from?" Nathan Holmes demanded as the exhausted soldier, Donna, Croft, and the others arrived in the assembly hall.

"A base just outside the city," he answered. He stood in the middle of the large room, gore dripping from his dirty uniform. "Look, is there any chance of getting any—"

"Was it you who was shooting yesterday?" Nathan interrupted.

"Not me personally, but—"

"And the engine we heard, that was you too?"

Cooper nodded, exhausted. He understood why it was happening, but this sudden interrogation was the last thing he needed.

"That was us."

"*Us?*"

"That's right."

"So where are the others?"

"Back at the base, I hope."

"And why are you still here?"

"We got separated."

"How come you can breathe?"

"How come *you* can breathe? We're all just lucky, I guess."

"Are the others immune?"

Cooper shook his head. "I doubt it. I only found out by chance. Look, could somebody please tell me exactly what happened here? I've been out of the loop for—"

"Aren't *you* the one who should be telling *us* what's happened?" Donna said. She walked across the room and positioned herself directly between Nathan and the soldier.

"I don't know," he replied. "None of us knew anything. We heard rumors, but nothing concrete."

"What rumors?" Jack Baxter asked, also moving closer.

"Like I say, no one knew very much. We heard talk of a disease. We knew it was widespread and that it had probably killed thousands, but nothing like what I've seen here."

"So where were you when it happened?"

"What?"

"If you didn't know that you were immune until you got here, where have you been hiding for the last few weeks? How come the rest of you didn't get infected?"

"We were in a bunker. Got sent down there when it all kicked off."

"You should be thankful you didn't see any of it," Bernard Heath said quietly, sitting down a short distance away from the others.

"Pardon?"

"I said you ought to be grateful you were out of the way when it happened," he continued. "It was more than thousands of people who died, it was millions. Millions of people just dropped dead where they were standing. Christ, I don't expect there's even a thousand people left alive."

"So what about the ones outside? Are they . . . ?" Cooper let his words trail away. No matter what he'd seen out on the streets, he couldn't bring himself to ask the impossible question which had been playing on his mind since he'd first arrived in the city.

"They're dead," Jack answered. "And if I hadn't seen it my-self then I wouldn't have believed it. They died on the first morning. A couple of days later they started to move again."

"But that's impossible."

"You go and tell them that."

"We don't know what caused it," Phil Croft said. "To be honest, there's no point even thinking about it. Won't do anyone any good now."

"Do *you* know what did it?" Paulette asked Cooper. The normally effervescent woman had been hanging on every word of the difficult exchange, hoping for answers. Her usually bright and energetic voice sounded uncharacteristically quiet and subdued. Cooper shook his head.

"No."

"But you must have some idea," Bernard protested. "You must have known why you were being sent down into a bunker. Did you not ask questions?"

"Orders are orders."

"Yes, but were we attacked? Or was it an accident, or . . . ?"

"I really don't know," he said. "I doubt it was a direct attack because you'd have seen or heard something. *I* would have heard something."

"What about the speed of it?" Donna asked before Cooper could respond. "I was nine floors up. I watched it move across the city killing everybody. How could that have happened?"

"I'm starting to wonder whether it was already here," Croft said. "There's no way a disease or a virus could spread that quickly, is there?"

"I really don't know anything," Cooper sighed. "Look, we're all in the same boat here. I've got no reason to hide anything from you and I swear, if I knew anything I'd tell you."

Wearily, he collapsed into a chair. Donna handed him a bottle of water and pulled another chair across the floor to sit opposite him. There was a look of intense concentration on her face. She wanted to know what had happened as much as the rest of them, but she had other questions to ask. Already her mind was working frantically, analyzing what he had so far said and wondering whether this unexpected stranger might be able to bring some stability and security to their increasingly dangerous world. He had, it seemed, arrived in the city from a protected oasis.

"So how many of you were there?" she asked.

Cooper drained the bottle of water dry, wiped his mouth, and cleared his throat before responding.

"Where? How many of us were out here yesterday or—"

She shook her head. "In this base of yours. How many of you are in the base?"

"Couple of hundred, I think. I'm not completely sure. Three hundred at the most."

"And are there more of them? More bases?"

He nodded. "There were supposed to be, but I don't know if anyone managed to get to them. I'm not even sure where they are. There's bound to be one close to the capital."

"You must have some idea."

"Why? I swear, I didn't know where our base was until I was in it. Look, these are the kind of places you don't know you've reached until you're standing right on top of them. I've heard that some of these bunkers are in the middle of cities, others are more remote. Christ, you might have lived next door to one for the last ten years and not known anything about it."

Phil Croft sat down next to Donna.

"So if we could get to your base," he began to ask, the tone of his voice tentative, "would you be able to get us inside?"

"You're out of your fucking mind if you think I'm burying myself underground with the army," Nathan said from a short distance away. "Completely out of your fucking mind."

Croft shot a disappointed glance in his direction and then turned back to face the soldier.

"Would they let us in?" he asked again. Cooper couldn't answer with any certainty.

"They might, but on the other hand they might not. Christ, they might not let me back in. It depends if the decontamination process works, I suppose. I left the base but I never made it back, and we were the first to go aboveground. The others who were with me might not have been able to get back inside. If they couldn't remove all traces of the contamination, then they'd have left them on the surface. For all I know they might have let it in when we left. The whole bloody lot of them could be dead by now."

"Are you serious? Would they really leave people outside like that?"

"If they were contaminated."

"To die?"

"I suppose. The lives of a few versus the lives of a hundred. Do the math."

"And did you know that when they ordered you to go outside?"

"No one said as much, but it doesn't take a genius to work it out, does it?"

"No wonder you're not rushing to get back."

"Part of the job," Cooper said nonchalantly. "Those are the risks you take. It's what you agree to when you sign up."

"And are you still on duty?" Croft quipped. The soldier shook his head.

"I quit," he said, deadpan. "I quit the moment I found out I could still breathe. You don't have to spend long out here to realize the whole planet's fucked. I figured I might as well try and make the most of the little freedom I've got left. They probably think I'm dead anyway."

31

Ignoring the potential dangers of being out alone, and with a sense of smug satisfaction warming him against the cold late-autumn breeze, Michael crouched down in the long grass on top of a bleak hillside and watched as another truckful of soldiers clattered down the overgrown track. He'd found the track again earlier in the day and had followed it as far as he'd dared on foot before heading back to the relative safety of the motor home. He and Emma had then driven to the point where he'd stopped walking. Michael guessed they were near to finding the base, and this sighting of the troops in their transport was proof that they were getting closer. Feeling more positive than he had for days, he turned around and put his thumbs up as a salute to what felt like a small but significant victory. The afternoon light was fading and rain was beginning to spit down. From the comparative warmth and comfort of the motor home a short distance away Emma watched and waved back, acknowledging his achievement.

Before returning to Emma, Michael stared down at the track for a while longer. There was a body walking along it now, a single rotting cadaver which pointlessly dragged itself along after the long-gone transport. Michael watched the lone figure with fear, hatred, and pity in equal measure. Although they had intentionally stayed as far away from the ruins of the rest of the world as possible, coming into contact with the corpses was an inevitable, daily occurrence. In the days immediately following the death of millions, they had studied the constantly changing behavior of the dead from the shelter of their farmhouse hideout, and they had since seen those changes continue unabated. Originally little more than empty shells, now these reanimated bodies were displaying increased levels of emotion and control. It was almost as if their brains had been anesthetized by the disease and the numbness was fading. Clumsy and unfeeling at first, the bodies seemed now to be developing a purpose. The ability to interpret and respond to basic stimuli had been the first thing to return, then something resembling base emotions. Were they driven by the need to protect themselves? Were they searching for a way to end their pain? More recently Michael had sensed a vicious inquisitiveness about the bodies, which frequently manifested itself as anger.

It was bitterly cold outside and he wasn't safe. He ran back to the motor home.

"Well?" Emma asked as he let himself inside and closed, locked, barred, and blacked-out the door behind him.

"More of them," he answered, out of breath.

"We're close, aren't we?"

He wiped the rain from his face and hair. "We must be."

Michael took off his wet outdoor jacket and kicked off his muddy boots. Now that he was safely indoors Emma busied herself with their nightly ritual—covering every window, vent, and door with wooden boards and heavy black material. They knew that even the smallest pinprick of escaping light might be enough to attract the bodies. Emma didn't mind the dark. It helped her to forget the cramped and squalid conditions that they were having to live in.

"Tomorrow morning we should try and get even closer," Michael said quietly as he sat down opposite her at the small table. "It doesn't matter how long it takes. One step at a time . . ."

"And are you sure this is the right thing to do?"

"Of course it is. Why?" Michael was surprised by her comment.

"Don't forget this is the army we're dealing with here," she explained. "Do you think they're going to welcome us with open arms? They might not have come across any survivors yet. And look at the state of us. They'll probably think that we're dead and that we've just—"

"Do you really believe that?" He sighed and looked down at the table.

"I don't know," she replied. "We're the odd ones out around here, aren't we? They're not going to be expecting—"

"They're not going to be expecting any fucking corpses to turn up in a camper van and knock their door, are they?"

"No, but—"

"But what? They'll see the van, they'll see us, and we'll be okay."

"What if they see you when you're walking?"

"Sounds like you're just trying to find reasons not to do this."

"Come on, that's not fair. I'm just worried that this won't work out."

"It'll work out."

"There are a hundred reasons why it might not. You told me yourself you thought they were wearing suits. They can't even walk out in the open. They can't breathe the air because it'll do to them what it did to the rest of the population."

"Yes, and that's our get-out, isn't it?"

"What do you mean?"

"If things don't work out the way we want, we can just walk."

"You think they'll let us?"

"You think they'll have a choice?"

"What if they want to cut us up? Make a vaccine from our blood or something like that? They might use us as lab rats."

"Now you're just being stupid."

"Am I? I'm sorry, Mike, I'm not trying to be negative. I just think we need to play this whole situation very, very carefully." She'd been trying to contain Michael's eagerness and excitement for days now. His cavalier approach and apparent lack of concern worried her. They both knew what was at stake. They had already lost just about everything they had. At the farmhouse they'd fought to build themselves a shelter to protect them from the rest of the world and, despite their huge physical and mental advantage over the plague victims, they had lost it all in the blink of an eye. One mistake was all that it had taken. And although sitting in a cold motor home in the middle of a field was far from ideal, at least they'd managed to wrestle some degree of control back again. Emma had an uneasy feeling in the pit of her stomach that they were dangerously close to losing it.

Every night felt like an eternity. The dark hours dragged endlessly. With no distractions or entertainment, Michael and Emma struggled not to dwell on the problems outside their thin metal door. Most of the time the heavy atmosphere in the cramped motor home was tense.

Conversation continued to be sparse and difficult throughout the evening. As the couple had quickly discovered, there was very little they could talk about that didn't lead back to everything they had been doing their best to forget. Going to bed sometimes brought temporarily relief, but much of the time it was of little help. They would either lie there restless, unable to sleep, or they'd manage to lose consciousness only to be jolted back into their bizarre reality by a dark nightmare or a sudden noise from the other side of the motor home's paper-thin walls.

The only true comfort that Michael had found in the days and nights since his life had been turned upside down was Emma. As they lay in bed together, holding each other tightly, keeping each other warm, he relaxed in the comfort of her closeness. He loved the sound of her voice whispering in his ear late at night, and the gentle tickle of her breath on the side of his face somehow managed to remind him that, no matter how it often felt, he was still very much alive. The smell of her, the feel of her body against his, the warmth that she brought to the long, cold nights—all helped reassure him that the effort of survival was worthwhile and that, despite the considerable odds stacked against them, there remained a faint glimmer of hope that things would eventually improve. He clung to the idea that, one day, the two of them might be free to walk out in the open again without fear. He knew it might happen. The bodies were deteriorating; they couldn't continue to function indefinitely, could they?

It was twenty past two in the morning. The wind was buffeting the side of the motor home, rain was clattering against the metal roof above them, and they could hear the squelching footsteps of a solitary body tripping and sliding through the mud outside. For a few precious moments none of it seemed to matter to Michael. He was close to Emma and, somehow, he was able to temporarily forget everything else.

32

Eight survivors sat together in semidarkness in one of the university lecture theaters and ate a scraped-together late-night meal. The atmosphere throughout the building had changed noticeably since Cooper's unexpected arrival earlier in the day. To many of the desperately frightened people gathered in the accommodation block, his appearance had brought a faint and unexpected glimmer of hope into their lives. To an equal number of others, however, his presence in the building had simply increased their unease and anxiety. Claustrophobic, monotonous, and uncomfortable their world may well have become, but with the rest of the country lying in ruins around them, this was all they had left and the soldier's sudden appearance proved disproportionately unsettling.

"We should get out of here now," Donna said, her mouth half-full of food.

"She's right," Sunita agreed. She didn't often sit in on discussions like this, and she contributed even less frequently. "We should go."

"Is this to do with what happened at the guild last night?" Croft asked her. She'd told him about the bodies when he'd gone up to her room earlier to scrounge a cigarette and had found her sitting in the corner, sobbing. Donna looked across at her, puzzled.

"Why, what happened last night?"

"I went looking for fags," she began, pausing when she realized everyone was staring at her. "I've been into the guild loads of times before and never had any problems, but last night there were bodies in there. They heard me in there . . ."

"That's not unusual," Bernard Heath said. "Perhaps you shouldn't have been there on your own?"

She shook her head. "This was different. I felt like they were hunting me out. They were quicker than before, more aggressive . . ."

"They weren't happy when I was trying to get in here earlier," Cooper said. He was right—the noise and commotion that had accompanied his arrival had whipped the crowds of bodies outside into an unprecedented frenzy. Even now, many hours later, the creatures were still fighting to get closer to the building, banging constantly against windows and doors with their rotting fists. "You think they're getting worse?"

"More violent," Donna answered, "and less predictable. If they're going to become more of a problem, then we're not going to gain anything from staying here. We should get out and head back to the base with Cooper."

"What's there for us?" Bernard asked anxiously.

"More than there is here," she replied before returning her attention to the remaining scraps of food on her plate.

"Who says I'm going back to the bloody base?" Cooper said, loud enough for all the others to hear.

"Whether we go to this base or not," Jack said suddenly, pushing away his plate of cold food and taking a swig from a can of drink, "isn't it time we started trying to make some decisions here? We can't just sit here and wait indefinitely, can we?"

"We can if we want to," Bernard disagreed. "It makes sense for us to sit tight and wait for—"

"Wait for what?" Donna wondered.

Sitting silently in the chair next to her, Clare looked from face to face in the low light. First at Bernard, then Jack, then Cooper, then Donna, and then back to Bernard again. She waited for him to say something. In the gloom he looked haggard, old, and weary, as if he was carrying the weight of everyone's problems on his shoulders. He tried to appear calm and controlled but she could see the fear in his eyes. He hadn't left the building since the morning he and Nathan had found her and Jack.

"What I mean is . . ." he stammered. It was obvious he didn't know what he meant.

"What are you waiting for, Bernard?" Donna asked again. "What exactly do you think is going to happen if we stay here and do nothing?"

Obviously uncomfortable and wishing he'd stayed quiet, Bernard played with his food and picked up a paper towel, which he screwed into a tight ball before throwing it onto his plate. He sank back in his chair and looked up for inspiration, but none came.

"The way I see it, something's got to give eventually, hasn't it?" Jack said.

214

"Like what?" asked Cooper.

"Well, things can't stay like this forever, can they? Nothing ever stays the same for too long. I mean, you turned up here today, didn't you? There will be more like you and—"

"There are more like me," Cooper said, "but as far as they're concerned this is a dead place. Don't assume they're going to come back."

"They might."

"Yes, they might, but on balance they probably won't. As far as I was aware we were sent out on a reconnaissance mission and that was all. If the others made it back to the base and reported what they'd found, then they'll know there's no real reason for anyone to come back here, won't they?"

"So what do you think they'll do?" Donna asked. "It doesn't matter where they go, chances are they're going to find the same thing everywhere."

"I really don't know. Like I said earlier, there were supposed to be other bases. If they managed to make contact with any of them then they might try and group together. But then again, maybe they'll just stay where they are, safe underground."

"Christ, imagine spending the rest of your life in a bunker," Phil Croft mumbled quietly.

"Better than not having the rest of your life," Clare said.

"You really think so?" Cooper asked. "You didn't see what it was like down there. And anyway, we don't know for sure if those are the only options. Whatever happened here might not have happened everywhere. I think it did, but it's always possible that there are some safe areas people could get to."

"I doubt it," said Croft.

"But do you see what I'm saying?" Jack continued, picking up from where he'd last ended. "You're talking about all these different scenarios, but the bottom line is that something's inevitably going to change, isn't it? It's damn unlikely that nothing's going to happen. The law of averages says that things will never stay the same."

"What the bloody hell are you talking about?" Richard Stephens asked from his seat in the darkness. Baxter stared across the room, but it was too dark for him to see exactly where he was sitting.

"Have you looked outside recently?" he asked, his voice suddenly cold and deadly serious.

"I try to avoid looking out of the window." Richard smirked. "Too fucking grim for my liking."

"Do yourself a favor and go and take a look out front, will you? There are thousands of those bloody things out there now and none of them are going anywhere. For whatever reason they're attracted to us and there are more and more of them arriving every hour. And like we've just been hearing, they seem to be becoming increasingly pissed off."

"So what's your point?" he asked.

"Seems to me there's going to come a time when the sheer volume of them outside is going to start causing us real problems."

"Why? Do you think they'll get in?" wondered Bernard, his voice low and nervous.

"They might," Jack replied, "but I don't think that's very likely. But what *will* happen is we'll need to get out. We're going to have to leave here for supplies eventually, aren't we? There's

216

only so much we can store here, and we haven't got anywhere near enough."

"He's right," Donna agreed.

"Much as I just want to shut myself in my room and not come out again, the more I think about it, the more I'm starting to think we should pack up and get out of here right now," Jack continued.

"There's also a lot to be said for sitting still and waiting," Phil Croft added. "Where would we go? Is it going to be any better anywhere else?"

"Jack's right," Cooper said.

"But the bodies are rotting, aren't they?" Bernard said. "They're going to become less of a threat, not more. No matter how determined or persistent those bloody things are, there's going to come a time when they physically won't be able to do what they're doing any longer."

"And how long's that going to be?" Donna asked, looking directly at Croft for an answer. "How long do you think it will take them to rot completely?"

"Six months maybe," he suggested although he was far from certain.

"We can manage that," Bernard said. "We could last in here for six months."

"We still need food and water, Bernard," Jack reminded him.

"Six months is my best guess," Croft said. "Might be longer. Might happen in half the time. We're dealing with a lot of unknown factors here."

"Such as?"

"The disease itself, for a start. We don't know what effect it might have on the speed of decomposition. And then there's the fact that they're aboveground. They'd probably rot quicker if they were buried, but then again, it might be that exposure to the elements and the physical effort of moving around wears them down at a faster rate. I just don't know for sure."

Donna suddenly stood up. The other survivors watched her.

"So we just need to find somewhere safe to hide out until they've decayed away to nothing," she said.

"Stay here," Bernard immediately suggested. "We can stay here until it's safe to move."

"You haven't been listening, have you?" Jack sighed at him.

"No, we need somewhere better than this, somewhere stronger and more isolated," Donna said.

"You need the base," announced Cooper, his voice filled with resignation.

33

He didn't know how he had let it happen. In just a few minutes he had experienced a full range of forgotten emotions—from glorious realization, joy, and fulfilment through to shame, utter despair, and regret. All of the confused and pent-up feelings which Michael had forced himself to keep suppressed for weeks had now, in a moment of rash madness, been allowed to bubble to the surface and reveal themselves. The situation he now found himself in was painfully awkward and unexpected. He felt frustrated and embarrassed, exposed, and naked.

It was early morning. Michael didn't wear a watch anymore because there wasn't any point, but he knew by the low level of light beginning to trickle in through the skylight in the roof of the motor home that it was about five or six o'clock, maybe even a little later. He'd managed to sleep for a while but, ultimately, the night had been as long and interrupted as most nights were. But the last few hours had been subtly different. Lying next to Emma (who, in comparison, had slept relatively soundly) he'd spent much of the night just watching her. She had rolled over to face away from him in the darkness. Instinctively he'd snuggled down behind her and put his arm around her body. His hand had brushed her breast. Both of them were fully clothed, but the unexpected sensation and the slightest caress of her soft bosom had been exciting. It had reminded him in an instant of feelings of desire and lust, which had been buried deep for what felt like forever. He had pushed himself closer to her in the darkness, pressing himself against her, praying that she wouldn't wake up but, at the same time, wishing that she would respond. He'd wished that she'd turn around and hold him and kiss him and stroke him and tell him that everything was going to be all right.

For a long time Michael had wrestled with his conscience. How could he allow himself to think about love and sex when the world outside was dead? What kind of a human being was he to even consider his own lust and sexual desires ahead of the devastation that had taken place beyond the fragile walls of the motor home? But regardless of how his brain and his conscience screamed at him and demanded that he should behave himself, his heart and other more basic, carnal instincts drove him to act differently.

In the semidarkness he reached down under the bedding and unzipped his trousers. Nervous at first, he began to touch himself in a way he hadn't since before the nightmare had begun. Initially uncertain, with each passing second his private excitement had mounted steadily and soon he was moving quickly, enjoying the unexpected freedom and holding on to Emma as tightly as he dared. She was the reason he was doing this. He knew he couldn't risk telling her how he felt about her and how much he wanted her but, for the first time, he finally allowed himself to admit and accept the depth of his feelings for the only other person left in his world.

His hand movements became quicker, faster and faster until he reached the moment. Caution and control gave way to sheer thrill and desire. He couldn't stop. He didn't want to stop. He knew that the silence and movement might betray him but he didn't care. He'd had a need—a physical lust—which had to be fulfilled. And then it happened. The movement stopped. There was a split-second pause and then an unstoppable rush of sheer pleasure.

Suddenly feeling paranoid and self-conscious, Michael did up his trousers and immediately began trying to work out how he was going to clean the bedding and his clothes without Emma asking questions or discovering what he had done. A once-familiar feeling of post-ejaculation regret bordering on disgust washed over him. What had he done? Christ, millions of people were dead outside and there he was, wanking under the bedclothes like some dirty little schoolboy. He felt ashamed, and that shame increased infinitely when Emma rolled over. She was awake. Worse still, he could tell from her eyes (not that he dared look into them for any longer than half a second) that she'd been awake for a while.

"You okay?"

Embarrassed, Michael nodded.

"Fine," he said awkwardly. "You?"

She smiled and rolled onto her back. A heavy silence descended on the motor home which seemed to Michael to last for hours but which, in reality, only lasted seconds. Covering his wet groin with his hand and a discarded T-shirt he got up quickly and headed for the confined bathroom space where he began to clean himself up, wincing with the cold as he sponged his clothing down with bottled water. How had he let it happen? Did Emma know what he'd done? Was it such a crime? Had he actually done anything wrong? Could she still trust him or would she now despise him? Did she think he was some kind of pervert? A potential rapist? All of his questions were answered when he finally plucked up the courage to return to the other room.

"It's all right, you know," she said softly. Even more ashamed than he had been when it first happened, Michael was now mortified.

"It's natural," she said, getting up from the bed and walking across the room to be closer to him.

"I just . . ." he stammered, not really knowing what he was trying to say. Sensing that conversation was going to be difficult, Emma instead wrapped herself around Michael, burying her face in his chest for a moment before looking up into his eyes and then gently kissing his unshaven cheek. She ran her hands up and down his back and squeezed him tightly.

"I understand."

"Do you?"

She kissed his lips. She had kissed him before, but this time the contact between them was undeniably stronger. She stared into his face.

"I know how you feel."

34

The vast crowd outside the university building was still increasing in size. Even now, several weeks after they had first fallen, still more of the deteriorating bodies were dragging themselves through the wreckage of the city center and out toward the university complex. For the survivors gathered in there it was impossible to appreciate just how obvious their presence had become. The rest of the nearby locality remained almost completely silent. The only sounds were either natural or accidental— snatches of birdsong, the noise of the wind gusting through brittle-branched trees, or staggering corpses colliding with random objects and sending them crashing to the ground. Even the slightest disturbance was amplified out of all proportion, and the reactions such disturbances provoked were similarly exaggerated. The population of this city had numbered more than a million before they had been struck down *en masse.* Of those killed, more than a third had subsequently begun to move again and each one of them had slowly regained the ability to react and respond to basic stimulation. Seeing one body react would cause another to lurch instinctively toward the first, and then another would follow and another and another. A single unexpected sound would frequently cause more than a hundred of the creatures to herd inquisitively in the same direction. The survivors, with their unintentional noises and occasional bonfire beacons, had succeeded in attracting the unwanted attention of a rotting crowd in excess of ten thousand bodies strong.

From a glass-fronted landing three floors down from the top of the building, Yvonne, the once prim and proper legal secretary, stood next to Bernard and gazed out onto the vast hordes below. It was early morning and, as usual, neither of them could sleep.

"What are we going to do, Bernard?" she asked quietly, pulling her thick overcoat tight around her to keep out the cold. As autumn took hold she was really beginning to feel the drop in temperature. Without power or gas there had been no heating in the building, and she'd lost weight as a result of living on little more than scraps of food for almost a month. Both she and Bernard were in their fifties and the physical strain of their ordeal was becoming painfully apparent. Yvonne in particular looked gaunt and pale, almost as pallid as some of the corpses outside. For no more obvious reason than their similar ages these two had become close and had spent much time in each other's company over the last few dragging days.

"I tell you the same thing every day," Bernard replied, staring intently into the endless crowds which stretched out in front of them. "I just don't know."

"Do you think they're right, the people that say we should

leave? I can't stand the thought of it. I can't bear the idea of being out there again with those things. There are hundreds and hundreds of them. How are we supposed to get through?"

Bernard didn't answer. He thought back to the conversation last night but deliberately said nothing. Instead he slumped forward and rested his head against the cold glass. It was raining outside, a heavy and continuous drizzle which soaked everything and which made the dull and lifeless world seem darker, colder, and ever more empty. Christ, he was so tired. He hadn't done any physical work to make him feel this way. Just trying to live through this nightmare required constant effort.

Down below, the bodies continued to surge closer toward the building. So many had arrived now that those at the very front which had been there almost since day one, had been completely crushed by the weight of the extraordinary volume of corpses behind. Despite their broken bones, their decay, and the lack of physical space, those creatures which were pressed hard against the windows and doors still tried to move even further forward. They had neither the strength, space, nor ability to be able to get inside the building, but they continually tried to claw their way through to the survivors on the other side of the university walls.

"You hungry, Bernard?" Yvonne asked. He shook his head.

"No. Even if I was, there's hardly anything worth eating."

He was right. Their food stores were running dangerously low. They had ransacked every square inch of the university campus and had so far been able to survive on what they'd managed to scavenge from canteens, restaurants, and vending machines. Although they had ventured into the city frequently

225

during the earliest days to get provisions, the risks had increased substantially since then and such excursions had virtually stopped. Even men like Nathan Holmes, originally full of bullshit bravado and contempt for the dead, were now reluctant to take a single step outside.

The longer Bernard and Yvonne stared into the rotting masses below, the more the complete hopelessness of their situation became apparent. Down to their right was the body of Sonya Farley, still somehow holding onto what remained of her baby. Sonya's body was decaying as quickly now as the corpses surrounding her. Deeper into the vile crowd, at the point where those bodies still able to move forward reached the many thousands rammed tight against the walls of the building, more basic animal instincts were being displayed. Yvonne watched with disgust as the occasional corpse ripped and tore at the others around it to get through, desperate to get closer to the building. She had never been able to stomach violence of any kind, and this sickened her.

Bernard was watching the behavior of the bodies too. As the others had said last night, they were changing constantly, and he wondered why they were reacting in this way. He was an intelligent man and he knew that the behavior of the creatures must have been following a logical pattern. As he peered down into the disease-ridden sea of shuffling figures, he considered the chronology of their decline. He'd thought about this countless times before but had come to few conclusions. The corpses were rotting, even from this distance that much was obvious, but it seemed that something inside them had survived the virus or disease. It was almost as if their brains had somehow been

226

frozen and were gradually beginning to thaw. The ability to move again had been the first sign, soon followed by the unwelcome ability to again react to external stimulation. Other basic needs remained unfulfilled—they apparently had no desire to eat or drink or rest, no flesh eating like in the films his son used to watch; instead they seemed just to exist in a permanent state of constant, pointless animation.

But there was another change now manifesting itself.

Bernard had noticed it as long ago as last week, and the comments he'd heard last night had confirmed his suspicions. The bodies were now more aggressive than they had been. There was a new determination about them. Physically they continued to deteriorate, but mentally they seemed stronger, more aware. He looked down into the area of the massive crowd where the bodies were struggling with each other again. More than the bloody determination Yvonne had noticed, now some of these creatures were actually beginning to fight.

"See what they're doing?" he said quietly. "Just watch them."

Bernard turned around and saw that Yvonne had gone. He hadn't heard her leave. Unconcerned, he looked back out of the window and returned his attention to the dead. Where emotionless apathy had previously prevailed, new energies were now beginning to reveal themselves. The bodies were exhibiting signs of rage and anger. They had so far swarmed around the survivors because, he'd presumed, there were no other distractions, but now he wondered whether they wanted more. Did they feel pain? Was their violence a result of feeling their bodies decaying around them? He remembered how he himself reacted to hurt. His first reaction was often to curse—sometimes even to lash out in anger and punch a wall or throw something. Perhaps that was what he was seeing manifest itself on the streets below? Perhaps their increasing ire was a direct reaction to their suffering?

There were more than ten thousand of the damn things out there. How violent and unpredictable were these creatures going to get?

35

The long day dragged, the tension made worse by many hours of arguments and counterarguments as supressed frustrations bubbled to the surface. The atmosphere in the assembly hall was deteriorating rapidly. By early evening tempers were wearing dangerously thin.

"Have you looked out of the bloody window recently?" the normally placid Jack shouted angrily. "Do you know what's out there?"

"More to the point," Donna added, "have you seen what's still in here? Have you checked the level of our supplies? I tell you this, we won't last long if we don't do something now . . ."

"She's right," Cooper said from across the room where he'd been watching the fight brewing. "Staying here isn't an option anymore."

"And what the fuck do you know?" Nathan yelled at him, his voice hoarse with anger. This argument had been raging for the best part of an hour with, it seemed, much of the venom directed toward him personally. "I'm sure you know a hell of a lot more than you're letting on. I bet you know exactly what caused all of this fucking mess."

"I wish I did," the soldier replied, struggling to remain professional and calm, "then at least I might know what to do."

Frightened faces peered out from every corner of the hall, illuminated by numerous candles, torches, and lamps. The light in the room was dull and uneven leaving even more people hidden in darkness. For once almost all the survivors sheltering in the building had gathered together—even the most reclusive of them having been drawn out of hiding by the events surrounding the soldier's arrival. Being alone in their rooms had become too difficult for most. Better to snatch a few moments of sleep in the company of others than to spend endless hours alone in the dark, wide awake and on edge. The only people not paying attention were the kids, who slept or continued to play, and the man in the corner who lay under his blanket and rocked as he always did.

"Look," Donna continued, "Doc Croft reckons that in six months' time the bodies will have rotted away to just about nothing. Isn't that right?"

She peered around in the darkness, trying to find the doctor. He was sitting on the floor just a few meters away, but had been trying to avoid getting dragged into the conversation.

"Something like that," he said reluctantly. "Give or take . . ."

"So we'll wait here for six months," Nathan announced. Donna shook her head in despair. Once full of macho pretense, the obnoxious man was now letting his true colors show. His plans to get out of the building and take what he wanted from the dead city had been long forgotten. He was as scared as everyone else, but he didn't have the intelligence or maturity to deal with his feelings, and his fear manifested itself as anger.

"Which part of this don't you understand, Nathan?" she said. "We haven't got enough supplies here to last six more days, never mind six months. We've got to go out into the city now."

"She's right," Jack said, stepping out of the shadows into which he'd subconsciously retreated as the argument had become more heated. "We don't have an option. If you stop and—"

"What the fuck do you know?" Nathan yelled. Donna intimidated him, but he knew he could handle Jack Baxter. Refusing to rise to his anger, Jack ran his fingers through his hair and stared at him through the shadows.

"I know about as much as you do, Nathan," he said calmly, "but if you forget about how you're feeling and take a look at the whole picture, it seems we no longer have any choice."

36

Several hours later and the raised voices that had filled the hall had been temporarily silenced. Nathan Holmes had disappeared into the depths of the building and with him much of the hostility had gone too. Apart from a few mumbled conversations and the dull but ever-present noise of the bodies outside, the assembly room was largely silent. Jack sat with his back against the wall doing his best to fade into the already drab and inconspicuous background. The benefit of darkness, he thought to himself, was that he could hide without having to move. He could observe things happening nearby while still managing to feel like he was a safe distance away.

Jack was sitting in a corner of the room near to Cooper, Croft, and Donna. Clare lay next to him on a makeshift bed made from folded blankets. She was sleeping relatively soundly. He frequently watched her when she was asleep, feeling an undeniable responsibility toward her, perhaps because he was the one who'd been with her the longest. She was a pretty girl with soft, delicate features which, for once, looked untroubled and relaxed. It wasn't often that she looked that way and—

"What do you think, Jack?" he heard Phil Croft ask. At the mention of his name he looked up quickly.

"What?"

"You're not with us, are you?" Donna said.

"Nothing against any of you," he replied, "but I wish I was anywhere *but* here with you."

"We're talking about getting to Cooper's base and whether they'd let us in."

"Problem is," Croft explained, recapping for Jack's benefit, "we're probably still carrying whatever it is that did all this. If it was a disease then we're going to be full of it. It'll be in our lungs and in our blood. They're not going to let us inside if there's even the slightest chance we're going to bring it in with us."

"Depends on how good the decontamination process is, then, doesn't it," Cooper said.

"And do you think it will be good enough?"

"I was a soldier, not a scientist."

"There's another problem, of course," said Croft.

"What's that?" Cooper asked.

"How exactly are we going to get there?"

"How many people are here?"

"Between forty and fifty," he answered.

"And how many will leave with us?"

"No idea. Got to work on the theory that they all will, I guess."

"We'll have to see what we can find in the city," said Donna.

"Such as?" Cooper asked. "We need to be sensible about

this. We're not going to be able to just drive out of town in a convoy of cars, are we?"

"So what did you arrive in? We heard it but we didn't see it."

"Armored patrol carrier. I could probably drive one of those if we had one, but you won't find anything like that around here . . ."

"You might be surprised," Donna said.

"Got something in mind?"

"There's a courthouse not far."

"And?"

"And around the back there's a loading bay."

"A loading bay?" Croft mumbled, unsure where her logic was leading.

"We could see it from the office where I worked. We used to watch them unloading when there was a big trial on," she explained. "The prison vans used to pull up around the back and reverse in to deliver and pick up the prisoners."

"So?"

"Think about it. Prison vans are designed to carry people. More than that, they're strong and they're safe. They're about as close to your bloody armored patrol carrier as we're going to get."

"Are there any vans there now?"

"How am I supposed to know? There's a good chance. You'd see at least one of them pulling up just about every morning. There's bound to be something there."

"I know the court," Jack said, "but how do we get there? It's halfway across town. I can't see how we're going to get past the crowds out there. And even if we did manage to get through, how are we supposed to get back here again? Christ, imagine what the noise of a load of prison vans will do to them."

Cooper took a swig from a cup of cold black coffee that he'd made almost an hour ago. He winced at its bitter aftertaste.

"Seems to me that whatever we do is going to drive them crazy," he said, "but there's no alternative."

"We could go out at night," Croft suggested.

"Not a good idea," Cooper responded. "I know what you're saying, but you've got to add up the risks and balance them out, haven't you? Whatever we do we're bound to attract attention to ourselves because of the noise we make, if nothing else. If we go out in the dark then we're just going to make it harder for ourselves. They'll still react to us so we might as well go out in the daylight and give ourselves the best possible chance."

"If we're really going to do this," Donna continued, "then we need to think very carefully before we put a single foot outside. We have to get everything we need in one trip."

"We can do it," Cooper insisted. "We just need to get enough of us out there, get what we need, then get back fast."

37

"What are you doing out here?"

Donna looked around and saw Nathan Holmes standing behind her. She was sitting on a wooden bench in the small enclosed courtyard just to the side of the assembly hall. She sometimes sat there when she needed to be alone and think, and after the long conversations of the last few hours she needed to clear her head. The five-meter-square area of concrete nestled deep between university buildings was as close as she could safely get to fresh air without being out in the open. She didn't want anyone's company tonight, least of all Nathan Holmes, so she turned her back on him again. Unperturbed, he sat down next to her.

"What do you want, Nathan?"

"Nothing. Just thought I'd come and say hello."

"And why would you want to do that? It's three o'clock in the morning, for Christ's sake."

He lit a cigarette.

"Why not? Nothing better to do," he replied, leaning back and looking up at a patch of dark, cloudy sky between the tall buildings which stretched up around them.

"I haven't got anything to say to you," she mumbled.

"You had plenty to say earlier."

"So did you. You asked for it, anyway. You're an arsehole."

Holmes shook his head in mock disapproval.

"Don't know why you've got it in for me. Just because I stand up for myself and don't want to risk—"

"Your fucking problem," Donna said, standing up and moving away from him, "is that you don't think about anyone but yourself. And worse than that, all the things you say and the decisions you make are based on fear. You're too damn frightened to even think straight."

"You don't know what you're talking about," he snarled. The tone in his voice had changed. He sounded angry and defensive. Donna had obviously touched a nerve. "You don't know anything about me."

"And I've told you before," she continued, "that's how I want it to stay. Let's be honest, the only reason you've been making such a noise about staying here is that you're too scared to leave. You can't face the prospect of—"

"Bullshit," he snapped. "Are you serious? The reason I'm staying here is—"

"The reason you're staying here is because you haven't got the balls to go anywhere else."

"I don't want to be attacked by a thousand bloody dead bodies, that's why I'm not moving."

"Rubbish."

"You take a single step outside and they'll swallow you up. There are fucking thousands of them, or hadn't you noticed?"

"So what would you do if they got inside?"

"They won't."

"They might."

"Then I'll deal with that when it happens. I tell you now, I'm not going out there to risk my neck unless I've got no other option."

"Seems to me that none of us have got any other options."

"*I'll* decide when I'm going to make my move. No one's going to tell me what to do."

"Then you'll never do it. You're a bloody coward, Nathan. You're going to sit here and rot until—"

"You shut your fucking mouth or I'll—"

"You'll do what? Come on, big man, what exactly are you going to do? You'll still be sitting in here when the rest of us have gone. You'll die in this fucking place."

Nathan jumped up from the bench and lurched toward Donna. She stumbled toward the door which led back into the assembly hall and collided with Phil Croft. He'd been standing in the doorway, watching.

"Everything okay?" he asked, grabbing hold of Donna's shoulders. She steadied herself, turned, and pushed past him.

"Fine," she said as she disappeared into the darkness.

Nathan and the doctor exchanged glances before Croft turned and followed Donna back inside.

38

The sound of leaden, rotting hands smashing against the side of the motor home woke Michael. It had happened before—maybe three or four times in the last few days—and he had quickly become adept at disposing of the nuisance cadavers. Most times it was just a single body that stumbled upon the vehicle by chance, but this morning he could hear at least two of them out there. Tired and cold, he sat on the end of the bed and pulled on his boots.

Through a slight gap in one of the heavy curtains he saw that it was a bright and sunny day outside. That was why the bodies had appeared, he decided. They often seemed to be attracted to the motor home when the cloud cover was light and the sun was shining. Michael had deduced that the sun reflecting on the metal and glass caught their attention. They were parked at the edge of a large field and there were no other man-made objects to attract or distract the dead.

Emma was shuffling in the bed, the noise having disturbed

her also. She covered her head with a pillow to block out the banging as Michael pulled back the curtain and peered out. He pressed his face against the window, trying to locate the bodies. One of them was close to the door (he could just about see it from where he was) and from the direction of the noise he guessed that the other was up toward the front of the motor home, banging relentlessly on the bonnet. Yawning, he got up and walked down toward the door, pausing only to pick up a crowbar which he'd left at the side of the little gas stove in the cramped kitchen area.

"Be careful," Emma said, sitting up quickly when she realised he was about to go out.

"I'll be fine," he replied as he opened the door and stepped out.

The morning air was bracing and fresh. The sky was deep, clear blue and it was relentlessly bright out in the open. Michael covered his eyes to shield them from the sun.

The first body was less than six feet away and it was already stumbling toward him, clumsy and ungainly but moving with unexpected speed. Michael just stood and watched it for a moment. It seemed to have been relatively young when it had died. A white, ginger-brown-haired male (he thought) dressed in the shabby remains of construction site worker's overalls, its face was a frozen death mask, its blue-green skin pulled tight over bone.

"Good morning," he said as he lifted the crowbar and wedged it deep into the body's right temple. He felt paper-thin flesh give way with hardly any resistance. As time marched slowly onward, Michael thought, so the rotting creatures were definitely becoming physically weaker and easier to destroy. Their intent and drive continued to ominously increase, but as each day passed the empty cadavers were becoming unsteady and frail.

The body tripped back, rocked on its heels, and then stood motionless for an instant before dropping to its knees in front of him. Michael pulled the crowbar out of its skull, then smacked it around the head. The diseased figure slammed face-first into the dew-soaked grass, its neck twisted around at a unnatural angle.

The second body was smaller (it had been a child but Michael forced himself not to think about that). Its unwanted interest was aroused by the noises accompanying Michael's brutal disposal of the other corpse. It moved awkwardly around the front of the motor home, then dragged itself closer. He marched quickly toward it, dispatching it with a single swipe of the crowbar to the side of its head.

Destroying the dead was becoming disturbingly easy. He only did it when he absolutely had no choice, but he could now do it whenever he had to, without hesitation. Even as recently as last week it had still been difficult. In spite of their condition, and as repulsive and alien as these things had become, it had been hard not to still think about them as people. But their situation was changing and the life he had once led—the pre-disease world—was a rapidly fading memory. This uncomfortable, scavenging routine had become their new normality. His previous, simple existence with all its trappings, routines, and trivialities now seemed distant and at times almost incomprehensible. He noticed that the farther away those memories felt, the weaker his emotional ties to the bodies became. Now they meant nothing. They were just an inconvenience, occasionally a threat.

241

He dragged the cadavers out of the way, dumped them under a tree on the far side of the field, then walked back toward the motor home. He was about to climb the steps and go back inside when he heard an engine. Emma heard it too.

"I'll go and check," he said. Emma nodded. A quick sprint toward the track they had spent the last few days following and Michael was able to look down and follow the progress of yet another transport full of soldiers. They were heading away from where he thought their base must be. No doubt they would return again later. He watched them until they had disappeared.

Today's the day, he decided. *Today we're going to follow them back.*

39

Croft, Donna, Jack, and the others had hardly slept. All the sudden talk about actually making a stand and trying to do something positive had forced them into action. During the morning the various rough ideas and half-baked suggestions which had been discussed in the darkness last night had been gradually shaped and formed into something beginning to resemble a coherent plan. Those who had volunteered to be directly involved knew the risks, but they also knew that what remained of their lives would hardly be worth living if they didn't take these chances. Cooper had put things into perspective for everyone when he'd told them earlier that their options were simple: either a) wait for the bodies to get inside the building, b) sit here and slowly starve to death, or c) risk (and possibly gain) everything by trying to get away from the city. And with the number of bodies outside still increasing, the probability that their shelter would eventually be breached was becoming more likely with each passing hour.

Donna was ready. Keeping well out of sight, she stood in a doorway and looked out across the marble-floored reception area toward the glass frontage of the building. No one ever came out here anymore, and it was obvious why. A thousand dead faces stared back at her. She knew she was sufficiently hidden by shadow not to be seen and so stayed where she was and studied the horrific mass of crushed creatures outside. It was a hellish scene. It was inevitable that a door or window somewhere would eventually give way under increasing pressure. The thought of what might then happen was almost too abhorrent to consider. The building would be filled with an unstoppable wave of cadavers in seconds. Donna already knew that they were doing the right thing by trying to get out. Looking deep into the rotting crowd only made her more scared.

The wall of corpses blocked out most of the natural light which would normally have flooded the reception area. It was difficult to make out individual faces and features within the endless sea of gray-green, decaying flesh but, if she stared at a particular area long enough, she could occasionally make out something recognizable. It was the movement that really disturbed her. The entire discolored mass seemed to be constantly shifting. Despite being pressed hard against the glass, the crushed bodies still twitched and flinched continually: eyes moving, lips sneering, tongues lolling in black, gaping mouths . . . Donna forced herself to look away.

The plan the group had collectively decided upon sounded relatively straightforward. Six survivors would leave the university via a back exit where there were usually fewer bodies. Using the subways which Cooper had used to get in (hoping, of course, that purposely slow movements and hidden emotions would still be enough to fool the dead) they would make their way back into town toward the court building. They were then going to force their way inside, find the loading bay, get whatever transport they could, and then get back to the university as quickly as possible.

And what if it didn't work? They all knew there were a thousand and one things that could go wrong. What if the subway was blocked? What if they got into the court building and found that there were no prison vans there? What if the vans wouldn't start? There was nothing they could do about any of these potential problems until they had actually happened and they were faced with dealing with the fallout. Going outside was still the biggest risk. The rest of the city was theoretically theirs for the taking once they were actually out there, and the more bodies that are here around the university, Jack had suggested, the fewer will be left elsewhere. If they didn't find what they needed in the courthouse, they'd just move on and look somewhere else. This was a vast city, and Donna was confident they'd be able to get what they needed eventually.

She slowly walked back to the assembly hall, sick with nerves. She tried to remain positive and focus on her part of the plan. Once the others had returned with sufficient transport, they had arranged to park the vehicles deep inside the university complex, away from the bulk of the bodies on an artificial turf football pitch which was surrounded by a tall wire-mesh fence. Donna's responsibility was to get the rest of the survivors organized so that they could get out of the building and into the vehicles as quickly and safely as possible.

It was going to be difficult trying to get any of these people to move. She walked back through the hall, looking at each of the silent, stony-faced survivors sitting around the edges of the room. A short time earlier Cooper and Croft had announced the plan to the rest of the group but there had been little visible reaction. She didn't know how many of them intended leaving the university and how many instead would remain within the confines of the building, paralyzed with fear and unable to leave. They couldn't force anyone to go. They were taking the children— it didn't seem right to leave them—but the others were free to make up their own minds.

It seemed to Donna that many of the emotionally-drained people cowering nervously in this building were increasingly beginning to resemble the bodies outside. Eaten up with pain and anger, devoid of all energy, and trapped in a seemingly pointless and endless existence, some of the living now appeared little better than the dead.

40

There were several nervous delays and false starts but, finally, they were ready and it was time. The six volunteer survivors stood outside at the back of the accommodation block in a small, sheltered alcove where several overflowing and foul-smelling waste bins were stored. There were no bodies around that they could see. Various building extensions, walls, fences, and other random obstructions had prevented the creatures from finding their way through to here.

"Ready?" Phil Croft asked. The others around him looked far from sure. The doctor did up the zip on the fleece he was wearing. Although bright, there was a threat of rain in the air and strong winds were carrying ominously heavy clouds over from the east.

"Suppose," Paul Castle replied when no one else did. "Never going to be a good time to do this, is there?"

"If you can't handle it, just go back inside," Jack said nervously. "Quit fucking moaning."

"I'm not moaning, I'm just—"

"Okay, that's enough," Cooper said, raising his voice to make himself heard over the gusting wind. "Stop bitching and shut up. Anyone speaks and draws attention to us once we're out there and we've had it. I tell you, those bodies aren't quick or strong enough on their own, but if you do something stupid and end up with a hundred of them coming at you, you're going to have a real problem."

Jack thrust his hands deep into his jacket pockets and leaned back against the redbrick wall. He was terrified. Perhaps that was why he'd overreacted when Paul had made his comment. He'd been close to throwing up with nerves before they'd left the building. He hadn't told the others, of course, trying hard to keep up the pretence. They'd all felt so sure of their plans when they'd discussed them last night and this morning. Doing this had seemed like a good idea until they'd actually been about to step out into the open.

A single body tripped across a footpath a short distance ahead. The six men stared at it in silence, collectively holding their breath and standing still, watching it intently until it had awkwardly moved away. Steve Armitage (an overweight long-distance lorry driver who had hardly spoken to anyone until today, but who had volunteered to do this because he could drive a truck and because he could no longer stand being trapped indoors) licked his dry lips and nervously lit a cigarette.

"Put that bloody thing out," Croft said. "We're trying to blend in here, you fucking idiot. How many of those damn things have you seen smoking?"

Steve dropped the cigarette down and stubbed it out with his foot.

"Sorry," he mumbled apologetically. "Not thinking. Bit nervous."

Cooper's military training was beginning to show. Although he may well have been as scared and apprehensive as the other five men, it was not at all noticeable. He appeared calm and collected, as if this was something he did every day.

"Don't worry about it, Steve," he said, doing his best to reassure the struggling lorry driver. "We can do this, you know. All we have to do is hold our nerve and stick together. Take your time, don't do anything stupid, and we'll be okay."

Bernard Heath was, surprisingly, the sixth and final survivor who had ventured out into the open. Although it seemed that his nerves had been steadily increasing during their confinement, he remained a rational man at heart. He had gradually come to accept that his earlier protestations and demands that they should stay inside were driven more by fear than any logical thought processes. Much as he still preferred the idea of staying locked away in the accommodation block, he understood that was no longer an option and, perhaps trying to make amends for the conflict and arguments he had helped prolong recently, he had volunteered to go outside. He glanced around at the faces of the others before Cooper led them out in the general direction of the city center. They began to move toward the dead heart of the city in slow, shuffling single file.

The door from which they had emerged had been hidden around the back of the building. As the vast majority of bodies had reached the university from the direction of the city, the survivors came across relatively few of them at first. Those corpses they did see were distracted—banging and scratching incessantly at the sides of the building, trying to get inside. Cooper kept his head low, doing his best to imitate the weary movements of the dead. Untrained, and having been shut away inside for some considerable time, the other men were unable to match his military-imbued self-control and found it difficult to suppress their emotions. They couldn't help but stare at the nightmarish scene into which they were now walking.

It was the noise they noticed first. The world outside didn't sound as they'd expected. Inside the university they had been insulated and had become used to the quiet. Out here, however, things were very different. There remained an eerie, vacuous quiet where the noises of traffic, the chatter and moan of thousands of people, and the rest of the day-to-day had once been heard, but now a low and constant humming and groaning filled the air instead—the sound of bodies dragging their feet along the ground and the buzzing of millions of insects gorging on the sudden proliferation of decaying flesh. The noxious smell of the rotting corpses was stifling. Jack felt the bile rising in his stomach. He didn't know if he was going to be able to handle this.

Cooper shuffled away in the general direction of the subway which he had originally used to reach the university. He didn't relish the idea of disappearing back down into that dark and foreboding hole again. The vast crowd had swollen to such an extent that it was difficult to be sure where the entrance actually was. In fact, now that he looked closer, it seemed that both the subway entrance *and* the exit had been swallowed up by bodies. He knew he had no choice but to stick with the original plan. He couldn't do anything else without talking to the others, and he couldn't risk communicating with them out here.

"Jesus Christ," he heard someone say a short distance behind him. The voice wasn't particularly loud, but in this dangerous and unpredictable environment even a whisper was too much. Cooper tried to subtly turn around to warn the others of the danger, but what he saw made him freeze with horror. The bodies were reacting. Too far away to have heard their voices, the corpses were beginning to make definite, conscious movements toward the six exposed survivors. Those on the closest edge of the massive crowd had lifted their rotting heads and were looking at the line of men slowly snaking toward the subway. A few of the bodies had already begun to stagger away from the main group and were now lurching toward them. As those corpses moved, so their sudden change of direction attracted the attention of others and then, in seconds, a deadly and unstoppable wave of movement had begun.

"What the fuck is going on?" Phil Croft demanded, forgetting himself. The sound of his terrified voice was enough to cause hundreds more of the vile creatures to peel away from the main bulk of the crowd and start moving toward them. "You said they'd ignore us if we acted like them."

Cooper knew there was no time to stand and argue. The behavior of the bodies had been changing constantly since the day they'd been infected, and even in the short time he'd been away from his base he'd seen them become more aggressive. A few days earlier slow movements and feigned lethargy might have been sufficient to fool the dead, but not any longer. Although still awkward and clumsy, they were now moving with an ominous speed and purpose.

"Run," Cooper ordered. "Just get to the fucking courthouse!"

Without waiting for any response, he turned and sprinted toward the city center. He led the way but, not knowing the city particularly well, he ran without direction.

"This way," Paul Castle yelled at him, running away to the soldier's left. The others followed, ever-swelling swarms of bodies building on every side. Paul glanced back over his shoulder as they ran from the bulk of the decaying crowd. Panicking and moving at speed, it was impossible to make out precise details. Instead he was just aware of a steadily increasing dark mass of cadavers following them. Terrified, he faced forward and smashed into a single random corpse, sending it flying to the ground and tripping over its flailing limbs.

Paul, Cooper, and Croft were relatively young and in reasonably good health. Jack and Bernard, although somewhat older, were also able to keep up. Steve, however, was struggling. The overweight truck driver lashed out at the numerous spindly figures which lunged toward him, the force of his large bulk enough to keep most of them at bay. It was difficult to keep sight of the rest of the group ahead, such was the number of ragged bodies which constantly crisscrossed his path and grabbed at him with decaying hands.

Reaching an unexpected, momentary pocket of space, Cooper turned around to look for the others. He couldn't see Steve, but he could tell where he was from the number of bodies gravitating around him.

"Over there," he yelled to the others, pointing over to his right. He needed to find shelter. It didn't matter what or where, they just needed to get out of sight for a time and disappear until the crowd's interest in them had dissipated. He pushed open the door to a small, glass-fronted bookshop and held it open for the rest of the men. "Go through to the back," he said as Paul, Croft, Bernard, and Jack crashed breathlessly past him. Cooper ran back out to where Steve was still struggling and started dragging the bodies off him. Thinking he was one of the corpses, the lorry driver swung a badly-aimed punch at him. Cooper caught his arm and pulled him back toward the bookstore, shoving him inside. "Get out of sight."

Croft dragged a bookcase and a low reading table across the door to block it once Cooper and Steve were safe. Bodies hurled themselves against the windows, a myriad of grotesque rotting faces already shoved up hard against the glass, trying to get at the survivors. Cooper pushed Croft deeper into the building and found the others waiting in a small, windowless office.

"What the hell do we do now?" Bernard asked anxiously. "We're screwed." He looked at Steve in despair. The red-faced man was slumped over a desk in the middle of the room, drenched with sweat, fighting to breathe. He was never going to make it to the court.

"We keep going," Croft said. "We don't have any choice. We can either turn around now and fight our way through a fucking huge crowd of bodies to get back where we started, or we do what we came out here to do, get some transport organized, and *then* fight our way back through a fucking huge crowd of bodies."

His attempt at humor went unappreciated. Regardless, the rest of the men knew he was right.

"Where exactly are we, Paul?" Cooper asked. "Where are we in relation to the court?"

"Not too far," he replied. "Probably be quicker if we go out through the back of this place. Five minutes, maybe. Half a mile or so."

"Fine," Cooper said. "We ready?"

Steve looked up in disbelief. "Give us a minute," he complained.

"You can rest when you're sitting behind the wheel, okay? Lead the way, Paul," Cooper ordered. Paul led them out through the back of the building, pausing when he reached a communal loading area shared with a number of neighboring shops. A narrow service road ran along the back of the buildings, then looped back around to the main road. As far as he could see there were no bodies nearby.

"We go right here," he whispered to the others, standing bunched in the doorway. "It's a few hundred meters once we hit the road."

"Okay," Cooper said. "This time we try and stick together and not a bloody sound from anyone, understand?"

Paul began to lead them away from the shop, pressing himself against the nearest wall and doing his best to blend into the shadows. In the middle of the group Steve silently cursed the state of his health and wished he could stop panting, scared that the sound of his wheezing might be enough to attract more of the bodies.

The service road continued for another fifty meters before turning a sharp right and rejoining the main road. Paul paused just before the junction.

"Carry on down this road and we'll reach a roundabout," he told the others, nodding toward the mouth of the service road. "Go left and the court's at the top of the main shopping street. No more than a couple of hundred yards."

"What's it look like?"

"Big, impressive-looking building, bronzed glass in all the windows, steps up to the door, couple of weird-looking statues out front . . ."

Cooper crept toward the end of the service road, stopping when he reached the point where it merged with the main road. Cautiously, he stuck his head around the corner and looked up and down the once busy street. There were plenty of bodies around, but considerably fewer than they'd seen before they'd taken shelter in the bookshop. He guessed that the disturbance they'd created back at the university might have caused many of the slow-moving corpses to gravitate around that area.

"There are a fair few of them about still," he reported back. "The only way to get through is to ignore them. Try and forget they're there. Run through them. They can't match the speed and power we've got."

"A few thousand of the bastards could . . ." Steve said anxiously.

"Yes but there aren't a few thousand out there," Cooper replied. "There are enough for us to handle. But if you panic we'll be screwed, so shut up, take a deep breath, and follow me."

Not interested in waiting for any further reaction, he headed back toward the main road. The rest of the group followed close, their nervousness increasing with every step. Bernard Heath took deep breaths of stagnant air in an attempt to fill his lungs with oxygen before they started running again.

Cooper paused and glanced back to make sure they were together, then sprinted out into the open, the others struggling to match his sudden, frantic pace. Almost immediately, the nearest straggling bodies in the street began lunging toward them. Cooper brutally battered them out of the way, forcing his way through. Paul was just a few steps behind, but was becoming dangerously distracted by what he could see all around him. A myriad of unexpected emotions ran through his mind. As the inhabitants of the city had rotted and decayed, so the city itself also appeared to have deteriorated. He'd known this place well and had naively expected little to have changed but, in the time he'd spent shut away in the university, the once-familiar sights that he'd seen hundreds of times before had subtly altered. Weeds were beginning to sprout through the cracks in the pavements. Motionless corpses lay in the gutter being steadily devoured both by rot and the passage of time, and also by scores of rodents and insects which fed off their disintegrating flesh unchallenged. A random body lashed out and caught him off guard. He grabbed it by the neck and threw it into a crowd of three more advancing cadavers.

"Left here!" he shouted at the soldier who, in his haste and desire to keep moving, had reached the traffic roundabout and was close to missing the turn. Paul changed direction, followed closely by the rest of the men who were all somehow managing to keep up a comparable pace. Bernard and Steve in particular were moving with unexpected velocity and newfound determi-

256

nation which belied their years and poor physical conditions. Pure adrenaline and fear combined to allow them to run like men half their ages.

Disorientated by its overgrown appearance and the sudden effort of the sprint through the streets, it took Phil Croft a while to recognize the court building. As he swerved to avoid another body with patchy long brown hair, a hideously deformed face, and wild, grabbing hands, his eyes locked onto the steep steps which led up from ground level to the court's imposing bronze-tinted glass entrance doors. He began to climb but snagged his foot on what was left of a gray-suited corpse and fell forward, hitting the ground hard and winding himself. Dazed, he shook his head and slowly stood up, then threw himself over to one side as Jack hurtled back past him and shoved away a body which had lumbered perilously close.

Cooper, Paul, and Bernard were already inside. They held the doors open for the others, then immediately slammed them shut and blocked them once they were all inside. Four of the men dropped to their knees, fighting for breath, but Cooper and Paul remained alert, both of them having already realized that there was advancing movement in the shadows all around them. Within seconds some fifteen ragged figures had appeared in the building's vast, marble-floored reception area. Countless more slammed into the door they'd just entered through and began to try and beat their way inside.

"Get rid of them," Cooper ordered. "Go for the head and try and take them out. We'll get this area cleared, then we can slow it down a gear."

Looking around for inspiration, he grabbed a freestanding

NO WAITING sign and turned to face the advancing body closest to him. What had once been a policewoman dragged itself toward him with willowy arms outstretched. Holding the end of the sign, he swung the long metal tube through the air and clubbed its heavy base into the side of the corpse's head. Crimson blood, almost black, began to ooze steadily from a deep gash above the body's shattered cheekbone, but it moved forward again undeterred. Cooper lashed out at it again and again, his fifth strike finally enough to make the pitiful creature crumble, leaving it lying motionless on the ground, its head a mass of shattered bone and wet decay.

The cadaver of an elderly man in barrister's robes stumbled toward Steve. It stared at him with empty, emotionless eyes and he stood frozen to the spot, exhausted and numb with fear. Suddenly too close to be avoided, the lorry driver screwed up his face in disgust and grabbed the pathetic figure with both hands, keeping his arms locked straight and preventing it from moving any farther forward. Although the body squirmed relentlessly in his grip, its negligible strength was no match for his. Suddenly more confident now that the vast physical gulf between him and the dead had become apparent, Steve swung the body around and slammed it into the nearest wall with angry force. The corpse dropped to the ground by his feet, then managed to haul itself back up and began to move toward him again. This time he grabbed hold of its grinding jaw in his right hand and then, releasing weeks of pent-up fear and frustration, he repeatedly smashed its skull hard against the wall, almost crushing it completely.

They were cutting through the bodies with incredible

258

ease—the lethargic movements, slow reactions, and comparative weakness of the cadavers was no match for the strength and coordination of even the most unfit survivor. In less than five minutes the reception area was clear.

"Good job," Croft said, wiping away splashes of gore. He was breathing heavily. Paul was pleased with himself, surprised by the way he'd just fought.

"Bloody hell," he said, "they were nothing, were they? Christ, we could have torn a thousand of them apart . . ."

"Only if they wait in line and come at you one at a time," Bernard reminded him, wiping his hands clean on a curtain. He too felt more confident now he'd actually got his hands dirty and fought.

"Don't assume that's all of them," Cooper said. "There will probably be more around the building. Just keep moving and don't let your guard down."

"Where now?" asked Steve, rubbing his grease- and gore-covered hands clean on the back of his trousers. Cooper gestured at a brass sign on the wall.

"Jurors' suite," he replied. His answer was met with blank looks. "Jurors sit on trials," he explained, "and trials happen in court rooms. Prisoners stand in the dock in courtrooms . . ."

"And?" pressed Steve, none the wiser.

"And the prisoners have to get from the prison vans to the dock, don't they? We'll work our way back through the building."

41

Having forced their way through the spacious and virtually deserted jurors' lounge, several connecting corridors, and staircases and a vast and grandiose courtroom, the six men worked their way back from the dock and eventually found themselves at the entrance to the cells buried deep within the bowels of the complex. The other five stood and watched anxiously as Phil Croft stretched his arm through the bars and struggled to remove a bunch of keys from the belt of a long-dead prison guard lying on the ground on the other side, just in reach. Croft pulled the dehydrated husk of the guard closer and eventually managed to yank the keys free. He stood up and began to try and unlock the metal barrier which was preventing them moving any farther forward.

"Come on," Paul said anxiously. He could hear more movement in other parts of the building around them.

"I'm going as fast as I can," Croft yelled as he systematically worked his way through the keys. His hands shook with nerves but, with a welcome click and a heavy thud, the seventh key opened the door. Cooper pushed past him and marched quickly down a narrow corridor which opened out into a gray office area with a chest-high reception desk straight ahead. This, he decided, was where the prisoners were probably booked in and out of the court. Secondary corridors ran off to the left and the right. To his right were the cells, to his left the way out. Through a toughened glass window in the exit door he could see a wide, open area reminiscent of the transport hangar back at the underground base he'd come from. It had to be the loading bay. "This way," he said.

With an unexpected flash of sudden, uncoordinated movement, a lone meandering body dragged itself through an open door and threw itself at him. In a single sharp, instinctive move, he clenched his right hand into a fist and threw a powerful punch at the obnoxious figure, catching it square in the face. For a moment it stood and swayed in front of him, the mangled remains of its rotting features having been rendered unrecognizable by the brute force of the soldier's punch. As dark, sticky blood began to seep down from the black hole where its nose had been, the creature dropped to the ground. Cooper shook his stinging hand clean and beckoned the men toward the exit.

The door which led down from the corridor into the garage and loading bay was ajar, conveniently propped open by the trapped torso of another guard who had fallen unceremoniously weeks earlier. He stepped over the body, then ran down a short flight of concrete steps.

"Close the door," Jack shouted back to Bernard, who was bringing up the rear. "Stop any more of them getting in." Bernard

261

did as he was told, screwing up his face as he dragged the obstructive body out of the way, then slammed the door shut. Panting nervously, he leaned against the door to catch his breath again. Several seconds passed before he could bring himself to lift his head and actually look around the loading bay. Had the risks they'd taken to get here been worth it?

"You okay, Bernard?" asked Croft. The doctor's question made him look up. He nodded, stood straight, then took a few tired steps into the main garage area. He had hoped to see it full of prison vans and other similar vehicles, but he was disappointed. There were two white lorries that he could see—one long enough to have several doors and a row of small square windows down the side, the other around half the length of the first—and a single police van. Steve was already climbing up into the cab of the largest lorry, settling into the seat and checking over the controls.

"Can you drive it?" Cooper asked. Steve looked down at him and scowled.

"If we can get it started then I can bloody well drive it," he replied, offended.

Bernard began to check the condition of the smaller truck while Croft concentrated his attention on the van. He found its last driver dead at the wheel, slumped forward with his face fixed in a grotesque masque of pain. The chin of the corpse and much of the dashboard of the van were covered in drops of coagulated blood. The doctor stood back and stared at the pitiful sight, trying for a moment to imagine the agony this poor bastard must have endured as he'd suffocated to death. As he began to yank the awkward cadaver out of the vehicle he was disturbed by the sudden sound of corpses beginning to smash against the outside of the huge metal loading bay doors, the survivors' raised voices and activity having alerted them to their presence. As much as the body he was shifting must have suffered, he thought, at least this man's torment was over. For the desperate creatures still moving (and, for that matter, for himself and the other survivors too) the fear, confusion, and disorientation seemed set to continue indefinitely.

Cooper left the loading bay and ran back to the reception area through which they'd passed just a few minutes earlier, looking for keys to the vehicles they had found. Grasped in the fingers of another dust-covered body sprawled on the floor in a small office behind the tall reception counter, he found the key to a slim metal cabinet mounted on the wall. Inside the cabinet were door keys, drawer keys, desk keys, and many other keys of countless shapes and sizes. He grabbed everything which looked as though it might belong to a car, truck, or van and ran back to the loading bay.

Having dragged the body away from the van, Croft turned his attention to trying to get the engine started. Fortunately he'd found the keys he needed in the footwell between the corpse's feet. He sat in the driver's seat and fumbled with the ignition. After a month of inactivity he didn't hold out much hope of them getting any of the vehicles going without a struggle.

"Jesus, can you hear them?" Paul asked anxiously. Croft glanced up at him then looked out through the windscreen toward the loading bay doors. He tried to imagine the size of the crowd battering the other side of the heavy metal shutter. He could see it rattling and shaking in its frame.

"Of course I can bloody well hear them," he said, forcing himself to concentrate on the van again. "More to the point, they can hear us."

He repeatedly turned the key in the ignition. The engine began to turn over, but then died pathetically each time. His last words rattled 'round his head as he tried the key again and again. The noise they were going to make getting these vehicles back to the university would be deafening. The grim reality of the situation was painfully apparent. It was clear that even without any engines, the noise they had already made had been enough to attract many bodies to the other side of the loading bay doors, and he knew that many more would follow. Take too long here and they'd be surrounded. Their options seemed to be becoming increasingly bleak: get out in the van and the lorries or don't get out at all.

Bernard had more success with the smaller truck. Having managed to find the right key from the collection Cooper had brought back with him from the office, he tried the engine a couple of times before, on the third attempt, it dramatically spluttered and burst into life, filling the loading bay with noise and belching out dirty black, floor-hugging clouds of fumes. Never before had the taste of carbon monoxide been so welcome, the university lecturer thought to himself as he accelerated the engine.

"Don't let it die, Bernard," Cooper shouted at him. "Keep it running."

Momentarily elated, Bernard watched as the needle on the fuel gauge slowly climbed across the dial, finally stopping just short of the three-quarters-full mark. He revved the engine again and again to keep it alive. Even over its throaty roar he could hear more and more of the bodies thumping against the door outside.

"Bernard," Steve yelled, "get over here. Pull up in front of me and we'll get this one started."

The lorry driver had also managed to locate the keys to his chosen vehicle. He watched from his cab as Bernard slowly drove the smaller truck forward then swung it around. Steve climbed down and ran over to an area in the far right corner of the loading bay which looked like it had been used as a makeshift garage or repair shop. Managing to locate a set of heavy-duty jump leads he ran back to the trucks, opened the bonnets, and started work.

Paul nudged Croft, who was still trying unsuccessfully to get the van's engine to fire. "Join the queue," he told him. "Wait till they've got the other truck going and then get them to do the same with the van."

Croft nodded. He gestured for Castle to move to the side and then released the handbrake, allowing the van to slowly roll a few feet forward. He turned the steering wheel and guided the vehicle as close as he could to the trucks.

Ten minutes later and all three vehicles were running. The six men stood together in the middle of the fume-filled loading bay and hurriedly agreed on their exit strategy. Much as the university had seemed the most cold, uncomfortable, and impersonal of prisons recently, every one of them desperately wanted to be back there now.

"Do we wait?" Bernard asked. "Should we shut the engines off and hope some of the bodies disappear?"

"No point," Croft answered quickly. "We might as well just go for it. The amount of bloody noise we've already made will have brought hundreds of them here. It'll take days for them to disappear."

"He's right," Cooper agreed. "We're not going to gain anything by putting this off."

"Are we going to fit everyone in these?" Jack wondered, thinking out loud. He stared at the three vehicles and tried to visualize how they were going to cram the survivors and their belongings in.

"We're going to have to," Croft said, his voice blunt and abrupt. "I'm not coming back here again."

The noise on the other side of the metal loading bay door continued unabated, a grim reminder that before they could think about getting out of the city, they first needed to get out of the court building. Cooper walked across the loading bay and studied the doors. Doing all he could to ignore the constant, violent battering coming from outside, he crouched and examined the locking mechanism. The doors were formed in a concertina style, and once they'd managed to unlock them they would slide open to the left. Equally keen to get out and get moving, and feeling increasingly useless and redundant because he couldn't drive, Jack also began to study the locks.

"Christ knows how we're going to get these open," he said. "These would have been powered doors. We'll be hard-pushed to get them open without any power."

"We can do it," said Cooper. "We'll take the locks out, free any restraints we can see, then force them open."

"Force them open with what?"

"One of the trucks if we have to, what else?"

He lay down on the ground and stared at the bottom of the door. Light was trickling in from outside and was being blocked intermittently by the constant movements of the mass of random bodies milling around on the other side. With an outstretched hand Cooper tried to feel the door mechanism and understand how it worked. He could feel a metal runner buried in the concrete and it followed that there would be something similar at the top. He stood up and returned his attention to the lock, which Croft was still examining studiously.

"Think you can get it open?" he asked.

"If I hit it hard enough I can open anything!" The doctor smirked. Steve appeared at his side with various spanners, wrenches, and other tools.

"Found these over there," he said, gesturing back toward the area of the loading bay where he'd found the jump leads earlier. Cooper took one of the heavier wrenches from him and began to smash at the lock. Croft stepped back. The noise the soldier was making was deafening, and the implications were obvious.

"Get into the trucks," Jack shouted to the others. As the only nondriver he felt duty bound to carry on working to get the doors open. "When we get this done there'll be thousands of those bastards dragging themselves in here."

Croft, Steve, and Bernard returned to their vehicles. Paul settled himself in the driver's seat of the smaller prison van which Bernard had started, the other man happy to let him take the wheel. Just ahead of them Cooper continued to batter the lock with the wrench, feeling it weaken with every deafening blow. Another thirty seconds and it was released.

267

"That it?" Jack asked. Cooper shook the door and tried to slide it open a fraction, but it wouldn't move.

"Must be other restraints," he said, taking a step back and looking up and down the edge of the door where it butted against the frame. He could see that there were two more locks or bolts, one about a third of the way up the side of the door, the other a third down. Jack gestured for Croft to drive the van over. The doctor edged the vehicle forward cautiously and stopped just short of the door. He scrambled up onto the bonnet of the van, then hauled himself up onto its roof.

"Give me something to get this open with," he shouted down to the others. Cooper passed up a heavy steel lump hammer with which Jack immediately began to batter the metal. His pulse raced as he smashed the hammer down again and again. His arm ached but he didn't stop. He could sense the vast crowd waiting for them on the other side of the metal door, but he didn't care. He wanted to be away from this place.

Directly below where he was working, Cooper was crouched in front of the van, trying to pry the one remaining restraint open with a metal crowbar. Although this was a secure door it was by no means impassable. It would never had needed to be impenetrable—there had been enough security both outside and around the courthouse to prevent or deter escape. He thought for a moment about the level of noise they were making and the distance the sound would have traveled. Bodies for miles around would by now be staggering relentlessly toward the courthouse. He felt almost as if they were ringing a bizarre church bell, calling a decaying flock to worship.

The door began to move. The bottom latch was free.

With the first restraint now released, Cooper moved out of the way and looked up at Jack, who continued to hammer relentlessly on the lock. Sweat poured from his brow and his right arm was tired and numb, exhausted by the effort of continually pounding against the door with the hammer.

"Almost there?" Cooper asked.

"Almost there."

The soldier readied himself to open the door. By default Phil Croft would be the driver leading the convoy and he tried to visualize his route back to the university. He never used to drive through town much and he struggled to think of the best route to take. It had always been so busy that public transport had been the easiest way to get to and from work.

"Got it," Jack finally yelled with relief. He threw the hammer to one side, the noise of it hitting the ground barely audible over the engines and the dead outside, and clambered down from the top of the van. Exhausted, he dragged himself toward the larger of the two prison trucks and climbed up into the passenger's seat next to Steve.

Cooper beckoned for Paul and Steve to move their vehicles as close to the back of the police van as possible in the limited garage space.

"Ready?" Cooper asked Croft, poised to throw the door open. The doctor nodded and leaned across the inside of the van to open the other door for Cooper.

The soldier opened the loading bay and, immediately, hundreds of bodies began to pour into the building, pushing themselves away from the dense, surging crowds behind and grabbing aimlessly at the stagnant air in front of them. Many fell and were immediately trampled by others pushing from behind. They flooded around the vehicles but Cooper was able to quickly cover the short distance to the van door and get in. He kicked and punched at the corpses that reached out after him, then pulled the door shut.

"Move!"

Croft jammed his foot down on the accelerator and sent the van flying forward, tearing through the rotting masses and obliterating those creatures unfortunate enough to remain in the way. The windscreen was immediately drenched in foul, dribbling, red and yellow stains, but Croft just kept increasing his speed, driving blind. Behind him the two trucks began to move, slower than the van but with even more strength and devastating force.

"Can't see a frigging thing," Croft shouted as body after body smashed into the windscreen, obscuring his view still further.

"Doesn't matter," Cooper replied. "Just keep moving. Just get us away from here."

The crowd was huge and, it seemed, apparently endless. Their relatively low driving position made it impossible for Cooper and Croft to fully appreciate the appalling sight which could be seen by the other four men from their higher vantage points in the cabs of the trucks behind. A never-ending sea of decaying bodies dragged themselves senselessly toward the court, then turned and stumbled after the vehicles driving hurriedly away. Thousands upon thousands of emotionless, empty shells lurched toward the sudden noise and frantic movement that had filled the otherwise empty and frozen world.

"Which way?" Croft asked, panicking and shouting to make himself heard over the sound of cold metal thudding into decaying flesh.

"I thought you said you knew this place," Cooper replied, annoyed.

"I did," the doctor yelled back. "Problem is I knew it before all of this happened and there were a million corpses filling the streets."

Croft glimpsed a familiar junction through a momentary gap in the crowd and turned right along a wide road which he knew would take them deeper into the city center. He clipped the curb, and the steering wheel was jolted from his hands momentarily. Despite being some distance from the court now, they seemed no closer to reaching the edge of the disease-ridden crowd. Unable to see anything much at street level, he looked up at the buildings which surrounded them on either side and managed to work out roughly where they were.

"Got it," he announced. "We'll go the wrong way down the ring road. That should get us back home."

A couple of hundred meters farther and they reached a large traffic island and flyover littered with bodies and the remains of cars, buses, and other vehicles. He managed to weave a path through the wreckage. With less control but considerably more power, the two trucks behind smashed their way through after him.

42

"Christ," Clare said as she looked down from a high window onto the remains of the huge crowd outside the university building. "Look at them! Just look at them!"

Donna had been sitting with her on the stairs, waiting anxiously for the others to return. She got up and walked over to where Clare was now standing.

"Bloody hell . . ." she gasped as she stared into the mayhem below. The bodies were moving with more force and speed than she'd ever seen before. Those nearest to the center of the city, on the edges of the crowd, were breaking away from the main mass and were stumbling away from the university complex. And as the first figures staggered away, so more and more followed. This was no random movement. They were reacting to something happening down at ground level.

"What are they doing?" Clare asked. Deep in the middle of the crowd she could see bodies beginning to fight with others to escape from the immense gathering. Donna didn't get chance to answer.

"They're coming back!" shouted another one of the survivors from a lookout position above them on the fourth floor of the accommodation block. The lookout's disembodied voice quickly traveled down empty corridors and into the various rooms where the rest of the group sat and waited nervously. Keith Peterson was the first to react. He jumped up from where he'd been loitering listlessly in the assembly hall and sprinted up the stairs. He hung out over a second-floor balcony on the side of the building overlooking the enclosed football pitch they'd arranged to use as a temporary lockup for any vehicles they managed to recover.

Donna appeared at his side and leaned precariously over the edge of the veranda, craning her neck to try and catch sight of the returning survivors while, at the same time, doing all she could to ignore the fear she felt hanging fifty feet above the crowd of corpses. She could hear some kind of transport approaching but the disorientating silence of the world made it impossible to be able to tell what it was, how far away it was, and from which direction it was coming. The noise the men had made by being in another part of the city had temporarily drawn a huge number of cadavers away from the university, maybe as many as a third of the total mass. It was obvious, however, that the return of the men would inevitably also result in the return of the huge swarms of corpses, possibly even more than before.

"I see them," Keith shouted. He'd climbed up onto the

metal safety barrier surrounding the balcony and was holding on to the frame of the door they'd just come through for support.

"Are they all there?" Donna asked anxiously.

"Can't tell. There are at least three of them. I see a van and two trucks."

The blood-splattered convoy slowly pulled into view, the once-white fronts of the van and the trucks now stained with gore and the dripping remains from hundreds of collisions with thousands of bodies. Inside the lead van Phil Croft steered toward the welcome sight of the university buildings, still trying to peer through the mayhem of countless random figures and hoping he'd be able to locate the track which would take them off the main road and deeper into the campus. Oblivious to the danger of the powerful vehicles, the pathetic corpses continued to herd toward them in massive numbers.

Croft spotted the entrance to the narrow service road and took a sudden sharp left. He glanced up into the rearview mirror and, among the carnage and confusion he'd left in his wake, watched as the two trucks turned and followed his route away from the main road.

"Not far now," he said, but Cooper didn't respond. Instead he turned around on his seat and stared up through the back window at the accommodation block which they were slowly passing. He was looking for the other survivors, wanting to be sure they knew they had returned. He saw Donna and Peterson first, and then noticed other faces peering out from different windows on different levels.

"So what do we do now?" asked Croft as they drove toward

the wire-mesh enclosed football pitch. They could already see that the gate was closed.

"Just keep moving," Cooper answered, swinging himself back around. "Just drive through the gate."

"But we'll . . ." Croft began to protest.

"I've already thought about it. Drive through, reverse up and we'll use the van to block off the gap once the others are inside."

"So how are we going to get back inside if we're going to block the fucking exit?"

"We're obviously not going to be able to do anything for some time," he explained, holding onto the sides of his seat as the van bumped and rocked as it ploughed through and over still more bodies.

"We could make a run for it."

"No point. We'll sit tight and wait for a while. Doesn't matter if we don't get back inside for a couple of hours. There will be fewer of them around by then."

Cooper braced himself as Croft accelerated toward the metal gate blocking the entrance to the football pitch. Steve Armitage watched from the larger of the two trucks following close behind.

"If he can't do it," the lorry driver grunted, "then I'll get through with this thing."

"And you'll take half the bloody fence with you," said Jack. He watched as the police van careered into the gate up ahead. The force of the impact was enough to twist it out of shape, leaving the buckled metal barrier hanging half open, held in place by one stubborn hinge. Croft reversed a few meters back and then drove forward again, this time smashing the mangled gate to one side and driving straight through onto the football pitch. The doctor turned the van around in a large arc and watched nervously as the bodies began to arrive. Some managed to spill through the gap; the diseased shells of countless others collided with the rattling wire-mesh barrier around the entire perimeter of the pitch.

"This is going to be tight," Steve said as he lined up the truck and drove through the space where the metal gate had been. An experienced driver, the sides of his vehicle missed the fence by little more than a few centimeters on either side.

Seeing that the first truck had entered the football pitch unscathed gave Paul Castle unjustified faith in his own driving ability. He forced the smaller truck forward and winced as the passenger side scraped along the gatepost, bending it out of shape even more.

As soon as the last of the three vehicles was safely on the football pitch, Croft accelerated again, then stopped the van across the width of the entrance, blocking access to the hundreds more staggering cadavers still dragging themselves toward the survivors. Steve parked his vehicle in the middle of the pitch across the center circle. After driving up and down and obliterating the fifteen or so bodies which had managed to squeeze onto the playing field as the vehicles had entered, Paul pulled up next to him.

"Get out of sight," Cooper ordered as he ran from the van toward the larger of the two trucks. "Get in the back of this one."

All around the football pitch, bodies continued to collide

276

noisily and clumsily with the fence. Where between ten and twenty had been moments before, now hundreds of bedraggled figures stood and smashed their rotting hands against the barrier, grabbing and shaking the wire mesh with gnarled fingers. Needing no further encouragement, the five other men followed Cooper into the back of the truck. Taking care not to fully shut the heavy, security-locked door, the soldier collapsed onto a nearby metal bench.

"Done it," he said quietly. The military authority and direction previously so clear in his voice had disappeared. Now he just sounded relieved.

"So what now?" Jack asked.

"Take it easy for a while," Cooper replied. "Nothing to do but sit and wait."

43

Michael sat anxiously behind the wheel of the motor home with Emma at his side. They had been in virtually the same positions for almost six hours, hardly daring to move in case they missed the return of the soldiers they'd seen leaving earlier this morning. The waiting was unbearable. Michael was beginning to wonder whether they were ever going to come back. Anything could have happened to the scouting party. He might have misread the situation completely. Their base could still be anywhere . . .

The motor home was parked in a field adjacent to the track they'd discovered. By nestling the large and cumbersome vehicle on the other side of a gray stone wall, underneath heavy tree cover, they had camouflaged their position and their relative invisibility was reassuring. The otherwise bright day had been interrupted by an unexpected sharp shower of rain a short while earlier and drops of water still fell steadily from the overhanging trees, dripping down onto the metal roof and providing an eerie, intermittent soundtrack to the afternoon. Apart from those few random sounds the world was deceptively quiet and peaceful.

Michael's stomach was churning with nerves. For what felt like the hundredth time in the last hour he turned and looked over his shoulder, peering back down the track in the direction the soldiers had disappeared earlier. He stared into the distance, hoping he would see movement but, at the same time, also strangely relieved that nothing was happening.

Emma slid across the front seats and put her hand around his shoulder. He didn't respond. She leaned over and kissed the side of his cheek. Still no response.

"I hate it when you're like this," she said, her face close to his.

"I'm okay," he replied, subdued. Much as he wanted her close, he also wished she'd leave him alone to think.

"What we need to do," she continued, "is find a—"

"Shh . . ." he interrupted.

"What?"

"Listen."

Emma pushed herself away from him and sat on the edge of her seat, listening carefully. She could hear the sound of an engine approaching.

"This is it," said Michael, and he turned the key in the ignition. The motor home's engine rumbled into life and he gripped the wheel tight with anticipation. He sat motionless in his seat and watched the road behind through the large wing mirror at his side. Although the stone wall obscured much of his view he was able to see the point where the track climbed and snaked away into the distance then disappeared.

The soldiers in their transport eventually appeared over the brow of a low hill, the bright headlights of their vehicle burning brilliant white in the increasingly gray gloom of late afternoon. He watched as they drove closer and closer until his line of vision was blocked by the wall. A few seconds later and they passed, the dark green roof of the transport just visible over the top of the stonework next to them. He began to cautiously edge the motor home forward.

"Don't get too close," Emma said nervously. "They don't know who we are. They might turn on us and . . ."

Michael wasn't listening. He inched out of the field, driving just far enough forward to enable him to see the transport working its way down the track. When it was almost out of sight he accelerated.

Michael followed the bright brake lights of the vehicle in front as it drove around to the right and then to the left. Several hundred meters farther and the track began to narrow and become even more rough and uneven. The sides of the road became steep banks, leaving Michael with no choice but to keep driving forward. The motor home wasn't designed for traveling over such rough terrain. One of the front wheels sank down into a muddy pothole and the vehicle lurched over to one side, its chassis scraping along the ground momentarily.

"Christ," Emma moaned, "this is a bad idea. As soon as we can we should get off this track and—"

"We're fine," Michael said, struggling to concentrate. "It doesn't matter what happens to this thing. It's not like we've got garage bills to pay or anything. As soon as we find where these soldiers are hiding out we can clear our stuff out and ditch it."

"I know, but we don't know how far away they are . . ."

Emma let her words trail away as they drove through an area of woodland. Overhanging, brittle-branched trees scratched at the sides of the motor home and the military transport up ahead. The track curved and twisted in unexpected directions and Michael was forced to slow down his unresponsive vehicle to little more than walking pace. A random body smashed against the side of the motor home.

"Jesus Christ," cursed Emma, surprised by the sudden noise. "Where the hell did that come from?" She stared at the figure in the side mirror and watched as, in silhouette, it turned and stumbled after them.

Up ahead, the transport disappeared from view momentarily. Michael was relieved to catch sight of it again as they emerged from the trees. He steered through a narrow gateway and over a cattle grid which shook and rattled the struggling machine. In the near distance the military vehicle began to slow down, finally stopping in the middle of an empty field. Michael gently eased off the accelerator.

"But there's nothing here."

"There must be," Emma said, struggling to see past three more bodies which were moving toward the front of the motor home. She noticed there were several more behind them also.

Without warning the soldiers' transport began to move again. With a powerful roar and a belch of noxious gray exhaust fumes, it began to race forward again with sudden speed. It drove up and over a grassy ridge that had been all but invisible in the low light, and then disappeared down a steep incline and out of sight.

"That's it," Michael said, forcing the motor home forward again. "That's got to be it."

He approached the ridge at a dangerous speed and with mounting trepidation. Both of them knew the importance of the moment.

"Careful," Emma said as the motor home dipped to one side, one of the back wheels clattering through a deep furrow. Michael didn't respond, concentrating instead on catching the soldiers, following the trails of mud and flattened grass. Not knowing what was on the other side of the ridge, he accelerated hard again. With his heart in his mouth, he pushed himself back in his seat as the front of their vehicle climbed up and then suddenly dropped down into the darkness like a stomach-churning fairground ride. At first all he could see were the lights of the soldiers' vehicle up ahead. Seconds later they were gone.

"Where are they?" asked Emma.

"How the hell should I know?" Michael shouted back at her. The velocity of the motor home increased as they sped down the incline. He fumbled with the switches at the side of the steering wheel, trying desperately to turn on the lights while still maintaining control of the vehicle. Moments later, the ground started to level out. The front of the motor home began to smash into shadowy shapes in the increasing darkness. One or two at first, then more, then a constant stream of them. Michael found the lights and switched them on.

There was no sign of the military transport. There was no visible sign of their base. Apart from a slight rise up ahead, for as far as they could see, the vast field they now found themselves driving through contained nothing but hundreds upon hundreds of bodies, crammed tight together out here in the middle of nowhere. Michael immediately slammed on the brakes and brought the motor home to a sudden skidding stop.

"Keep going," Emma yelled at him. "For Christ's sake, don't stop here."

She was right, but it was too late. He tried to accelerate again but the loss of traction on the wet, churned-up grass and the mass of dead flesh surrounding the vehicle combined to stop them from going anywhere. The wheels spun freely in the mud, digging deep grooves and failing to grip. Michael looked out over the sea of rotting heads, desperately hoping to catch sight of something man-made among the decaying flesh. But there was nothing. He switched the lights off again and silenced the engine. As the nearest creatures began to smash their rotting fists against the sides of the motor home he instinctively grabbed hold of Emma's hand and dragged her into the back. Pulling a blanket off the mattress to cover them both, he threw her down into a small space between the foot of the bed and the table—a place where they'd hidden numerous times before. He held her tight as the deafening noise around them increased.

They were surrounded.

44

Donna ran through the university complex with Clare following close behind. At speed they worked their way through a labyrinth of dark, featureless corridors they hadn't used before, remembering details from a campus map they'd studied and hoping they'd be able to remember the way back to the others. After running the length of several empty, interconnected buildings, as far as they thought they could get without going outside or finding bodies, Donna stopped.

"This'll do," she said breathlessly, slowing down to walking pace and resting her hands on her hips.

"Where do we do it?" asked Clare.

Donna looked around. There was an exit door to her right. Through a safety glass panel she could see a narrow concrete pathway which led out to a detached prefabricated storage building. That was what she'd been aiming for. She'd seen it from her bedroom window.

"Perfect," she said as she opened the door and stepped out

into the night. The path between the main university complex and the storage building was completely enclosed with fences on either side and, apart from a single withered and gnarled corpse lying motionless on one side of the path, she couldn't see any bodies. She waited until she was completely sure there was no movement nearby, then ran the length of the path and broke into the stores, Clare close behind. Her eyes quickly became accustomed to the shadow and gloom as she looked around the musty building.

"Sheets," Clare said, pointing at a metal rack on the far side of the narrow rectangular room. She walked over and began unfolding them, making a pile in the corner farthest from the door. Donna added a stack of papers and wooden furniture to the mound.

"That's enough," she said as she disappeared into a second room. Obviously some kind of laundry stores, the shelves on the walls of this room were loaded with various bottles, tubs, and cartons. Bleach, disinfectant, and countless other chemicals used by cleaners and janitors no doubt. She looked through a small window in the back wall, out toward the center of the city.

Clare backed up toward the entrance door as Donna reappeared carrying a bottle of an acrid-smelling liquid marked FLAMMABLE, which she began emptying over the pile they'd built. She then crouched down and struck a match which she used to set light to the corner of a pile of once-important invoices, bills, and paperwork. The paper instantly began to burn. She lit another match and did the same again a little farther into the pile, shoving more linen onto the flames. The orange glow ate quickly into the tinder-dry paper and cloth, and in less than a minute the room was filled with bright flickering light and wispy gray

285

smoke. The fire grew in size rapidly. Donna stood back and waited a few seconds longer until she was sure that the blaze was properly established. She watched with satisfaction as the fire quickly ate through the linen and wood and then began to lick at nearby curtains and up the wall. A noticeboard caught light, leaflets and posters immediately curling up and starting to smolder. She knew the entire building would be completely ablaze in next to no time.

"Think this is going to work?"

"Should do," Donna replied as she ushered Clare out of the building and back down the path into the main campus. As they walked she could hear the crackle and spit of the fire behind her taking hold, and she could see the reflection of tall, dancing flames in nearby windows. "All we want is a distraction," she continued, "just enough to start the crowd moving in this direction. As soon as they're away from the trucks we can think about trying to get out of here."

Less than a quarter of an hour later the entire university was rocked by a sudden explosion. Donna sprinted to the nearest window to see what had happened.

"Bloody hell," Nathan Holmes said, "what did you two just do? You were only supposed to start a fire, not blow the bloody place up."

Clare laughed nervously, almost embarrassed. Donna peered out as a second, slightly smaller explosion ripped through the night, rattling the glass. The blaze they'd started in the storage building had been allowed to burn unchecked. It had only been a matter of time before the flames had reached more flammable

286

materials, resulting in the kind of blasts they'd just heard. She'd hoped it would happen. The bigger the distraction, she thought, the more chance they had of getting over to the trucks and getting away.

Outside in the back of the prison truck, Cooper and the others heard the muffled explosions too. Croft stood up and peered out through one of the truck's small, dark windows.

"Christ," he said quietly.

"What is it?" Steve asked, immediately concerned.

"Fire," he answered. "Look, over on the far side of the university. Something's on fire."

"Where?" demanded Cooper, barging past and craning his neck to look out through the window. "Shit."

For a moment no one spoke, each of them privately contemplating what had happened and fearing the worst. Croft was the first to try and make sense of the situation.

"They've started it on purpose, haven't they?" he said, turning back around to face the others. "They must have. No one's been up there where the fire is. They must have started it deliberately."

"But why?"

The doctor sighed. "Isn't it obvious?"

It clearly wasn't.

"Jesus, look at the bodies," Jack said excitedly, daring to open the door slightly and lean outside. "They're moving."

"Of course they are," Croft continued. "They're distracting them so that we can get back in."

The chain reaction which Donna had been counting on

causing was slowly beginning to spread through the rotting crowds still surrounding the perimeter of the football pitch. Slowly and awkwardly, almost the entire diseased mass appeared to be staggering toward the searing heat and bright light at the far end of the university complex.

"Time to go," Cooper said.

"We should give it a while longer," Bernard nervously protested. "There are still hundreds of them around. If we go outside now we'll be—"

"Time to go," Cooper said again. "They're moving away from us. We'll have an advantage if we're running through them from behind. By the time they realize we're there we'll already be gone."

"What do we do about the van?" Croft asked, remembering that, on Cooper's instruction, he'd left it parked across the entrance to the pitch.

"Someone will have to stay with it," Bernard suggested.

"Two should stay, just in case," said Cooper.

"I'll do it," Steve volunteered. "I'll only slow you lot down. I've already done enough running today, more than I've done in years."

"I'll stay," Paul said, the thought of sitting with the van and trucks seeming slightly preferable to going out into the dark night unprotected.

"We'll move the van back out of the way," Steve said, "then block the exit again as soon as you're all through, okay?"

By the time the lorry driver had finished speaking Cooper was already out of the truck and on his way over to the van. Croft handed Steve the keys and followed Cooper out.

"Back to the door we used this afternoon, okay?" Cooper reminded the others as they nervously grouped by the remains of the mangled metal gate. Steve climbed into the van and looked down at Croft, Cooper, Jack, and Bernard. He started the engine, sending a sudden splutter of noise and fumes belching out into the cold night and causing a swathe of bodies to turn and start moving back toward the football pitch. Realizing that he needed to move fast, he slammed the van into reverse and skidded back a few meters to open up a narrow exit. As soon as the gap was large enough, the four men ran out into the darkness. Steve drove forward again and blocked the entrance.

Still sluggish and clumsy but now with clear intent, a mass of corpses stumbled toward the van. The darkness provided some cover and the comparative speed of the four survivors was such that most of the creatures were not aware of them until they were close. A half-naked cadaver lashed out at Croft and knocked him off balance momentarily. Bernard, running with his shoulder dropped, charged body after body out of the way, not about to let anything stop him from getting back inside.

The ground was wet and uneven, and Cooper slipped and fell. By the time he'd realized what had happened six bodies were already within a meter of him. He dragged himself back up and ran on, leaving them surging after him. He was the last of the four to reach the sheltered area and the door they'd used earlier. Croft was already there and was ushering the other men inside.

"Get in," he shouted to them. Cooper pushed past and relaxed as the door slammed shut behind him.

45

Time to leave.

The crowds around the building were larger and wilder than ever. By leaving the building to fetch the vehicles and then lighting the fire to try and draw the bodies away from the trucks and the area around the main accommodation block, they had succeeded in making every last one of the vile creatures throughout virtually the entire city aware of exactly where they were hiding. Donna and Clare's well-meaning but ultimately uncontrolled distraction had become an unwanted complication, creating the kind of obvious beacon they'd previously tried to avoid. More bodies were appearing constantly. The earlier question of "Should we go?" had, for most people, now been replaced by "When do we go?"

Donna ran along the long corridors of bedrooms, checking each room one last time before they moved out, making sure everyone was either already out or definitely aware this was their very last call. She'd just left Yvonne sitting alone in her room.

She hadn't wanted to go. "I was born here, I've lived here all my life, and I want to stay here until . . ." she'd said to Donna, not able to bring herself to reach the obvious conclusion to her sentence.

Donna turned the final corner to head back downstairs and ran headfirst into Nathan coming the other way. For a moment both of them waited for the other to speak.

"Seen Rich?"

"In his room, waiting for you," Donna answered. She slipped past him and moved toward the staircase, not wanting to waste any more time here. Nathan started toward the bedrooms but then stopped and turned back.

"Donna, I . . ."

"What?"

He fumbled.

"I just—"

"Save it, Nathan," she said. "I don't want to hear it. We've all heard your great plan, and we all know exactly what you are and why you're doing it. You're a coward. You think we don't have a hope in hell out there, but you're wrong. You're so wrong."

For a moment he didn't react, looking surprised like she'd just punched him in the face. Then he slowly shook his head.

"It wasn't that," he said quietly. "I just wanted to wish you luck, that was all. I do think you're wasting your time, but I hope you're not."

Working quickly and with real purpose, those survivors who had elected to leave collected up their useful belongings and gathered in the long, dark corridor near to the door that Cooper and the others had used to get in and out of the building. Standing by the door and waiting anxiously, Jack counted about thirty men, women, and children and tried to visualize how they were going to fit them and their supplies into the two prison trucks and the smaller police van. Christ, he thought, he hadn't even seen some of these faces before now. They were going to be tight on space, and many of the bags and boxes that each survivor carried would have to be left behind. Food and supplies could be replaced. These people couldn't.

The vast majority of the bodies continued to swarm around the raging fire at the other end of the campus and it made sense to get out now and make the most of the distraction before it either burned itself out or spread closer. The nervous survivors, many of whom hadn't dared take even a single step outside in almost a month, prepared themselves to run through the darkness toward the vehicles waiting for them on the football pitch.

"You ready?" Cooper asked quietly, disturbing Jack, who was still trying to work out how he'd managed to get himself stuck at the front of the queue. He glanced back along the line. A row of frightened faces stared back at him in expectation, but he couldn't give any of them any reassurance.

"Now's as good a time as any," he said, eventually replying. "Might as well do it."

Cooper moved across the corridor so that he could be seen and heard by the rest of the group. Donna watched him anxiously from near the back of the line.

"Okay," he began, looking up and down the faces in the semidarkness, "if you don't think you can go through with this, disappear now and find somewhere safe to hide because you're on your own. As soon as we open this door you need to start running. Run faster than you've ever run before. Push your way through the bodies and don't try and fight. Just hit them hard, keep moving, and you'll get through."

Standing a little way farther down the line, Phil Croft spoke up.

"Don't stop if you start to get tired because you won't make it. Whatever happens, keep going and don't let your speed drop. You can rest when you're in the truck."

Jack rested his hand on the door handle and waited for the signal.

"What if they don't see us?" a nervous and young-sounding woman asked from somewhere around the middle of the group. He tried to find her face in the gloom. Sheri Newton, he thought her name was.

"Who?"

"The blokes in the van—what if they don't see us coming?"

A ripple of concern worked its way along the line.

"Then the one who gets to the van first bangs on the bloody window and screams at them until they realize what's happening and shift the damn thing, okay?" Cooper replied.

"But what if they—"

"Don't worry about it," he interrupted. "They'll see us."

"But what if they don't? What if—"

Cooper sensed that the numerous questions being fired in his direction were just delaying tactics. He ignored them and nodded at Jack.

"Do it," he said, his voice loud enough for them all to hear. "Open the door."

Knowing that if he hesitated he'd lose his nerve, Jack slammed the handle down and threw the door open. For a moment he simply stood still and stared out into the night. Cold wind and a light rain blew into his face. He could see the football pitch and the van blocking the entrance, but in the darkness it seemed an immeasurable distance away. And worse still, between him and the vehicles he could see bodies. It looked like there were hundreds of them, shuffling, staggering, and limping across the scene in silhouette. Unmistakable with their stilted, pained movements and lethargic, but still threatening, determination and dogged persistence, the nearest few had already turned and were moving toward the building.

"Go, Jack," Cooper shouted. "Move!"

Jack immediately began to run. Full of thoughts and concerns for the others while they had all been safe indoors, he now sprinted across the grass and tarmac pathways in selfish isolation, only interested in his own survival. He knocked one body out of the way, then another and then another. Within seconds his heart was thumping hard in his chest and his lungs were on fire. Another few seconds and some of the younger, fitter survivors had overtaken him. That damn van didn't seem to be getting any closer.

The rest of the survivors pushed their way out of the university building, jostling with each other to get through the door. Loaded up with bags of belongings, they forced themselves through the swarming crowds. Men and women, young and old, all moved forward together in absolute terror, praying they'd get through, terrified that if they slowed down they'd be swallowed up by the diseased masses. Toward the back of the group some of the stronger men and women carried the smallest children. The delighted squeals coming from a two-year-old boy were muffled by the groans of effort and moans of fear coming from Erica Carter, the middle-aged woman who had taken it upon herself to carry him on her back.

Paul and Steve sat in the front of the van, oblivious. The hours since they had volunteered to stay behind and look after the vehicles had dragged unbearably. Still surrounded by corpses remaining from the earlier noise and activity, and with no idea when the survivors would be able to make their move, the two men had sat together in absolute silence, not daring to move or even talk to each other. Sitting in the front passenger seat, Paul struggled to keep his tired eyes open. His head lolled forward as he drifted off, and thumped against the glass. He sat up with a start and glanced out through the window. It took a couple of seconds for what he was seeing to register.

"Bloody hell."

"What is it?" Steve asked, immediately concerned.

"Oh, Jesus," he whined, "they're coming for us."

"What?"

"Loads of fucking bodies," he continued to wail pathetically. "Christ, Steve, they're coming . . ."

Steve leaned across the width of the van and shoved him out of the way so he could see through the steamed-up window.

"You fucking idiot," he said angrily, sitting back in his seat and starting the engine as the first survivors slammed against the door. "That's our lot."

Paul peered deeper into the darkness. A sudden movement and the ominous thump of another body hitting the side of the van next to him made him recoil with fright and surprise. The screaming face at his window, although he didn't recognize it, definitely belonged to a living human being, not one of the corpses. The panicked, obscenity-ridden tirade suddenly being yelled at him was proof positive.

The noise of the engine spluttering into life again whipped the rotting figures which remained near to the football pitch into a feverish frenzy. They began to clatter against the fence, some grabbing hold of the wire mesh with bony fingers and pulling and shaking it furiously. The night air was filled with light and noise as Steve flicked on the van's headlamps and reversed, allowing the first survivors and an equal number of corpses to flood onto the football pitch.

"How am I supposed to know when they're all in?" Steve asked nervously.

"There's Cooper," Paul eventually replied. He watched as the soldier stopped at the gate and ushered in the remaining stragglers. Feeling suddenly useless he jumped down from the van and ran around to help him fend off the dead hordes still trying to push their way inside.

"Can't see anyone else—I think that's it," Cooper shouted as he pushed away another lunging cadaver and grabbed hold of Sunita by the scruff of her neck. Paul didn't need to be told twice. He ran onto the football pitch and dived out of the way as the soldier signaled for Steve to move forward and block off the entrance again.

The pitch, quiet and empty until just a few minutes ago, had suddenly become a frenzied melee. Diseased corpses mingled with survivors who, in the cold gloom of the night, struggled to tell one from the other. Sensing the confusion, Steve climbed out of the van and ran over to the nearest of the prison trucks, pushing several bodies out of the way as he did so. Hauling himself up into the cab, he fumbled in the dark for the keys. Eventually managing to find them, he turned them a notch and switched on the headlamps, immediately flooding part of the football pitch with bright light. He did the same in the second truck and then, suddenly able to distinguish fellow humans from the empty shadows of corpses again, the survivors began to clear the pitch. Fragile and weak cadavers were beaten and smashed beyond recognition by frightened men and women. Others—the old and the very young—cowered in fear around the prison trucks. With their weight considerably reduced as much of their flesh had either withered and decayed or dribbled out through various wounds and orifices, Cooper and several others were able to pick up the wiry-framed creatures and literally hurl them over the fence and back out into the darkness. Donna watched with fascination and disgust as one corpse landed at the feet of a group of five more which immediately set about it, tearing it apart, oblivious to what it was.

Sheri Newton screamed, finding herself surrounded by bodies in a corner of the playing field. Even more grabbing hands reached for her through the fence, tugging at her clothes and pulling her long hair through the wire mesh. She fell to the ground and covered her head as the first corpses dropped down and began to thump and smash at her with leaden, uncoordinated fists. Donna and Baxter ran across to help and pulled the bodies away from her. Standing a short distance behind them, Keith Peterson and another man disposed of the cadavers over the fence.

297

Croft stared into the darkness ahead of him. He was aware of constant movement all around but he couldn't see who or what it was. Dark, shambling figures crisscrossed in front of him. Living or dead? It was impossible to tell. He froze as he felt rough hands on his back. Spinning quickly around, he grabbed the collar of his assailant's loose, ragged clothing. In the confusion he slipped in a greasy puddle of something which was once human and fell on his back, a heavy black shape landing on top of him.

"Bloody hell, Doc," Jack gasped, surprised to find himself dragged onto the ground. "Take it easy."

"Sorry, mate," the doctor replied as he pushed the other man away. "Didn't know it was you."

Jack grinned at him, his face now visible in the light from the headlamps of the prison trucks. By the time the two men had scrambled back onto their feet the pitch was virtually clear.

"Get into the trucks," Cooper shouted as he started to bundle terrified survivors into the back of the prison vehicles. Desperate people forced themselves into the transports which they prayed would soon take them to safety. Seventeen climbed into the back of the first vehicle and another twelve into the smaller. Steve made for the larger truck and Croft took the wheel of the other. Donna, Jack, Sunita, and two others headed for the van. Cooper clambered into the driving seat.

"You sure you can remember the way back?" Donna asked. He nodded and slammed and locked the door. He wound down the window at his side.

"Ready?" he screamed into the night. Two sets of bright headlights flashed back at him in acknowledgment. He put the van into gear, turned around in a tight circle, and then drove out of the football pitch, heading back toward the road. Donna looked over her shoulder and watched as the two trucks began to slowly trundle after them.

Fighting hard to concentrate and keep moving in the right direction, Cooper put his foot down on the accelerator as masses of bodies hurled themselves in front of the van.

46

Standing together in silence, looking out of the window of a first-floor bedroom, Nathan Holmes and Richard Stephens watched the convoy of survivors disappear into the night.

"Bloody idiots," Nathan said. "They're wasting their time."

Richard didn't respond. He turned away, trying to hide the fact that he was crying. Nathan glanced over his shoulder and looked at him momentarily before turning back to stare out of the window again. He could see the fading taillights of the trucks and the van in the distance, hundreds of staggering bodies following pointlessly in their wake, no chance of ever catching them. To his far right the huge blaze at the other end of the university complex was continuing to draw thousands more cadavers to the scene. He looked back at Richard again.

"Okay, mate, you ready?" he asked. Richard nodded and sniffed back more frightened tears. "Going to be a good night, this is. Best night out ever."

Nathan picked up an outdoor jacket which he had left

draped over the back of a nearby chair. He put it on and did up the zip. Still crying, Richard pulled on a warm fleece.

"Sure you're up for this?"

"I'm desperate for a drink. Anyway, no choice now."

The two men left the room and walked down the dark, echoing corridor to the staircase. They then made their way down to the ground floor together and entered the farthest room along.

"Pub or club?" Nathan asked as he pried open a window. Richard managed half a smile.

"Start with a pub and see how we go. We can always move on later."

"The Crown or The Lazy Fox?"

He thought for a moment. "The Crown. It's closer."

Grinning, Nathan leaned out of the window and looked up and down along the outside wall of the building. He climbed up onto the windowsill, swung his legs around, then jumped down into the middle of an overgrown flower bed. Richard followed close behind. Terrified, and knowing that this would almost certainly be his last night alive, he stopped walking suddenly. Nathan looked around again, then took a step back and rested a hand on his friend's shoulder.

"Don't be scared, mate. Think about it this way: that lot that left here tonight, they've got nothing left to look forward to except more and more grief. You and me, though, we've got it made. It's going to get harder and harder for the rest of them, but it's going to get easier for us. No more running. No more hiding."

Nathan crept forward until he reached the edge of a narrow pathway.

"Nathan, I—" Richard started to say.

"Trust me, mate," he interrupted, and with that he turned and began to jog away from the university.

The two men emerged from a side street out onto a section of the ring road which was swarming with bodies. As the number of corpses around them increased, so they increased their speed. They pushed their way through the crowds, smashing the cadavers away before they had chance to react.

After reaching the far side of the carriageway, Nathan turned left into another wide street and headed for the dark remains of The Crown public house, a large pub which had occupied a prominent position on the corner of two once-busy main roads. Panting with exhaustion he crashed through the swinging entrance door, followed a few seconds later by his friend.

"You okay?" he asked.

Richard bent over double with his hands on his knees, fighting to get his breath.

"I'm okay," he answered, wheezing.

The now familiar dull thud of bodies smashing against the outside of the door made the two men look up. Nathan immediately began to pile up tables, chairs, cigarette machines, and anything else he could find in front of the entrance to prevent the odious creatures from forcing their way inside. Richard walked deeper into the building, looking around at his instantly familiar surroundings, feeling unexpectedly nostalgic and sad. The pub was empty. It had been closed when the disaster had struck. Thank God it hadn't happened late on a Saturday night, he thought to himself.

"What are you drinking?" he asked as he walked around to the back of the bar, stepping over the body of a dead cleaner.

"Anything you can lay your hands on," Nathan replied as he finished blocking the door. "Bottle of beer, spirits . . . whatever's easiest." He peered through a gap in the mountain of furniture he'd just created and watched as the cadavers in the street continued to try hopelessly to force their way forward.

As Richard busied himself behind the bar, Nathan dragged two leather armchairs across the room and set them in front of a fireplace, one on either side. He smashed up a table and stool and built a fire in the hearth with the splintered wood, using liquor to help fuel the flames. Richard carried several bottles of spirits and beer over on a tray and sat down. He poured them both a drink.

"Cigar?" Nathan asked, suddenly disappearing across the room and grabbing a handful of cigars and boxes of matches from a display at the back of the bar.

"I don't smoke," Richard said.

"Then maybe you should start," he grinned. "It's your last chance, mate."

Richard helped himself to a single cigar, threw away the cellophane wrapper, sniffed it, and then lit it. Nathan did the same. The two men sat back in the dull orange glow and began to drink.

"You do know this is as good as it's going to get, don't you?" Nathan said quietly, his voice carrying none of antagonism and venom that had been so prevalent throughout their previous days and weeks of confinement. "All you have to do now," he continued, "is drink and smoke and relax. Make sure you drink enough because they're going to get in here at some point and it'll be easier if you're drunk. And if we manage to make it through to the morning, we'll just drink some more."

Richard was crying again, but the drink soon began to take the slightest edge off his pain. "Bloody hell," he said, "they're already at the windows."

Nathan looked up and saw that a multitude of dark shapes were milling around on the other side of the frosted glass. He could still hear the bodies banging against the front door too. If their noise doesn't attract even more of them, he thought, then the light from the fire almost certainly will.

"Drink up," he said, "and think yourself lucky. Tonight, everyone else is either dead or on the run. No one else is like us, enjoying a civilized drink down the pub. We're in the best place we could be."

Richard didn't know if he agreed, but the more booze he forced himself to drink, the more he realized he didn't care.

It took several hours for the crowd out on the street to build to such a size that the pressure of their numbers forced the doors open and allowed them to flood inside. A street-level window behind and to the right of Nathan and Richard also smashed, sending glass flying in all directions and allowing countless more bodies to spill into the pub. Already too drunk to react or fight or even care, the two men sat in their chairs and continued to drink as the building steadily filled with rotting flesh.

47

For several hours, Michael and Emma had lain motionless on the floor of the motor home. Their bodies ached but they hardly dared move for fear of attracting the corpses again. There were still hundreds of them nearby—the two survivors could sense their closeness—but their interest in the vehicle and its occupants finally seemed to have dissipated. For a while the relentless rocking of the motor home had stopped. The clattering of another sudden downpour of heavy rain on the roof temporarily drowned out all other sounds.

"We can't just stay lying here," Emma whispered in Michael's ear. "We have to do something."

"What else can we do?"

"Try the engine again. See if you can get us moving. Christ, a bit of noise won't make things any worse, will it?"

Michael didn't answer. Instead he just stood up very slowly, every bone aching from hours of inactivity. The rainwater running down the windows blurred his view of the outside world.

The sudden lack of visibility combined with the unexpected but welcome noise of the relentless rain gave him enough cover to be able to risk moving around. He worked his way around the sides of the motor home, blocking the windows with heavy curtains and boards as they did each night. Emma sat up and watched in silence from the floor.

"This is a real fucking mess," he said under his breath as he leaned forward and closed up a narrow crack of light around the edge of the nearest window. "There are thousands of bodies here."

He walked the length of the motor home and sat down in the driver's seat, then cautiously lifted up a corner of material covering the windscreen and stared outside. All he could see were corpses. Soaked by the heavy rain and tightly packed together, they were crammed into the field, pressed up hard against the motor home on every side.

"There must be something we can do," Emma said.

"We've got to be right on top of the base," he said, not answering her. "There must be an entrance near here. There wouldn't be so many of them hanging around if there wasn't something attracting them. We're out in the middle of nowhere, for Christ's sake."

"So what do we do?" she asked again. Michael said nothing. He was distracted, his attention caught by a group of bodies fighting with each other to get closer to the motor home. One of them, slightly less decayed than many of the others, forced itself forward, grabbing wildly at the cadavers in front of it and literally ripping rotten flesh from their bones. An unstoppable reaction to the sudden outburst quickly spread through a wide swathe of the huge crowd.

"All we can do is wait," he replied, transfixed by the violence outside. "We either wait for the soldiers to appear again and try to get their attention, or we wait until this crowd starts to thin out and try and get away from here."

"And when's that likely to happen? Come on, Mike—"

"No idea. Sometime in the next six months, I should think."

"I'm serious," she said angrily. "We can't just sit here indefinitely, can we?"

"What else are we supposed to do? I don't think we have any choice."

48

Cooper wished he'd had the time and resources to try and set up some kind of communication system between the van and the two prison trucks. It was a stupid oversight on his part. Even a couple of basic two-way radios would have been sufficient, but they had nothing. As if the effort of driving through the remains of the country wasn't enough, he was also having to contend now with appalling weather conditions, and keep his speed low enough so that he didn't lose the two trucks which labored slowly after the van. It wasn't going to be easy to find the base again. He knew the general route, but the early morning light was dull and everything seemed to have changed immeasurably since he'd last driven there. The world around him had continued to crumble and decay, rendering it frequently unrecognisable. The relentless rain today only added to the confusion.

The huge, dark shadows of the city which had imprisoned them for weeks were now just distant specks on the murky horizon behind them. The convoy made slow progress away from the dead town, speeding up slightly as they moved deeper into the countryside. Cooper drove along the hard shoulder of a macabre motorway scene. The three lanes of the wide road in both directions were strewn with the tightly packed wrecks of thousands of crashed cars, all of them having lost their drivers and gone out of control at the same time at the peak of the country's final rush hour. Once one of the busiest stretches of motorway, the road was now a bizarre, almost surreal sight: a rusting, rotting, never-ending traffic jam graveyard.

Cooper rubbed his eyes and massaged his temples, his head pounding. Immediately concerned, Donna leaned forward to speak to him.

"You all right?"

"Fine," he answered abruptly as he wrenched the wheel and steered hard around the remains of a car which had smashed into the back of another, leaving its boot jutting out into his path. He glanced up into the rearview mirror and watched as Steve Armitage plowed into the back of the vehicle he'd just avoided, ramming it into another car, sending it flipping up into the air then crashing down onto its roof, crushing the still-moving bodies trapped inside.

The underground base was some thirty miles outside the city and by his calculations they had probably already traveled almost two-thirds of the distance. Although unsure of its precise location, Cooper did remember the names of the villages nearby and was fairly confident of finding his way back to the general vicinity, then working his way to the bunker when he found

309

something he recognized. The vast installation was buried in a remote and inconspicuous area of land. By its very nature it was always going to be hard to find.

The sound of a truck's horn blasted through the air. Donna turned around and peered through the back window of the van. A short distance behind them, Steve Armitage had slowed down and was flashing his lights furiously.

"Shit," Cooper cursed, slamming on the brakes and bringing the van to a sudden stop.

"What is it?" Jack asked anxiously.

"Don't know," he replied, reversing back quickly along the hard shoulder, the van's engine groaning with effort. "I can't see the other truck from here."

Once Cooper had stopped again, Jack opened the rear of the van and ran back down the road. When he reached the truck he climbed up onto the driver's footplate. Steve wound the window down to speak to him.

"What's the matter?" he asked, wiping spitting rain from his face. Steve gestured back over his shoulder.

"Not me," he replied. "They're stuck. I think a car I hit has blocked the way."

Jack peered farther back into the semidarkness. Steve was right. The car he'd caught and flipped over had landed across the narrow stretch of road at the side of the motorway along which the convoy had been moving. Cooper suddenly appeared at his side.

"Too much noise. Kill the engine, we're attracting attention," he said to Steve, who immediately did as he was told. Steve saw that Cooper was right. Although not in anything like the massive numbers they were used to, bodies were approaching. They moved painfully slowly through the maze of twisted metal, some finding their way forward blocked at every turn, others managing by chance to find a clear path through. On the other side the progress of the dead was slowed by a steep, grassy embankment. They tried relentlessly, but their decaying limbs struggled with the severe angle of the muddy slope and most remained mired at the bottom.

"He'll have to try and smash his way through," Cooper said. "There's nothing else we can do and we can't manage without his truck. We're tight enough on space as it is."

Steve nodded and jabbed his thumb back behind him. "This lot are beginning to suffer," he said quietly, talking about the people in the back of the truck. "I couldn't take any more in here even if I wanted to." The vehicle hadn't been designed to carry this many passengers. The survivors and their belongings had been crammed into an uncomfortably tight space.

"I'll tell Croft," Jack said to Cooper. "You get back to the van."

Cooper sprinted back, teeming movement all around him. He glanced down the embankment and saw that the number of corpses was increasing. Several had managed to crawl more than halfway up the incline, climbing over other fallen corpses and using them to get a foothold.

Jack ran to the other truck, focusing on its headlamps and ignoring everything else around him. He tripped, stubbing his toe in a pothole, and slammed up against the wreck of the nearest car, almost smacking his face against its cracked windscreen. Inside the car, still anchored to its seat by its safety belt, a corpse lunged toward him. "Fuck me," he cursed as he staggered back with surprise. For a few seconds he just stood there and stared. The longer he looked into the endless line of crashed traffic, the more frantic, trapped movement he could see.

"Just put your fucking foot down," he shouted when he finally got to Croft. "You've got to try and smash your way through. Nothing else we can do."

"I'm sorry, I'm just not used to driving anything this big. I don't know how far I can push it and—"

"Just shut up and do it!" Jack yelled, sidestepping a cadaver which lunged at him. He shoved it down the embankment, watching it land on several others and knock them back down to the bottom. "Worry about it when it goes wrong, not before."

Jack turned and ran back to the van, not wanting to be outside any longer. Croft did as he was told. He struggled for a few seconds to select a reverse gear, then sent the truck careering back along the hard shoulder, unintentionally obliterating several more bodies and causing panic among his terrified, claustrophobic passengers. He accelerated hard and plowed into the wreck which was preventing him getting through, trapping it under his bumper, carrying it along in front of the track and throwing up a shower of white-hot sparks. It scraped along the road for a few meters before finally working its way loose and tumbling down the embankment, wiping out another clutch of corpses still struggling to get up. Finally able to drive freely again, Croft accelerated to catch up with the van and the other truck.

49

As grimy gray daylight gradually began to creep across another cold, and foreboding morning, so Cooper's orientation and recollection of his surroundings slowly returned. Landmarks and familiar place names helped crystallize his thinking and reassure him that he was leading the survivors in the right direction. They passed through a lifeless village which he clearly remembered. Dead for more than a month, many of the cottages and homes which lined the main street had burned to the ground, others were scarred by smoke, dirt and decay. Sudden movement surrounded the convoy as the noise of their engines caused bodies to emerge from the shadows and surge toward the road. Their reactions were still slow and the bulk of the lethargic creatures didn't appear until the vehicles had already gone. A lone corpse, however, stumbled into the road a short distance ahead of the van. Cooper accelerated and obliterated it with a brief moment of effort and absolutely no remorse.

They drove through the village and back out onto an

exposed country road which twisted and turned precariously as it worked its way between fields and hills. The narrow road began to climb a steep gradient with a sudden turn at the very top. Now completely sure of his surroundings, Cooper turned the steering wheel to the right and sent the van careering through a gate and down an even narrower, even steeper downward slope along a track which was virtually invisible from the road. With his heart in his mouth Steve Armitage followed, slowly coaxing the cumbersome prison truck down the track while, at the same time, taking care not to lose sight of the soldier ahead. Steve was used to driving trucks. The doctor driving the third vehicle was not. His pulse raced and his hands were clammy with nervous sweat.

"Fuck," he shouted, pushing himself back in his seat and panicking as his truck began its unsteady descent. The size of the bulky, angular bonnet in front of him and the steep angle meant that for a few meters he was virtually driving blind. More through luck than judgment he managed to keep the vehicle on course, the truck's tires eventually finding the grooves in the ground left by other, even heavier, vehicles before them.

The track straightened out quickly, running below but parallel with the road they'd just left. Donna sat in the back of the van behind Cooper and wondered just how many hidden routes like this existed. How many places like this had she been close to and not known about? They would never have found this place if they hadn't had the soldier with them. If he'd chosen to stay behind in the city then they'd have had to do the same. Whether they liked it or not, they each owed him a debt of gratitude.

A hairpin right, quickly followed by yet another descent,

and then the track suddenly cut across a wide field nestled at the foot of a steep and otherwise inaccessible valley. Huge hills loomed up on either side, hiding them from view. Donna felt safer in the shadows.

"You never know where these places are until you're there," Cooper said, concentrating on following the hidden road but occasionally glancing back and checking on the two trucks.

"So if we're going to have trouble finding it," Donna said, peering over his shoulder, "then this base of yours should be pretty safe."

"You'd hope so."

The track climbed briefly and then dipped down again, crossing a wide stream at a shallow ford. The three vehicles powered through the water, sending low waves rippling away on either side. Cooper could see the tops of a copse of trees ahead and he knew they were close. The sides of the track became steep banks and he increased his speed.

Phil Croft wiped his face and forced himself to concentrate on the uneven road which stretched out in front of him. He was becoming used to the size and handling of the prison truck now, but driving a machine of such power was something which didn't come naturally to him. The larger truck in front was being driven with obvious skill and precision by Steve and an uncomfortable gap had opened up between them. One of his wheels sunk down into a water-filled pothole and Croft overcompensated, sending the vehicle skidding across the uneven surface of the track, lurching alarmingly over to one side. He could hear the nervous reaction of the survivors in the back but he ignored them. They'd all been through much worse to get this far.

315

At the front of the convoy Cooper turned right, following another sharp bend in the track. The steep banks on either side had dropped away again, leaving him with a clear view of the narrow roadway as it disappeared into a dense forest of brittle branched trees. Would the trucks be able to cope with this terrain? With concern he looked into his mirrors and watched as Steve slowed down to a virtual stop, teasing the heavy truck around the tight bend.

There were more dips, furrows, and twists in the track as it wound its way through the trees. There were bodies nearby. Steve noticed them first from his high vantage point. They were staggering through the undergrowth, tripping over rocks and half-buried tree roots and then scrambling back up again, converging on the road. The truck driver wasn't concerned. His vehicle was huge. He knew that a few diseased cadavers posed no threat.

The last faint traces of doubt and uncertainty disappeared from Cooper's mind as he drove through a familiar-looking narrow gate and over a cattle grid which violently shook and rattled the van and its passengers. As the trees around them thinned away to nothing he allowed himself to put his foot down on the accelerator and steam ahead. The track cut through a another field and then quickly climbed toward a slight rise. The base was on the other side.

"Must be getting close now," Steve grumbled as he followed Cooper out of the forest. Once through the gate and over the cattle grid he increased his speed to match that of the van just ahead of them. Behind him, Croft reacted to the sudden increase in the speed of the other two vehicles. Afraid of losing sight of them (although he knew there was no way that he would) he too slammed his foot down on the accelerator pedal. The truck began to lurch and sway uncomfortably.

"Bloody hell, mate," Paul said, "slow down, will you."

Croft wasn't listening. He kept his speed constant and lined himself up to drive through the narrow gate. The front wheel of the truck hit a moss-covered boulder and was forced up into the air. Momentarily unbalanced, the back of the overloaded vehicle clipped the gate post. For an instant the truck balanced precariously on two wheels, until the weight of the people in the back, blind to what was happening and being thrown around violently, caused it to topple over. It crashed over onto one side and slammed onto the ground, the speed at which it had been traveling causing it to skid a little farther along the muddy track, stopping only when it hit the trunk of a tree.

Dazed, Croft lay still, slumped forward heavily in his seat, held by his safety belt and hanging in midair. Beneath him lay Paul Castle's dead body. He'd been thrown out of his seat and smashed against the windscreen by the force of the impact. He lay facedown in a pool of blood and broken glass, neck snapped.

Drifting in and out of consciousness, Croft managed to lift his head and open his eyes momentarily as the first few corpses began to beat against the shattered windscreen to get to him.

50

Michael was slumped forward over the steering wheel of the motor home when a sudden noise made him jolt upright in his seat.

"Jesus Christ," he cursed as the van driven by Cooper thundered past, carving a bloody groove through the field full of corpses and just managing to swerve around the rear of the motor home in time to avoid hitting it. "Where the hell did that come from?"

Emma ran to his side and watched in disbelief as the van continued to tear a path through the mass of wandering bodies. Before she could speak the prison truck appeared.

"Follow them," she eventually managed to say. With his hands shaking, Michael started the engine and attempted to move the motor home forward. All around them bodies were reacting with ominous strength and fury to the sudden activity. Some staggered after the van and the truck, others turned and lurched back toward the motor home, their unwanted interest aroused by the sudden engine noise. The van skidded to a halt about a hundred meters ahead, the once-white (but now muddy brown and blood-soaked) truck a few meters farther on. They watched as a man hung out of the side of the truck and began to gesticulate furiously to the people in the van. He was waving back in the direction of the incline that they had just appeared over. The reversing lights on the back of the van came on and the vehicle sped back toward the motor home, its engine whining and its wheels churning mud, gore, and rotting flesh into the cold morning air. The driver slammed on the brakes when the two vehicles were parallel. There was a gap of less than a meter between them. He wound down his window and shouted over to Emma.

"Any room inside?" Cooper yelled. Still stunned, Emma could only nod in reply. "How many of you are in there?"

"Just two of us," she stammered.

"One of our trucks has gone down in the forest," the soldier shouted back. "I need to go back for them. Can you take my passengers?"

Who were these people? She struggled to work out what was happening, then realized it wasn't important. These people were survivors, the first they'd seen in weeks, and that was all that mattered.

"There's a side door," she shouted to him, gesturing back. "I'll open up."

Without waiting for his response, Emma ran to the door and threw it open. Michael appeared at her side and immediately began kicking, pushing, and hitting out at the vast number of badly decayed cadavers which suddenly threw themselves toward them. A meter and a half away, the back of the van flew

319

open. Four figures jumped down into the field, slipping and sliding in the muddy confusion. Emma reached out and grabbed hold of Donna, hauling her quickly to safety as Michael continued to hold back the dead. Between the two women they dragged the other three inside, then slammed the door shut.

Jack pulled the van door closed, then watched through the window until he was sure the others were safe.

"They're in," he yelled to Cooper, who immediately began to drive forward again, plowing down more bodies. The already rough ground had been churned up by the numerous military vehicles that had driven to and from the base recently and the van struggled to get traction. The constantly swarming bodies made it almost impossible for Cooper to keep it moving forward safely. He slowed and then stopped moving altogether, the vehicle's wheels spinning but going nowhere. The soldier took his foot off the pedals and let the heavy vehicle roll a short distance back down the slight slope.

"We're never going to get back up there," Jack said, climbing over into the passenger seat and looking up at the hill they'd driven down to get here.

"We'll go around," Cooper replied, glancing from left to right and trying to work out which side of the hill to attack. He chose right and drove forward again. The ground was slightly more level and, to his relief, the tires finally gripped and allowed him to build up some speed. He continued to accelerate steadily, pushing rag-doll bodies away rather than completely obliterating them, increasing his velocity gradually until they were moving fast enough for him to risk attempting the climb again. Jack held on to the sides of his seat as Cooper swerved back around to the left and forced the van through the farthest edges of the crowd and up over the top of the ridge. Their speed slowed and the engine groaned with effort until they reached the top of the climb.

"Bloody hell," Jack said as they leveled out and powered along the flat, approaching the prison truck lying stranded on its side, surrounded by corpses. "What a mess."

Cooper stopped the van a short distance back and tried to decide on a plan of attack. The number of bodies already surrounding the crash meant that they couldn't risk getting out and attempting a rescue on foot. Although the majority of the dead remained in the field near the hidden entrance to the base, trapped there by the steep undulations of the land, many more had obviously been congregating nearby. The front of the truck was obscured by a dense throng of some thirty cadavers.

"How the hell are we going to do this?" Jack asked. Cooper didn't answer. Instead he drove forward again, turned the van around in a tight arc, and then reversed back toward the truck's overturned cab. Distracted by the sudden noise of the approaching vehicle, almost as one the bodies turned and began to stagger toward them.

"Open the back doors," he yelled as he leaned out of the window and steered the van backward. Jack scrambled out of his seat and crawled to the far end of the van. He threw the doors open, then jumped back as the van thumped into the cab of the truck. A random body, trapped by broken legs pinned between the two vehicles, thrashed its arms furiously. Before Jack could react Cooper was next to him. The soldier swung a single punch at the dead creature, the force of his fist almost ripping its head off its shoulders.

The cab of the truck lay sideways on, leaving Cooper and Jack just enough clearance to be able to squeeze through and clamber up and over its beached bulk.

"We'll get them out from the back and bring them over the top," Cooper explained, wiping his bloodied right hand on the back of his trousers. "We'll get Paul and Doc Croft out first."

Carefully choosing his spot for fear of causing further injury to the two men, Cooper lifted his boot and kicked the center of the cracked windscreen. Already weakened, the window gave way after just a few blows. Jack leaned forward and looked down at Paul Castle's bloody body.

"Too late for Paul," he said. "The poor fucker's had it."

Cooper nodded as he worked to unfasten Croft's seat belt. Once freed, the unconscious bulk of the doctor dropped into his arms. He pulled the injured medic free from the wreckage and laid him down carefully in the back of the van. The bloody irony of it, Jack thought as he watched—the only survivor who had the medical knowledge to treat injuries like these was the poor bastard who was lying there in front of him half-dead.

"Get ready to help them in," Cooper shouted as he climbed out of the van again, up onto the truck. He hauled himself onto the upward-facing driver's door and then ran the vehicle's length. There was a door almost exactly halfway between the front and back. He yanked at the handle but it wouldn't move. He could hear the people trapped inside thumping on the walls, trying desperately to get out.

"Get me the keys," he yelled back to Baxter, who was watching helplessly. The older man did as instructed, reaching in through what was left of the broken windscreen and twisting his arm around the steering column until his outstretched fingers made contact with the keys. From his awkward angle he tried to tease them free and succeeded, only to drop them again. They landed in the puddle of coagulating blood around Paul Castle's lifeless face. With equal amounts revulsion and sadness he closed his eyes and grabbed them, shaking them dry and wiping them clean on his jacket as he lifted them up.

"Here," he shouted, throwing them up onto the side of the truck. Cooper caught them and immediately dropped to his knees by the door. There were many keys on the bunch and it took several attempts before he found the right one. Eventually the lock clicked, the door opened outward, and the arms, head, and body of the first bruised and bloodied survivor emerged.

"Get ready, Jack," the soldier yelled, "they're on their way to you." He leaned down and pulled a middle-aged woman he didn't recognize out of the truck. Helped by more survivors pushing her out from inside, she was soon free. "Get yourself over to the van," Cooper told her as he reached down for the next person.

On her hands and knees, the woman shuffled toward the front of the truck. As she moved she looked down at the increasing crowds of bodies gathering on either side. Sensing her unease, Jack coaxed her forward.

"Come on," he said, "nearly there."

Back on top of the vehicle, Cooper had pulled two children and another woman free. He peered back inside and counted another seven people still waiting. He could also see a corpse. It was Keith Peterson. He lay facedown on the ground, crushed by the others in the sudden impact and crash.

Jack climbed out onto the truck to help the children down. As he guided more survivors into the van, Cooper shouted more instructions to him.

"Get behind the wheel."

"I can't," Jack replied frantically. "I can't drive."

"You're fucking kidding me?"

"Do you really think I'd joke at a time like this?" he yelled, stomping on the outstretched fingers of a corpse which reached out for the survivor he was trying to help into the van.

"Then find someone who can drive," Cooper ordered, "and do it now. We need to get moving."

"I'll do it," the first woman they'd rescued volunteered, her voice trembling with nerves. "You'll have to tell me where to go because I can't—"

"What's your name?"

"Jean," she replied. "I just don't know if I can—"

Jack wasn't interested.

"Get in the front and I'll tell you when we're ready to move," he said, pushing her forward. "Follow the tracks. You'll know where to go."

Jean climbed into the driver's seat, recoiling as a corpse slammed a rotting fist against the window. She looked up and froze. A densely packed crowd of grotesque faces stared back at her, their clouded eyes filled with hate. She looked down at her feet, looking anywhere but up, struggling to keep control and not panic. The bloody things were banging on the glass all around her now, covering the windows with smears and stains.

"Last one," Cooper yelled from on top of the truck. Seconds later the final survivor appeared, half-climbing, half-falling into the van. Cooper was close behind him. "Tell her to pull forward so we can get the doors shut," he ordered.

"Start moving forward, Jean," Jack repeated. Forcing herself to look up again, she gently pushed down on the accelerator pedal and eased it slowly forward, pushing steadily into the rotting crowd. As soon as they were far enough from the remains of the truck, Cooper jumped down, then scrambled up into the van. He pulled the doors shut behind him, then pushed his way through to the front.

"Drive!" he ordered, pointing in the direction he wanted her to move. "Just fucking drive!"

Back in the middle of the field Michael sat nervously behind the wheel of the motor home, trying to get the wheels to grip and move forward.

"This isn't good," he said quietly to Emma standing just behind him. "I think we should go and—"

He stopped talking when the van powered over the ridge and began a dangerously fast, barely controlled descent back into the densely-packed field of bodies. The van overtook, and Cooper, his face pressed against a window, gestured for Michael to follow. Steve Armitage accelerated after the van, the sole remaining prison truck belching clouds of noxious exhaust fumes into the morning air already polluted by the stench of death. Starting to panic, Michael pressed down on the accelerator again and again but was still unable to get any traction.

"Try a different gear," Donna suggested, clutching at straws. He did as she said and the motor home stalled, lurching forward and coming to rest with a corpse under one of its rear wheels.

Michael restarted the engine and revved it even harder. Through a combination of the higher gear and the body under the tire, the motor home finally started to move.

Around the back of a small and barely noticeable rise, completely hidden from view from virtually all other approaches, was a ramp leading down to a huge gray door, obscured by its position relative to the ground. Bodies swarmed around the three vehicles with frantic energy and bile, riled again by another sudden burst of noise and activity.

"Hit the horn!" Donna screamed as soon as she saw the door. "Let them know we're here."

"It's a fucking bunker," Michael said. "They're hardly going to hear us, are they?"

"Got any better ideas?"

Michael slammed his fist down on the horn. Steve Armitage did the same, as did the woman driving the van. The air was filled with noise, and that noise continued to whip the massive crowd into an uncontrollable fury. He stopped the motor home just meters away away from the concealed entrance.

"What now?" he demanded. "For Christ's sake, what are we supposed to do now?"

From every direction the horrific creatures surged toward the three vehicles, fighting with each other to get closer, tearing each other apart, pushing themselves against the metal and glass and slamming their rotting fists down again and again and again.

"Keep the noise going," Cooper said to Jean. "It'll distract them."

The soldier pushed past Jack and the rest of the survivors

326

crammed into the back of the van, then opened the back door and started to get out.

"What the hell are you doing?" asked Jack.

"Letting them know we're here," he answered. "Can't believe the dumb fuckers haven't already seen us."

He was halfway out of the van when he stopped, booted a corpse back out of the way, then pulled himself back in again and slammed the door behind him.

"What is it?" Jack asked, unable to see anything through the ever-increasing mass of corpses surrounding them. Without warning, the bunker's heavy entrance doors finally began to slide open. The two sides of the barrier began to part painfully slow, and as soon as a wide enough gap had appeared a stream of soldiers in protective clothing emerged, every inch of their faces and bodies hidden. They aimed their weapons into the crowds and began to fire, pushing back the dead. The space left by each fallen corpse was immediately filled by several more.

Without waiting for instruction, as soon as there was a wide enough space, Michael accelerated between the van and the truck and drove down into the base. It was immense—a vast cavern illuminated by artificial light as bright as the day outside. He'd never seen anything like it. The prison truck followed the motor home with the van close behind. Cooper dejectedly looked around at his surroundings as they began their descent, his exhaustion and relief immediately replaced with an uncomfortably familiar unease.

The sound of gunshots continued to fill the air as the protective-suited soldiers closed the doors and picked off the last few bodies which had managed to get through, using a digger to scrape and shove their remains back out into the open before the entrance to the base was resealed.

Still sitting in their vehicles, Michael, Emma, Donna, Jack, Bernard, and the rest of the survivors looked around the cavernous hangar in disbelief. Only Cooper got out. He stood in front of the van and raised his hands. The countless weapons which, moments earlier, had been pointed at the bodies outside, were now all aimed directly at him.

51

One of the soldiers stepped forward. Cooper tentatively lowered his hands and took a similar step forward to meet him.

"Sir!" he snapped attentively, saluting and standing to attention. He couldn't see who was behind the soldier's protective face mask.

"Cooper?" the faceless officer said. Despite his voice being muffled and distorted by the heavy breathing apparatus, his surprise was clear. "Where the hell have you been, soldier? We thought you were long gone. Welcome back."

The weapons were lowered.

Under continuous armed guard, the survivors were crammed into a room alongside a decontamination chamber. Their initial relief and euphoria soon faded and were replaced with nervousness and uncertainty. They were trapped, but they were safe. Exhausted and empty, they sat and stared into space. The lucky few managed to sleep.

Emma lay on a hard wooden bench, her head resting on Michael's lap. She looked up into his face and wondered what would happen to them now. Would the questions they'd both been asking since the first morning of the nightmare finally be answered by someone in this cavernous base? Would someone be able to explain to them what had happened to their world?

As the hours crept slowly by she drifted in and out of consciousness. Although still restless and uneasy in these new and alien surroundings, for the first time she was able to move and speak freely without fear of being hunted out and attacked by vicious bodies. No matter how highly trained they were, these soldiers with their guns and masks seemed to be nowhere near as much of a threat as what remained of the dead population outside. These people, she hoped, were rational and controlled. The millions of decaying bodies on the surface were not.

In order to conserve power, the main lights in the room were eventually switched off and dull yellow backup lights used instead. Emma curled up with Michael and waited silently for the next day to arrive. Although she wasn't completely sure, she thought it would be Friday. Almost four weeks since it had begun. Almost two weeks since they'd lost the farmhouse. Maybe tomorrow would be the day when everything would start making sense again?

In the arms of the man who had come to mean everything to her and surrounded by more survivors than she thought she'd ever see, Emma relaxed and slept and began to feel human again.

Outnumbered 1,000,000 to 1, a small band of the living face down the walking dead

Book 5

Book 4

Book 3

Book 2

Book 1

"A marvelously bleak dystopian future where the world belongs to the dead."
—Jonathan Maberry, *New York Times* bestselling author of *Patient Zero*

 St. Martin's Griffin   THOMAS DUNNE BOOKS

WARNING:
YOU WILL KILL TODAY

BOOK 1

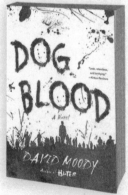

BOOK 2

BOOK 3

OWN THE ENTIRE CRITICALLY ACCLAIMED HATER SERIES

AVAILABLE WHEREVER BOOKS ARE SOLD

St. Martin's Griffin   THOMAS DUNNE BOOKS